The Fake

A **Smart Jocks** Novel

REBECCA JENSHAK

The Fake

Also by Rebecca Jenshak

one

Nathan

"Of all the asinine, stupid, foolish, goddamn selfish, ridiculous…" Coach's tirade continues as he stands and faces the wall behind him, muttering his expletives in that staccato fashion that he slips into when he's really, truly good and pissed. My heart punches my chest, matching the rhythm.

I glance to my buddy Wes, who stands with his arms crossed, leaning against the wall to my left, hoping for some solidarity among friends, but he's in hardcore assistant coach mode and his expression is as angry as Coach Daniels'.

Their disappointment sits heavy on my shoulders, and I switch my gaze to the floor. How did it come to this? The answer isn't simple, but it's not all that complicated either.

A knock at the door brings my eyes up. Matt, another of the four assistant coaches, waits for Coach Daniels to turn around before he gives him a thumbs up signaling that my drug test was clean, which I already knew and swore to the fact an hour ago when Coach called me into his office, but it's a relief anyway. One less disappointment to the man who's been like a father to me since I arrived at Valley U.

Matt walks away and Coach lets out a long breath and takes a seat back in his creaky desk chair. He runs a hand over his clean-shaven jaw. It's a few weeks before the season starts, and he still has that hopeful, optimistic look in his eye and fresh, put-together appearance... or he did.

"I'm not going to ask you any questions because it doesn't matter and frankly, the wrong answer could put you in a whole heap more trouble." He picks up the open textbook where my pills and weed are stashed inside a cutout in the middle of the pages. He snaps the book shut and tosses it to Wes. "Flush those, would you? And destroy the book." He mutters a few more remarks about how goddamn stupid I am before he adds, "I need a few more minutes with Nathan."

Wes offers a tight smile as he nods to Coach and steps out, shutting the door behind him.

"By the look on Wes' face, I'm guessing your teammates weren't aware of this any more than I was?"

"No—"

He holds his hand up for me to stop speaking. "Please don't say anything. If you tell me those drugs are yours, then I have to call the athletic director and maybe the police." He pins me with a hard gaze. "You get how

2

serious this is?"

This time, I keep my mouth shut.

"I don't understand why you'd risk it all with something like this. You're a bright kid, Nathan, well-liked, and a huge asset to this team. Now, I know basketball is probably the last thing on your mind right now, but we're going to need you this year. Losing Zeke, Wes, and Malone all to graduation leaves us with a lot of re-building to do. I'm hoping you want to be a part of that."

I think he wants me to answer this time, but my throat feels like I swallowed cotton. At the risk of my voice croaking like a twelve-year-old boy, I nod firmly. He's wrong about basketball not being on my mind— it's the *only* thing on my mind. I cannot lose my scholarship. Without it, there's no way I can pay for school or stay in Valley.

Even with it, I've only survived thanks to my friends looking out for me. Joel stocks our pantry with food I know he doesn't even like, and Wes is always covering me at the bar and giving me his old textbooks to sell for cash. The one coach just handed him was one of his own. Ain't that some shit. My friends mean well, and they try to play it off like it's nothing, but every handout chips away a little more at the normalcy of my life.

"Good." He leans back in his chair. "Until further notice, I want you to report in with Coach Matt every week for testing."

"But—"

He holds up a hand, and I fall silent.

"Weekly drug testing until I'm convinced today's negative result wasn't a fluke, and..."

Here it comes. I brace myself for the suspension I'm sure is coming. *Goodbye, Valley.*

"I'm making you co-captain." His jaw flexes.

Mine hits the floor, and my heart sputters. Excitement, confusion, dread—I run through the gamut as his words sink in. I'd been uncertain about making captain before, unsure I even wanted the responsibility. The moment I walked through the door and saw my stash on his desk, that uncertainty went up in smoke. And surprisingly, I'd been sad about it. Being named captain is a huge honor that's only put on the best and brightest on the team. I've proven time and again that I'm not either of those, but I guess a part of me still strives for it.

"Why would you do that?"

He smiles for the first time today. "Because it's the best way I know to teach you some responsibility." The expression on his face quickly falls back to anger. "This isn't a *three strikes and you're out* situation, Nathan. Next time, I'll be forced to take much more extreme measures that won't be good for you or the team. You hear me?"

I nod and try to swallow but my mouth is so dry.

"Do you hear me?" he asks again more sternly.

"Yes, sir."

When Coach dismisses me, I shuffle out of his office on shaky legs and collapse in the chair in front of my open locker. The contents, mostly dirty clothes and toiletries, lie on the floor scattered around my feet.

What a shit-tastic start to the week. It's the final week before classes start, and I was pumped to enjoy the last days of summer getting back into the swing of things before the campus, including Ray Fieldhouse, is overrun with students.

I know I should probably feel relief that I'm not kicked off the team or out of school or in fucking handcuffs, but instead, what I'm feeling is more like panic. Without those drugs, I'm not only out of a job, but I'm also out of money. I broke rule number one in dealing—don't get caught. I can't exactly go back to it with Coach watching over my shoulder. I may not have liked how I felt about selling drugs, but it provided money I need to survive and keep my little brother from falling into a similar situation.

Angry footsteps interrupt my spiraling thoughts and Wes' brooding frame casts a shadow over me.

"Didn't happen to save any of it, did ya?" I ask without looking up. "If I were going to start doing drugs, now seems like the perfect time."

"How can you possibly joke at a time like this?" he snaps.

Instead of answering him, I stand and scoop my shit off the floor and toss it in the locker, slamming it shut when I'm through. I head out of the locker room with Wes hot on my heels.

"Dude, stop."

I don't.

"Nathan."

Stilling, I count to three and school my features before I face him. Wes' expression has gone from angry to looking like I kicked his dog. He shoves both hands in his pants pockets and lowers his voice. "Are you alright?"

Laughter bubbles in my chest, and a strained chuckle escapes. "Nah, man, I don't think I am."

"Do you want to talk about it?"

I don't know if this is my buddy asking or assistant coach Wes, but he looks about as excited to have a heart to heart as I do to dump my problems on his lap.

"Can't. I gotta go figure out how I'm gonna make up for the money I just lost."

"Wait. Just... wait a minute." Wes shifts his weight from one foot to the other and lets out an exasperated groan. His blue eyes darken, and he pulls at his dirty blond hair. "Will you talk to me? Tell me what the hell is going on?"

"What's going on is I needed the money from selling the shit you flushed down the bowl." I lift a shoulder and let it fall. I could explain further, but he won't understand, no matter how I break it down. "Now, if you'll excuse me, I need to go see if I can sell plasma or sperm or maybe an organ."

He looks like he wants to say more but doesn't know what, and I don't give him time to come up with something. I leave him standing there without the answers I know he's looking for that'll explain it all away. If only it were that easy.

Outside of the fieldhouse, I take off in a run, sun beating down on me, and I'm sweating instantly. It's late morning but the summer temp is still hovering above one hundred degrees. I live just across the street, but I don't head there. I pump my legs hard in the opposite direction of the gym. It's not until I've hit the mile mark that the burn in my chest dulls everything else and I can think straight. I slow as Joel's Tesla comes into view.

"I should've known," I mutter as the car screeches to a halt beside me.

Joel tilts his head down so his eyes peer over the top of his sunglasses. "Get in, loser. We're going shopping."

I look past him to Wes sitting in the passenger seat. He avoids my gaze, but it doesn't take a genius to realize he ran straight to Joel and told him what happened.

"No thanks, and shitty Regina George impersonation, bro."

Joel chuckles. "Don't be an asshole, that was spot on *Mean Girls*. Now get in the car. We're going day drinking."

With a defeated sigh and a tiredness I feel deep in my soul, I give in and slide into the back seat and sink into the leather. The comfort annoys me. I don't want cushy. I want to erase the pain with pain.

Joel takes off, glancing in the rearview mirror as he does. "Sooo… how's your day?"

"Awesome. My day is going awesome."

He looks from Wes to me. "Hey, anyone got any weed or Xannies—could really help take the edge off, ya know?"

Wes glares.

"Too soon?" Joel smirks. The tightness around his shit-brown eyes gives him away though. He knows I've screwed up royally, and this is just his way of being here for me. I appreciate it… or I will when I'm not so angry at myself for letting things go this far.

No one speaks again until we're at the Prickly Pear, a dive that's more popular with townies than college students. It's early, so the place is empty except a lone guy sitting at the bar.

I slump into a chair at our usual table while Joel and Wes get drinks. I can't afford to buy my own beer and for the first time, I don't give a shit if they cover me. This was their idea. If they want me to drink with them and pretend this is just another day hanging with friends, they're gonna have to pony up.

Wes drops a pitcher in the middle of the table and divvies out the mugs. Joel's three steps behind carrying six shots precariously in his hands.

"Dude, we have the athletic mixer tonight." Wes raises both brows and his tone is all serious and adult-y. He's become a total bore since he graduated and became an assistant coach.

"It's barely noon. Lots of time to sober up before then." Joel lifts a shot glass and reluctantly, Wes and I do the same. "Bottoms up."

two

Chloe

*C*racking open your textbooks a week before classes start has to be some sort of warning sign. *Caution: fragile emotional state* or *Caution: bored completely out of her mind.*

Maybe I'd been that eager freshman year but definitely not since then. Senior year starting over at a new school… not how I planned it.

I flip the page in my new Applied Communications book and skim a couple of paragraphs before I give up and toss it aside and resign myself to death by boredom. *Caution: prone to dramatics.*

The last one isn't strictly true, but it's another side effect of being cooped up with no one to talk to. I'm all in my head with no outlet. Volleyball practices don't even start for a few more days, so I have nothing to occupy my time.

I could call my bestie back home, Camila, but admitting how worried I am that I made a huge mistake in coming here will only make her feel sorry for me. Besides, she's probably off having fun with our friends and teammates back at Golden U soaking up the sun on the beach. I guess *former teammates* now.

My current teammates, three of them anyway, are in the common room of our suite. I can hear them through the wall that separates it from our bedroom. That's another thing I never thought I'd do again—dorm living.

I grab another textbook and flip through it without even looking to see which class it's for. Bri's voice gets louder and more animated and then there's laughter.

I miss laughing. I miss talking. I miss that feeling in your chest when you're so in the moment everything inside expands and tightens and somehow makes you feel light, too. Good conversation, I definitely miss that.

Closing the book with my thumb holding my place, like it's really imperative I keep my spot for all the reading I'm not going to do, I rest it on my stomach and close my eyes, trying to hear them more clearly and imagine what it'd be like to be out there with them.

Bri's voice is the only one I can make out word for word. Her high-pitched disdain carries through the thin walls, and I can picture her blunt-cut bob swinging around her face as she shakes it disapprovingly. "It's a total waste of time. I can think of a million better ways to spend the night than prancing around in dresses as eye candy for alumni who couldn't care less about us. They're just here for the football and basketball teams."

"Well, I'm excited. It'll be a good chance for all of us

to hang out before classes start. Plus, we can check out all the new recruits."

I smile at Sydney's retort. She's the opposite of Bri in every way. From her long blonde hair to her sweet, gentle voice, and, more importantly, her desire, or lack thereof, to make my life as miserable as possible.

Transferring to Valley for my senior year after being kicked out of my previous school doesn't exactly make the type of impression that beckons people to welcome you with open arms. I get that, but I hadn't expected it to be quite this bad five hundred miles from home. I mean, it's not like I tried to buy my way into Valley. Technically, *I* didn't buy my way in anywhere, but that's not how the media portrayed it.

Untalented Wannabe Begs Mommy and Daddy to Get Her a Spot on Top-Ranked Beach Volleyball Team. That's almost word for word the headline from one of the nastier writeups. They didn't use the words untalented or wannabe, but they all but implied it by highlighting, in excruciating detail, every fault I've made in my entire volleyball career.

In some ways it was great that they'd focused more on me and less on my dad, the hotel mogul. He's had a record high year. Go figure. People seem to be more forgiving of rich CEOs than of their college-aged daughters or maybe that's just my perspective.

I had hoped that coming to Valley would be a fresh start, but Bri is standing squarely in the way of that. It's one thing to dislike me; it's another to make sure the rest of the team alienates me. She has made it very clear that talking to me is in direct violation of their loyalty to her and the team.

She might be a total bitch, but she is one of the best blockers in the conference. She also happens to be the captain of the Valley U beach volleyball team. Also, I don't really think she's a bitch to anyone but me. Overbearing, yes, but I seem to be the only person to get her full wrath.

"What are you two going to wear?" Bri asks them. "I think we should keep it simple and classy. Nothing too flashy or short. Let's see your dresses."

I register Bri's request and Sydney's footsteps too late. The door to our room flies open. I fumble with my book, open it, and pretend I'm reading as Sydney enters. Her big, brown eyes flit to me, and a guilty expression crosses her face. She gives a small smile, bites on her lower lip, and then disappears into our closet.

If it weren't for Bri and her fiery hatred of me, I think Sydney and I could be friends. Close friends even. We haven't spoken much at all, but I can usually tell within a few minutes of meeting someone if they're my kind of people, and Sydney gives me all those vibes.

When she comes back into view, she's carrying two dresses. Standing in front of our full-length mirror, she holds the first one, a short black cotton dress, in front of her. Then she drops it and holds up the other option. Her face automatically pulls into a smile at her reflection.

I admire her adventurous fashion sense with the neon pink and green band dress that shouldn't look good on anyone but will on her because she could duct tape a neon green poster board around her body and pull it off. Sydney is gorgeous and even more so because she doesn't seem to realize it. Long blonde hair, giant brown eyes, tall and thin with an athletic frame. She's a knockout in anything.

"I like that one," I tell her, giving up any pretense that I'm reading and not watching her with rapt interest. Also, I'm tired of the silence.

And I really do like the dress. Bonus that I know it'll make Bri's head spin. She has certain ideas about how we should look and conduct ourselves to best represent the team. I get it, kind of, but this is a college mixer we're talking about not tea with the queen.

She's even instituted a dress code for practices just in case anyone decides to drop in and watch, which I'm told next to never happens. But on the off chance, we're to be in standard-issued Valley blue and yellow only. You'd think she's the one who grew up with parents who wanted everything to appear perfect. Perfection is non-existent. She'd be happier if she accepted that. I'd offer her that tidbit if I thought she'd actually listen.

Sydney lets the dress fall to her side and tosses it on her bed. "Thanks." It's no more than a whisper and then she hurries out of our room carrying the black dress. I give the neon dress an apologetic smile. Poor dress. I've probably just ensured it never gets worn again.

Our room is set up with each of our twin beds pushed against the far walls and there might as well be a piece of tape dividing our halves for how much either of us has crossed into the other's space. Bri and Emily share a room on the other side of the suite with a similar setup.

I shove off my bed and decide to plan my own outfit for the night. The athletic mixer is mandatory for the entire team—free drinks and appetizers, mingling with alumni and boosters. Under normal circumstances, I'd be excited about a night of dressing up and going out, but since I have zero friends here, I'm not jumping for joy about being the social leper standing in the corner all night. It's embarrassing enough to hide away in my room, but I've never walked into a party alone like I know I will tonight.

I close the closet door behind me and pull the cardboard box labeled *Misc Junk* from the top shelf. Settling on the floor, I tug the flaps open and let out a sigh at the contents. Every overpriced piece of clothing I own is carefully folded and safely stored inside a plastic, zippered bag.

When I transferred to Valley, I thought it would be best if I left all traces of my life in California behind. It's not like I was walking around campus in couture, but I had nice, designer brand clothes, an off-campus apartment in an area that college kids shouldn't be able to afford, and money to blow on pretty much anything I wanted thanks to the allowance my parents transfer to my checking account like clockwork on the first and fifteenth of every month.

I don't fancy myself some sort of saint for attempting to rough it at college by wearing cheaper clothes and only buying necessities—this is all about self-preservation, but I'm sort of proud of how easy it's been to give up the things I thought I couldn't live without just a few months ago.

That being said, a whirl in my favorite dress might be just the bright spot I need in an otherwise crappy start at a new school.

I lift the dress, a beautiful light pink lacy Dolce

Gabbana number that is feminine and sexy, and with my summer tan still intact highlights my blonde hair and green eyes perfectly. I empty it from its protective bag, shove the box to the top of the closet, and then head back out to the room and lay the dress on my bed.

Grabbing my shower caddy, I prepare to face my roommates. There's only one way to the bathroom, and I've gotta go by them to get to it.

The common living room between our bedrooms is small but comfortable. The girls already had a blue couch and a TV when I moved in. My first day in Valley, I made my initial mistake when I went out and bought a floral print armchair, a rug, and a lamp to contribute to the room. I'm sure they'd already pinned me as the spoiled princess type from the rumors and news articles, but I found out real fast that flaunting my money was not the way to win them over.

Bri sits where the armchair should be, but it's pushed against the wall, and she's on the floor with her back to me. Sydney and Emily are on the couch with their dresses held up in front of them. Emily avoids eye contact with me altogether, hiding behind her blonde curls. Sydney smiles and then catches herself and looks away faster than I can return the gesture of friendliness.

I'm two steps from the freedom of the hallway when Bri calls, "Are you coming tonight or is this type of thing too lowbrow for you?"

I fight back a witty and cutting remark. "Yep, I'll be there."

I slip out and head to the ladies' room. Freddy dormitory is a co-ed dorm, but the guys and girls have separate bathrooms. It hasn't stopped me from walking in on the random guy coming out of one of our toilet stalls or spotting two pairs of feet under shower stalls, but mostly, everyone seems thankful for our separate spaces.

Freddy is where the majority of the student-athletes are placed at Valley. All the volleyball girls, with the exception of a few who live off-campus, are here. Before we arrived, all of our doors were decorated with our names in cutesy cutouts that matched our sport. Volleyballs, soccer balls, tennis racquets, and so on. There's at least one person from every sport living on my floor.

It's busy for a Wednesday afternoon. Doors open and shut all down the hallway, laughter and conversations filtering out and giving the place a fun and party-like vibe. It feels decidedly less depressing walking the twenty steps to the bathroom than it does being in my own room.

I spot a sophomore soccer player who lives across the hall coming out of the shower with a big fluffy yellow towel wrapped around her. She's one of the few friendly faces I've met, and I don't have to force the smile that comes when she walks toward me. She's one of those people who seems to know and like everyone.

"It's a madhouse in here," I say after waving hello.

"Give it another thirty minutes, and there'll be a line for the shower. I bet the guys' bathroom is a ghost town. They won't start getting ready until fifteen minutes before the mixer starts." She rolls her eyes.

"I didn't realize everyone was going tonight. I thought it was just a few teams."

"Ah." She squeezes the ends of her wet, red hair.

"Yeah, it's mandatory for everyone. It's a big deal. Lots of local media on top of the alumni and season ticket holders."

My stomach sinks with the new information. The last thing I need is more PR. I fake excitement. "Can't wait. I guess I better snag one of those showers before everyone else gets the same idea."

I stand under the hot water until my skin is pink from the heat and the stress tension I've been carrying in my neck disappears. When I step out, sure enough, a line has formed for the showers and a dozen more girls are using the mirrors to do their hair and makeup.

With my robe on and caddy in hand, I head back to my room. I take a deep breath before I enter the suite, feeling my neck muscles tighten at just the thought of facing Bri. I relax when I find the common room is empty and the door to Emily and Bri's room is closed.

But the tension comes screaming back when I walk into my room. Bri sits on my bed. Dark brown hair falls into her face, blocking me from seeing her expression, which I'm positive is smug. Her ass is planted on my comforter and both feet are pulled up on top of my dress while she paints her toenails a bright blood red. I'm not sure what's more shocking—the audacity to blatantly disrespect me or her choice in nail polish color.

Sydney's face turns a rosy shade as she glances between us. "Chloe's back now, Bri."

"Sorry, just finishing up here." She takes her time giving the toes on her right foot a second coat before screwing the lid on the bottle and swinging her legs off the bed. "Oops, looks like I got a little spot on your dress. You weren't going to wear this tonight, were you?"

My blood pressure spikes, and I feel a little woozy that her words might be true but force myself to calmly move to the bed and grab my pink dress to hold up for inspection. She wouldn't. The Dolce and Gabbana dress was on sale, but it's still the single most expensive piece of clothing I've ever owned. I bought it for a Golden team event not so different than the one we're attending tonight. It's so beautiful, and I'd felt just as beautiful in it. *Was* too beautiful.

Little red smudges mar the pink lace fabric along the bust of the dress. I clutch it to my chest and feel my eyes start to burn. "You ruined my dress."

She laughs. "Oh, relax, Mommy and Daddy can just buy you a new one, right? Just like they bought your way into college. *Twice.*"

"They didn't—" I stop myself from sticking up for them or myself. She doesn't want to hear the truth. "Stay out of my room and don't touch my things." I hurry into the closet, shut myself in, and press my back against the door.

Moving to Valley might have been the worst idea I've ever had. I know there's no escaping your past, but is it too much to ask for a second chance?

three

Nathan

*W*e're a damn mess as we make our way through the crowd at the mixer. We need to check in with Coach so that he knows we were here, but I'm thinking him seeing us like this would be worse than missing it altogether.

The event is an annual thing. There's a lot of handshaking and speeches about having another great year and winning seasons, yadda, yadda, yadda. I fully support my team and want the best for all the teams on campus, but I could do without the flashy show of support. The free drinks and food are welcome, though.

"This is bad," Wes says and sways to the left. "My first official event as an assistant coach and I'm drunk. Coach is going to fire me before the season starts."

"Oh, relax, you're not getting fired." Joel pulls a pack of gum from his pocket. "Here. Try and cover the beer breath until you've got a drink in your hand. Coach is busy schmoozing, so it's our chance to be seen without having to stop and chat."

Joel looks from Wes to me. "Ready?"

"Go ahead. I need to make a call first."

"Make sure you check in with Coach," Wes says, slipping right back into his assistant coach voice.

"Can't I just check in with you?"

He flips me off but then straightens as if he just again remembered he's a member of the faculty.

The event is held outside between the fieldhouse and the baseball field. It's a grassy shaded area with tall, skinny cypress trees that make the spot a scenic backdrop. I know this because every year they force us to stand in front of it for a photo op.

Staying on the outskirts of the party, I find a quiet spot to make my call. My brother answers on the third ring.

"Hello." Heath's tone is sullen and disinterested, but I try not to take offense. He's eighteen so the only thing that has his interest right now is girls and hockey. In that order, too. Also, he's voiced his opinion on talking on the phone several times. You can fake a lot through text, though, so I keep calling him to check in periodically in addition to texting.

"Hey, what's up, little bro?"

"Same ole." He curses under his breath, and I hear the sound of a video game in the background.

"How's camp? Your old skates working out okay?"

"They're tight as fuck, but I'm managing for now. I'll need new ones before the season starts though, and the team is ordering new warm-up jackets."

The Fake

I bring my thumb to the middle of my forehead and press in like it might relieve the stress rising up and trying to swallow me whole. "I sent money for the jacket. Mom didn't give it to you?"

"She probably spent it on bills. She quit the cafe, said the long hours alone were making her depression worse."

I jab harder against my skull. "I'll talk to her. I'm sure she just forgot to give it to you."

"The country club is hiring. I could get a part-time job to help out."

We've had this conversation a dozen times. I know it annoys Heath to depend on me and Mom for money—neither of which are all that reliable. Especially now. Fuck. I need to let Frank know what happened and tell him I'm done dealing. I push all that off to worry about later. One problem at a time.

Heath can't work, at least not during the season. Maybe he could find someone to work around his schedule and he could get an hour or two a week, but the paycheck wouldn't make much of a difference.

"You know you can't work and keep up with practices. Coach will either bench you or kick you off the team." I shake my head. "I'll figure something out."

"Okay."

We fall silent, and I listen to my little brother play Xbox. The noise from his thumbs stabbing at buttons and the sound effects of whatever game he's playing. It's such a normal, innocent thing to be doing that just sitting here listening to him helps me remember that against all odds, Heath isn't totally screwed up. Not yet anyway.

I know selling drugs to pay for hockey equipment seems extreme, but it's the only shot he's got to get out of Michigan and away from our mother, who is spiraling faster with each lost job.

When our dad died, I was just finishing high school and heading to Valley. I got out, excited to leave behind memories of the happy family that didn't exist anymore. I was selfish, only thinking about myself. I left Heath to fend for himself and it kills me to think of the things he's had to deal with while I was out partying and acting like life was grand. Especially since it's my fault Dad's gone.

Mom was okay at first. She was sad, as we all were, but she was functioning. Then... I don't know. One lost job turned to two, bills started to go unpaid. I didn't even know about it for a while. Heath and I barely spoke my first year at Valley so it's no shock that he didn't reach out until it was already pretty bad.

It was the beginning of sophomore year the first time he called and asked for money. I hadn't gone home that summer so I didn't see how bad it was. We've never been rich, but there'd always been money for what we needed. It must have taken some guts to call and ask me to help. Guts or desperation.

"How's everything else? Is Uncle Doug still stopping by on the weekends to check in?"

"Yes." He sounds glum. "I don't need a babysitter. He just makes things worse. He rags on Mom and makes her feel worse than she already does. Then he leaves, and I'm left to deal with her crying all night."

"Is it that bad?"

"It's fine. I know how to handle her. I'm eighteen.

I'm not a kid anymore, bro."

My chest breaks with a chuckle that I keep silent. He reminds me so much of myself at that age. Headstrong and independent, ready to take on the world like I knew it all. The difference is I had two parents keeping an eye on me and knocking me down a peg or two when I needed it.

"Yeah, alright. Listen, I'm at a team event, so I gotta go, but text or call me if you need anything. And if it's an emergency, call Uncle Doug."

"I know, I know."

"Stay out of trouble."

"I'm hanging up now."

"Love you, bro."

"Love you, too."

The conversation sobered me up something awful. Every muscle in my body is coiled tight as I pocket my phone and head toward the party. Coach Daniels still has people all around him, so I walk in front of him slowly until he spots me. He tips his head in acknowledgment and I do the same.

Obligations for the night complete. Tomorrow, I'll go back to stressing about Heath and my mom, try and figure out how to solve my money issues on the up and up, and start worrying about how bad I'm gonna screw up being co-captain, but for tonight, I just want to forget it all.

At the bar, I grab a Jack and Coke and circle the party. I don't see any of my teammates, but I spot some of the guys from the baseball team.

"Hey, Mario." I lift my glass in greeting. He and a few other baseball guys live just down the street so we're tight. He opens his stance up to let me into the circle. The other guys are all huddled around someone's phone.

"What's up, Payne?"

"Not much, man." I point to the guys. "Some chick make the unfortunate decision to send one of you nudes?"

Mario shakes his head. His gelled blond hair holds perfectly in place and I run a hand through mine, wondering if I look as rough as I feel. "Nah, nothing like that. One of the girls on the volleyball team is some sort of heiress."

"Freshman?"

"Transfer. Got busted for buying her way into school in California."

An heiress at Valley? Buying her way into college? My brows pull down in disbelief.

"I think that's her over there in the red dress." Mario looks over my shoulder, and I turn to face that direction.

She'd be easy to spot even if she weren't wearing a dress the color of a fire engine, but as it is, there's absolutely no way to miss her. Long, tan legs and blonde hair that hangs in loose waves, she looks more California surfer girl than rich bitch.

She's the only person at this event standing by herself. She's holding a glass in one hand, perfectly poised and put together but slouched like she's given up any pretense of pretending to have a good time.

"She's hot. Hot enough I'd let her be my sugar momma," Clark, one of the guys standing nearby, says as he steps into our conversation.

"I'd give twenty bucks to see you try," Mario says

with a shake of his head.

Clark tips his beer to Mario's and clinks the bottles together. "You're on."

"This should be entertaining."

I nod in agreement and watch as Clark weaves through people to get to Surfer Princess. He tosses a smirk back our direction when he's a few paces from her and then goes for it.

She's tall and the heels she has on make it so that I can see over Clark's big head and watch her expression as he gives what I can only imagine is the worst pickup line ever. Clark is a good guy but about as smooth as a cat's tongue.

A hint of a smile overshadows the slight discomfort I detect as she shifts her weight from one leg to the other. Her lips move in response to Clark and then she lifts her drink and takes a sip.

I can pinpoint the exact moment things go horribly wrong for ole Clark, though I haven't a clue what he could have said to have the girl in front of him bristle in such a dramatic way I can spot it from twenty yards. Her mouth draws into a tight line as she nods and then takes off. She doesn't even wait for Clark to move, just pushes past him and hightails it to the far side of the party.

"Crash and burn." Mario chuckles as Clark turns back to face us wearing a sheepish grin and shrugs.

I laugh along with him, but I can't shake the horrible day to offer a real one. I need more booze and maybe a lobotomy. "I'm gonna get some air."

"We're outside, man."

I'm already two steps away when I respond, "Air other people aren't breathing."

I get stopped no less than five times, get forced into a photo with the team, and spend twenty painful minutes talking to an alumnus who has food stuck in his teeth before I can slip away from the party.

I pull the flask I stashed in my pocket and unscrew the cap. The burn of liquor is fresh on my lips when I spot her. She's double-fisting it now, champagne in both hands as she leans against the side of Ray Fieldhouse. It's the side entrance, only accessible with a badge given to staff and student-athletes.

Surfer Princess is hiding, not that I blame her. If the baseball guys knew about her, that means everyone else does too or will shortly.

She stills when she sees me, her haven invaded. Taking a step like she's going to leave, I stop her. I'm not sure why, except she seems like the only person who might be having a shittier night than I am. "You don't have to run off. You have dibs, being here first and all. I'll just kick rocks."

To my back, she says, "Wait."

Color me surprised, I turn back to her, and she shifts uncomfortably on her tall heels. "Got something good in that flask?"

I shake my head. "Nah, it's not good." I close some of the distance between us and hold it out to her in invitation. "But it's effective."

She walks slowly until she's within an arm's length away. Up close, she's even more beautiful, which seems like it should be impossible because she looked pretty damn good from a distance. She hands me one of the flutes, takes the flask, puts it to her lips, and tips it back without so much as a sniff or sip to test it first. She's taken a healthy amount before she hands it back, eyes closed, and mouth twisted in displeasure. "You're right on both counts."

"Damn." I take another, much smaller, drink. Who is this chick? I mean, I know who she is, but... damn. "That was impressive."

"You say that now, but I might be sleeping right here tonight." She shudders and coughs. "What was that?"

"Mostly Everclear. Little bit of Mountain Dew."

"It tastes like rubbing alcohol." She holds her hand out for the flask despite her obvious dislike for it.

"One hundred and twenty proof."

She takes another drink.

"Go easy."

When she hands the flask back this time, I pocket it. I know my limits, but I'm not sure she does. Lifting the champagne flute I've been holding for her, I ask, "This one for me?"

She shrugs. "Seems fair, I guess."

I take a seat on the bottom step, one of three that leads up to the door. The sun just went down and there's a nice breeze. I don't know this girl, but this is the most at ease I've felt all day.

"Hiding from anyone in particular?"

"No. I'm hiding from everyone."

"I feel that."

She eyes me suspiciously. "Did Bri send you over here to mess with me?"

"Who's Bri?"

She sighs and takes a seat next to me. "Roommate, teammate, captain, arch-nemesis."

"Bad combo."

"Who are you hiding from?"

"Myself. Everyone. No one." I drain the rest of the bubbly in my glass and pull out my cigarettes. "You mind?"

She gives her head a little shake and watches as I light up.

"You want one?" I ask after I take my first drag and feel her eyes still on me.

"No. I just haven't seen anyone smoke in… forever. You know what those things do to your lungs, right?"

I chuckle.

"Guess that rules out track."

"What's that?" I ask. Glancing over at her, my gaze is drawn to her green eyes—the color of summertime in northern Michigan where I grew up.

"I was trying to guess which sport you played."

"Not track," I confirm.

"Baseball?"

"Nope."

"Football? Quarterback maybe?"

I shake my head. "I could just tell you."

"What fun is that?"

My soft chuckle lingers between us, and we smile back at one another. It's the first real smile to come from me all day. I put the cigarette in my mouth and extend my hand. "Nathan."

"Chloe."

four

Chloe

"Wanna tell me why your roommate hates you or do you want me to guess?" Nathan leans back on an elbow, his long jean-clad legs splayed out in front of him. Most of the athletes here tonight are dressed up, but he pulls off the dark jeans and black t-shirt like he's red carpet ready.

I shift my weight, giving one butt cheek a reprieve from the hard ground. We've been sharing information for the better part of two hours, or rather, we've been trying to guess information about the other. So far, I haven't learned much, but he's been surprisingly accurate in his assessment of me.

He takes my silence as an indication I want him to guess.

"You slept with her boyfriend?"

"Oh, my God, no, of course not." I laugh, and he joins in.

"Kidding." He considers me for a moment, his blue eyes scrutinizing me in such detail, I feel the blush creep up my face. "She's jealous of you."

"No." I roll my eyes at the thought of Bri being jealous of anyone. She's captain of the team, she's beautiful, she seems well-liked, if not a tiny bit feared. It's more like the other way around. I'm jealous of her. Of her position on the team—one she earned—and the respect and friendship of her teammates. *Our* teammates. I'm jealous that she doesn't have to start over with a new college, different city, and an altered perception of the past three years.

"You're gorgeous. In my experience, that's all it really takes for other chicks to be jealous."

"That's not it," I say more adamantly. He cocks a brow like he doesn't believe me. "I got kicked out of my last school for fraud or bribery. Honestly, I'm not sure what the official ruling was."

I cannot believe I just told him that. Maybe he already knew. That douchebag who tried to hit on me earlier with some sugar momma pick up line certainly did. Nathan's face gives nothing away. He doesn't speak so I keep going.

"I didn't know. Not that it seems to matter to anyone, but I had no idea it's how I got into college. Anyway, I'm pretty sure that's why Bri hates me. She thinks I don't deserve to be here or maybe she just doesn't like having someone with a scarlet letter on her precious team."

I slam my lips shut to keep from blubbering on, but

he's looking at me so intently, I can't not say more. "I'm sorry, I've totally ruined the moment."

I go silent again and stare down at my hands, wishing I could sink right into the concrete.

"I might have heard something about that floating around earlier," he says. Screw sinking into the concrete, I want to run far, far away. "I'm sorry."

"You're sorry?" I ask, meeting his gaze and finding it sincere.

"Yeah, I know all about screwing up. It changes the way people treat you. Doesn't matter your culpability or even the reasons behind what you did—they only see how it affects them."

"Thank you." Something like shock or relief washes over me at his understanding.

One side of his mouth pulls into an awkward smile, and he shrugs like it's no big deal, but it means everything to me. Absolution, even from a near stranger, brings a little more of my old confidence to the surface.

"I bet you get along with your roommates." I check his face to see if I'm right and he nods.

"Off-campus?"

Another nod.

"Okay, tell me something real about you since I just unloaded all my baggage."

His body visibly tenses, and I'm afraid I've ruined the mood for good this time. We're in this bubble, partially alcohol-induced, but I haven't felt like this in a long time.

Finally, he smirks and lifts the flask. He's run to get us fresh drinks twice, but we're down to just the ridiculously strong liquor again. "I'm gonna need more booze soon."

"I'm serious." I shove at his shoulder playfully, but the contact makes me intensely aware of the heat of his skin and the hum coursing through my veins.

"I'm *really* having a good time. Been the best part of my day." He sits up and brings his flask to his lips, tips it all the way up and then frowns. "Empty."

Both of us fall silent as we stare in the direction of the party. We're just out of view, but the noise has died down so my guess is it's dying off. I had my picture taken with the team and walked around by myself for half an hour dodging reporters so I don't feel the least bit guilty about disappearing. Plus, it feels amazing to be having good conversation. I've got that light feeling in my chest, and it's not all thanks to the drinks.

"Well, I guess it's time to call it a night."

Neither of us moves and I scramble for ways to keep us here. I don't want to go back to being ignored after being seen again.

"We could go back to my place. I don't have any Everclear, but I've got a couple of bottles of wine stashed under my bed." I can barely believe I've offered, but I really don't want the night to end. There's something about Nathan I can't quite put my finger on. He seems to get me, and I'm not even sure I get myself these days.

"What about the evil roommate?"

"If she's going to hate me before I do anything to deserve it, I might as well do what I want."

"Let's do it."

The Fake

We take our time walking back to my dorm, talking about nothing and everything. His fingers brush up against mine accidentally, and I cast a side glance in his direction. He tosses that sexy smile back at me and my stomach flutters.

His hair is the color of sand and sticks up around his head in an unkept but not homely way. If I were to describe Nathan's style, I'd call it the I-don't-care-about-my-appearance look. And he's very much pulling it off.

The halls of Freddy are quiet, and I let out a sigh of relief when I open the door to my suite and find it empty. I didn't have a plan for dealing with the roommates if they were up, but it looks like I'm in the clear. Both bedroom doors are closed and all the lights are off the best I can tell.

I flip on the light in the common room and Nathan takes a seat on my floral chair. He's probably the first person to sit in it, which seems sorta fitting. "Give me just a minute. I'm going to grab the wine from my room."

I kick off my heels and hold them in one hand as I slip quietly into my room. Sydney is asleep and the lights are out, making the room pitch black. We've taken to falling asleep with music playing to drown out the deafening silence between us.

Khalid plays softly and it's enough that I don't worry that my rummaging under my bed for the wine will wake her.

He's scrolling through his phone when I return with two bottles, a wine opener, and one cup.

"I could only find one of these in the dark." I hold up the hot pink cup.

I waffle on where to sit until he slides down to the floor. The way he moves, so effortless and comfortable in his skin, strikes me. It's attractive for a man to be just so... himself.

I sit across from him between the couch and coffee table. "Red or white?"

He smirks. "Can't guess which I like better?"

Both bottles are some cheap bottom-shelf brand. Neither can taste that great, but considering the nasty alcohol he had on hand earlier, I go with the dryer option and grab the red.

"Lucky guess."

I scoff. "That was not luck. If I've learned nothing else about you tonight from this weird back and forth guessing game, I took note of your choice in alcohol. Potent and rough around the edges."

Sort of like him.

He wraps his long fingers around the bottle and slides it closer to him while grabbing the opener with the other hand. He has the cork out and the cup filled quickly and offers it to me. "Ladies first."

Just the very tip of our fingers touch as I grasp the cup, but I can tell by the way his eyes lock onto the contact that he's as aware of it as I am. His presence in my dorm is heady and relaxing all at once. The first real friend I've made in Valley.

"Cheers," I say before taking a drink.

The wine hits me hard after the various types and

large consumption of alcohol I've had. I'm giggling and smiling at Nathan as we continue our guessing game—bouncing from favorite foods to middle names. My face actually hurts from smiling. And the more I learn about Nathan, the less I care about the answers and the more I realize just how good it feels to be sitting on the floor of my dorm sharing a cup of wine. Though, he's pretty interesting too. And not at all hard to look at as we've established.

"Alright, Chloe, give me the important details. Name, age, hometown, major." My name on his lips is the final shot to do me in.

"Chloe Marie Macpherson, twenty-one years old, originally from California, senior, communications major," I rattle off the facts that make up who I am and yet say so much less than we've already shared. I set the cup down in front of him. "Your turn."

"Nathan Robert Payne, twenty-one years old, from Michigan, senior, business."

"Soccer?" I ask, returning to our earlier conversation.

"No, and you're running out of sports." His eyes narrow on me again as he delivers a question I didn't expect. "Single?"

I nod because I'm holding my breath and I'm afraid if I speak, it'll come out all breathless and needy.

He moves closer with that sexy smirk and fingers a strand of hair. "Good." He leans in so his lips hover over mine. He smells of liquor and wine and awesomely bad decisions. "I don't have to guess if some dude is gonna track me down tomorrow for doing this."

five

Nathan

For the last several hours, I've been thinking about kissing Chloe. I'm not usually the kind of guy who wonders what it'd be like to kiss a girl. I think about getting them naked, of course, and it's not like I don't enjoy kissing. Kissing is great, but it's usually just the required first step to my end goal.

I wonder if she'll taste like Everclear, champagne, or wine? A combination of all three, maybe?

But when my tongue sweeps inside her mouth, she doesn't taste like any of those things. She tastes like summer. Sunshine, lazy days, carefree nights, endless possibilities—things that I'd have sworn only moments ago don't even have a taste.

Slow unsure kisses turn long and deep and somehow, she ends up on my lap. I can't remember if I put her there or if she climbed on top of me, but now that she's here, I've got both hands tight around her waist to keep her in place.

It doesn't seem like she's going anywhere, though. Her hands thread through my hair and then slide down my back. I let her make the first move to naked town. She lifts my shirt over my head, and those green eyes roam over my chest and abs with blatant appreciation.

When her mouth finds mine again, it's with a desperate moan that has me wondering if maybe we should have taken this back to my place where we'd have more privacy. Hell, maybe she wants to get caught. I worry about it for all of three seconds until she presses her chest against mine and I can feel her nipples poking through her dress.

I need to taste them. I have to know if they taste like summer, too. I ask her, and she laughs and then shocks me a little when she stands and unzips her dress. It falls to the floor, and she's standing in front of me naked except for the smallest red panties imaginable.

"No need to guess. Find out for yourself."

So I do.

I kiss every inch of her, starting with her lips. *Sunshine.*

Working my way down her neck, my lips caress her collarbone and then dip lower to taste one pink nipple. *Lazy days.*

I give the other the same attention and then kiss down her stomach. *Carefree nights.*

She quivers and moans as I nip at her hipbones. *Endless possibilities.*

And when my tongue finally licks up her pussy, it tastes exactly like summer, but something else, too. It tastes like new beginnings.

Six

Nathan

"*O*h, my God."

I open my eyes and find Chloe, still as stunning as the night before but her face twisted into an expression of horror, peering down at me. She's clutching her dress in both hands, holding it in front of her gorgeous body. Her very *naked* gorgeous body.

"Already saw what's underneath," I tell her, voice gravelly from too many drinks last night.

"Oh, my God," she repeats and grabs a pillow from the couch and tosses it at my dick. "You have to get dressed and go."

I stand and run a hand through my hair, trying to get my bearings. "Everything alright?"

She's not paying any attention to me, though. She's wrapped herself like a burrito in a blanket from the couch and turns in circles, picking up all the evidence from our night together like it's a crime scene. Condom wrappers, wine bottle corks, panties.

She picks up my shirt and tosses it to me, our eyes finally locking before hers travel down. I glance at the time on my phone. Shit, I gotta get going. "Can I get your number?"

She doesn't answer, just moves past me to straighten the coffee table and pick up the empty wine bottles.

"Here." I try and take one of the bottles. "Let me help."

Her grip tightens. "I got it. You should go. My roommates will be up any minute."

"Yeah, alright." Nothing like being kicked out of a girl's room first thing in the morning.

I'm turning my shirt right side out when a door opens and two girls step through. Both tall, one with wild blonde curls and the other a brunette with straight hair and a sharp angular face that's probably pretty when she smiles. As it is, her cold expression gives new meaning to the term resting bitch face. Sooo, this is the evil roommate.

Confirmed when she steps fully into the room and takes in the scene. Her eyes go from shocked to taunting. Her tone is condescending as hell when she says, "Good morning, Chloe. Who's your friend?"

My surfer princess stiffens.

"You did catch his name, right? A one-night stand, really? Or is he from a service?"

A service? Hell, no. Did this girl just insinuate I'm a prostitute?

After pulling the t-shirt on over my head, I step

40

forward and extend a hand. "Hi, nice to meet you. I'm—
"

"Nathan Payne," she finishes. Her eyes have gone from narrowed slits to wide saucers. "Oh, my God. Hi. Welcome. I didn't recognize you without your shirt on."
Welcome?
She looks to Chloe like she expects an explanation. "How do you two know each other?"
We met last night and hooked up seems like the wrong answer so I stay quiet.
"Actually." Chloe's green eyes flit to me and then her spine straightens with some sort of resolve. "Nathan is my boyfriend."
I let out a chuckle of surprise and then do my best to hide it behind a cough.
"*You're* her boyfriend?" The brunette's wide eyes snap to me.
I nod.
"I'm Emily." The blonde with bouncy curls places her hand in mine. "It's so nice to meet you."
"Nice to meet you, too."
The other roommate continues to stare at me in shock, so I move to Chloe. "Well, I should get going." I drop a kiss to her cheek. "I'll catch ya later, *girlfriend*."
I feel three sets of eyes following my every move out the door. Chloe catches me before I reach the stairs. Her red dress from last night pulled back on and bare feet, she looks like sex on Christmas morning.
"Thank you for covering for me back there. I panicked."
"No problem."
She nods. "Listen, about last night. It was…"

"Awesome? Hot? Unexpected?" I call out adjectives like dirty mad libs as images from last night flash through my mind. The night's a bit blurry in places, but those long legs wrapped around me and her blonde hair falling around her shoulders as she rode me, taking her pleasure and rocking my damn world, are fucking vivid.

"A mistake," she finally says. "I don't do things like that. Ever." She shakes her head with what I can only imagine is revulsion at what I thought was a pretty good night.

"You did it pretty well for someone who doesn't."

She blushes. "I—"

I cut her off before she can destroy any more of my fondness for last night. "I get it. Last night was fun. Let's just leave it at that."

"Thank you."

"Yep." I turn and head down the stairs.

"Tennis?" she calls after me.

I shake my head without looking back. "Basketball, princess."

Joel's in the kitchen when I get back to the house. "What's up, buddy? I was just about to send out search and rescue."

Sitting on one of the barstools, I take the muffin he tosses at me. It's still warm. "Momma Moreno?"

"Yeah, you just missed her."

"Too bad," I tease my buddy. His mom is

ridiculously hot, and we all like to give him shit about it. He gives me the finger. "We need to figure out who we're going to ask to take Wes and Z's rooms this year." "Feels weird replacing them." Both Wes and Zeke graduated in May, and we've been dragging our feet to get new roommates.

"I'm thinking Shaw and Datson. Get our starters under one roof."

"What about Wickers?"

"Nah, he's got a place off-campus already with his girlfriend." Joel's phone vibrates on the counter. "That's Katrina. I'm heading over to her place before practice. Think about it and if you're cool with it, we'll let them know today."

After Joel leaves for his girlfriend's place, I grab a Powerade from the fridge and head up to my room. I plug my cell phone in and lay down on my bed. When it has enough juice to turn back on, I read through the texts I missed last night.

Wes: Local paper wants a picture of starters.

Wes: Dude, where are you? We're waiting on you.

Wes: ?

Shaw: Wes is about to blow a gasket. Where are you?

Well, that sucks. Day one of being co-captain, and I'm already screwing it up. I keep scrolling, respond to a text from Gabby about hanging tomorrow, and then I brace myself to open the final message.

Frank: Come over at five so I can set you up for the week. Got some new stuff to test out, see if there's any interest in it.

I still haven't told Frank about getting busted. I don't know why I'm dragging my feet. I know I'm lucky I didn't get caught sooner. Almost two years I've been selling. Somewhere along the way, it stopped being such a big deal. Not getting caught will do that to you—make you believe what you're doing isn't hurting anyone.

It isn't like I was proud of it, but Heath and the guilt... that's harder to live with than the logistics of how I was making my money. And I guess that's really why I haven't texted Frank yet. Once I'm out, the money will stop, and I have no clue how I'm going to survive the guilt.

One problem at a time. Right now, I need to get rid of this hangover so I can make it through practice today.

The next afternoon, Gabby and I are floating on matching unicorn floaties when I give her the rundown of my colossal fuck up.

She's quiet for too long. Something distinctively un-Gabby-like. My best friend is never shy about voicing her opinion.

"Say something. Please."

"I think I'm in shock." She reaches over and takes my hand. "Why?"

"I needed money. You know what it's been like with my mom and Heath."

She gives me a look that calls bullshit. She's the only person I've confided in about things back home, or most of it at least, but her face tells me it's not a good enough reason. "Selling drugs has to be the worst way to make money. This could have ended so much worse, Nathan."

"I know. I know. Honest. I do."

The thing about Gabby is that even when she doesn't understand my choices, I know she still cares about me. She's honest to God the best friend I've ever had. A few months ago, I thought my feelings for her might be more than friendship, but then she hooked up with my buddy and teammate Zeke. Seeing how happy she is now makes me realize things worked out exactly like they were supposed to.

"I can't have a regular job—my scholarship comes with all sorts of stipulations."

"I'm pretty sure no dealing drugs is somewhere in the fine print," she mocks.

"I was desperate and dumb. I thought it'd just be the one time. I'd make some quick cash to send home and be done, and then... well, it wasn't."

"How long?"

"Two years."

Her mouth falls open, and I know that look will haunt me. It's not judgment; it's pity.

"But you're done now?"

"Yeah."

She fixes me with a gaze that's all worry and concern.

"Really. I'm done, I already told Frank, but I gotta pay him back for the weed and Xanax that Wes flushed. Plus, I still need to figure out a way to make sure my brother has what he needs to get through the next year."

She chews on her bottom lip like she's forcing herself to hold back.

"What?"

"Is Heath playing hockey really that important that you'd risk your own future?"

"It's not just about hockey; it's making sure he has the same opportunities I did."

"I could lend you some cash. I don't have a lot, but—"

"No way. I'm not dragging you into my mess. I got myself into this, I'll figure a way out."

"I could talk to Brady at The Hideout. Maybe you could pick up some shifts."

"Thanks, but between practice and school, I don't know how many hours I could put in. It'd take me forever to make the money working a day or two a week, and that's assuming Coach would even sign off on it, which I highly doubt."

Which is exactly what led me to Frank in the first place.

Later that night, I wake with a start, drenched in

sweat. My chest heaves as I gulp air like I've been underwater for too long. Scanning the room, I take in the damage. Mattress is half off the box spring, bedding is on the floor, as well as the pillows.

The stillness of the house tells me it's the middle of the night even before I check the time. I contemplate trying to fall back asleep, I'm tired as hell, but I grab my phone and a fresh shirt and head downstairs to work out.

More nights than not, this is where I end up—in the living room at two a.m. lifting weights. Gabby told me once she works out for the endorphins and that feeling she gets when she's done like she could take on the world. I work out to chase away the ghosts. Maybe ghosts hate endorphins or maybe they like them and steal all mine because I don't feel anything like world domination when I'm done.

seven

Chloe

$\mathcal{S}$chool starts and I've never been so glad to have an excuse to get out of my room and focus on something besides myself and my teammates, who are still treating me like I'm all that's wrong in the world. Although, the outright insults have stopped. They've been replaced by intense stares that I'm positive have everything to do with Nathan Payne.

They haven't asked, but I can see the questions every time they look at me. Turns out he's kind of a big deal. According to Emily and Sydney, and my stellar eavesdropping skills, the entire basketball team are like gods around here. If they all look like Nathan, I can understand why.

The Valley campus is smaller than my previous college in California and easier to navigate, but I still find myself walking into both my Monday morning classes just as the professors started. The campus map I studied for an hour is harder to remember while trying to avoid the stares of my fellow students. I know it's probably paranoid to assume they all know and hate me, but the thought crosses my mind every time someone holds my gaze for a second too long or dismisses me without returning a smile.

I head to University Hall after my morning classes to grab lunch. I find a table in the corner to sit. Earbuds in, I FaceTime my best friend Camila.

"You are alive," she answers the phone, her black hair and olive complexion filling the screen and making me miss home with such ferocity my chest aches. "How's Arizona?"

"Awful. Save me."

She rolls her eyes. "So dramatic." Camila looks me over carefully. I can feel her scrutiny even through the screen. "Did you just get done with practice?"

"No. Our team workouts are in the afternoon. I just got done with my morning classes."

"You wore that to class?"

I glance down at my plain white t-shirt and cut-off jean shorts. "Yeah. What's wrong with it?"

"Nothing. It's just so… casual for you."

"I'm trying to blend in."

"Blend in where? At a monster truck rally? Honey, it's the first day of classes you always go all out."

Thinking back to some of the outfits I wore to classes at Golden, I can't argue that I've gone more casual, but it feels good, feels like me.

"Tell me about Valley. How are classes, how's the

team, how are the boys?" She emphasizes the last one with a smirk.

Nathan's face flashes in my head and my face heats. "Classes are good, the team still hates me, and I don't have time for boys."

She rolls her eyes.

"I'm serious. No distractions. I'm going to prove I'm one of the top volleyball players if I have to eat, sleep, and dream volleyball."

"You don't have to prove anything. Your record last year speaks for itself, Chlo."

"No one believes I earned any of that and you know it. Everything I accomplished at Golden is tainted. *This* is my chance to prove I can do it all on my own." I shake my head before she can argue her point any more. "I don't want to talk about me. Tell me about you. How's the team shaping up?"

I listen to her go on and on about my former team, and I'm filled with such longing and sadness I forget to guard against the onslaught of emotions, namely anger, that comes when I remember why I'm not there finishing out my college volleyball career on the best team in the country. The niggling doubt that maybe I never really belonged there isn't easy to push away either.

Maybe I earned my spot at Golden, maybe I didn't. Even I'm not sure anymore. If my parents were willing to buy my way into the college, who's to say they weren't also making sure I was getting to play? I hate that I don't know for sure if I ever truly belonged there in the first place.

"Tenley isn't you, but she's doing alright." Tenley is

The Fake

the girl who took my place as Camila's new partner.

"Thanks for saying so even if it's not true. I hate the idea of someone else being paired with you."

"That makes two of us." I watch the background change as she walks through campus. Valley's not so different, but it's not home.

"What are your weekends going to be like? Any chance you can come visit in a few weeks?"

"I'm not sure," I tell her honestly, but I leave out my misgivings about going back. Camila knows I didn't have anything to do with the scandal that got me kicked out, but not everyone is as understanding as her. And the only people who dislike me more than my teammates at Valley are those people at Golden who blame me for my parents' actions.

"I gotta go," she says. "I just walked into class. Think about visiting. I miss you."

"Miss you, too."

She puckers her lips to the screen and then she's gone.

I take what's left of my sandwich and eat it on the way to my last class for the day. I find it without getting lost, and I'm so relieved to be in my seat before the professor starts talking that I slump into my chair and let out a sigh.

I feel eyes on me and look over to see Sydney and Emily a few seats down. I give them a small wave and notice Emily staring from me to a spot just behind me with a strange expression. I turn in my seat just a fraction and look over my shoulder and right into Nathan's cocky grin.

Those lips say everything without forming a single

51

sound. Starting with *fancy seeing you here* and ending with a thousand impossibly dirty reminders of our night together.

It's been five days, and I think he got hotter somehow. Memories of the other night play in my mind like a porn highlight reel and I can't peel my eyes away from him. One-night stands are so not my thing. I don't mean that in some judgy way either. Sometimes I think I would be better off if I could treat sex as a casual endeavor, but I've never been able to really enjoy sex unless I'm super into the guy. It's a real travesty, I assure you.

Which is one of the million reasons I can't wrap my head around the multiple orgasms. I don't know if it was the Everclear or if my vagina just imprinted onto Nathan's penis, but I enjoyed the hell out of it. Or what I remember.

Plus, since the scandal at Golden, I've started to view my actions like they might end up front-page news and *Transfer Student Gets White Girl Wasted and Sleeps with First Guy She Meets* isn't how I want to start out at Valley.

I try and smile naturally at him, not letting him or my roommates see how frazzled I am. I say hello, voice wavering. He returns my greeting, keeping that cocky smirk plastered on his face as he lifts two fingers from the desk in a casual wave. He's totally pulling it off while I'm pretty sure I look like I walked into a surprise party completely naked.

A plain blue t-shirt the same color as his eyes, jeans, and that hair… messy hair shouldn't be this attractive. He's seated next to two other guys that I can now assume are basketball players. Now that I know that's his sport, I can totally see it. Tall, muscular but not bulky, and long and lean fingers that make heat bloom in my face when I remember what he did with them.

Professor Sanchez directs our attention to the whiteboard, and I'm all too thankful to have a reason to look forward.

"Welcome to Business Communications. I am Professor Sanchez. Let's get right to the important stuff, shall we? Attendance is not mandatory, *but* if you miss more than three of my classes, I will dock you a percent for every additional class missed."

A collective groan sweeps over the class. Classes with an attendance policy are the worst.

Professor Sanchez continues, "Ten percent will come from weekly quizzes, fifteen percent from homework, and that leaves…"

Someone up front finally says, "Seventy-five percent."

"Yes. Exactly." He picks up a stack of papers on his desk and hands them to the front row. "Take one and pass them around. Seventy-five percent of your grade in this class will come from the semester group project outlined in detail in the syllabus coming around. You will work in groups of two or three to create a pitch for a product not geared toward your demographic. You'll each choose a product from the basket. Find a partner and then one of you come up front to select your product."

Panic to find a partner has everyone glancing around the room.

"Go ahead. You'll have the rest of the class to get these details ironed out, and we'll reconvene on

Wednesday."

I turn my head just enough to see Nathan hasn't moved and he's watching me with amusement. Oh, God, now what?

Emily and Sydney are already huddled together reading the project syllabus and if I ask to be in their group, they're going to know I lied about Nathan and they may very well say no anyway.

I do a quick perusal of the entire classroom, but everyone is already pairing off. When I glance back at Nathan, the guy next to him elbows him and lifts the syllabus. Nathan says something in response that I can't make out, but when his blue eyes meet mine, he tips his head to the empty chair on his other side in an unmistakable invitation to join him.

Every step closer to him makes my heart hammer faster in my chest. "Hey, ummm, do you maybe wanna be partners?"

He tries and fails to keep from smiling. "That depends. Are you asking as my girlfriend or as the girl who kicked me out of her room before I'd even got my pants on?"

My face flushes and I freeze, grappling for how to respond.

"Relax, I'm kidding." He motions again to the chair next to him.

I sit. "I'm so sorry."

"For which thing?"

This time, at my loss for words, he doesn't try and hide the giant grin on his face. "This is gonna be fun."

He picks up the syllabus from his desk and starts to read. I'm still gawking at him a minute later when he says, "If you keep staring at me like that, though, I might get a little creeped out."

"Sorry." I duck my head and hide behind the paper. I skim the project guidelines, noting mostly how much time Nathan and I are going to be forced to spend together. If he's at all put out by the idea, he doesn't let on. Leaning back in his chair, one leg is stretched out at an angle to accommodate his height. His hair is a little too long on top, but the messy look suits him. So does the scruff.

"So, what do you think?" he asks as he sets the paper down.

"Fine."

He smirks.

Get it together, Chloe. "Do you want to exchange numbers? It looks like we're going to need to work on this outside of class."

Two long seconds pass before he scribbles his number on a piece of paper and passes it to me. "Knew you'd change your mind about wanting my number."

He stands and shoulders his backpack, giving me a wink before he heads out of the class.

"What about picking our product?" I call after him.

"You pick, let me know what we got when you text me."

I'm still jittery from my encounter with Nathan when I make the walk from campus to practice. It's going to be a very long semester seeing him in class three times a week. He's ridiculously hot and charming and everything I don't need in my life right now. Volleyball has to be my focus. The other night was... well, it was pretty spectacular, if I'm honest, but it can't happen again. Not until I've proven myself. I need to know that I'm capable of doing it all on my own.

But working beside Nathan all semester is going to be a sweet kind of torture.

I get to the courts one minute before practice— perfectly timed to avoid being in the line of Bri's wrath for longer than necessary. Standing off to the side by myself while my teammates chat, I strip off my shoes and grab my sunglasses before tossing my bag in the sand.

Coach won't arrive for another fifteen minutes, giving our captain the responsibility of getting us warm and loose.

"Three laps," Bri calls out and the team shuffles to the perimeter and begins the run around the courts. I step in line, clearing my head of the day and ready to get to work, but Bri's voice yelling my name is like nails on a chalkboard. "Chloe. You've brought opponent colors to practice." *Shit.* I glance toward my Golden team bag. Valley and Golden colors are similar, but I get it. It's disrespectful, and I hadn't even done it on purpose. "Since you're such a fan, today you can practice with the bag."

She can't mean I have to carry my bag all through practice. But the icy stare she gives me tells me just how serious she is. I walk back toward my bag with anger radiating. I wouldn't be surprised if there was steam coming out my ears. Anger at my bitchy captain. Anger at myself for being so stupid. And anger at my parents for my being here.

I loop the bag over my shoulder and step into line a full lap behind already.

The Fake

After practice, I walk back to the dorm slowly. I'm so tired I don't even care that no one looks up or speaks to me when I head through the common area to my room. I stop at the sight of the Valley Volleyball backpack on my bed.

"Hey." Sydney pokes her head in before walking all the way into our room. "Do you like it? I managed to get you one of the new ones instead of the hideous ones from two years ago that are some awful purply-blue color."

"Thank you, I should have thought of that." I start transferring the essentials to my new bag.

"There's a supply closet in the locker room at the fieldhouse. I only grabbed the bag, but there are shirts and water bottles and some other stuff too."

I face her and see nothing but sincerity. I want to hug her, but I hold back. Someday, I hope we can get there. Just one more reason I need to focus on volleyball. If I prove myself on the court, I think my teammates will be more inclined to accept me. "Thank you. I appreciate it, really. I didn't even think about bringing my old bag to practice."

I've carried it for the better part of three years. So much that it feels weird when I pick up the Valley one and try it out. It's bigger and made just different enough that it feels unnatural.

She shrugs and looks like she might want to say more, but Bri calls for her from the living room. Sydney smiles apologetically. "You're welcome."

Tuesday is far less eventful. I don't have any more run-ins with Nathan, and I give Bri absolutely no reason to yell at me during practice. I'm in full Valley gear, and I work my ass off. Coach even comments on my performance, telling me to keep it up.

Wednesday afternoon, I head to class early so I can grab a seat before Nathan gets here. I try and busy myself with my phone, but I'm still aware of the exact moment he walks in. His deep voice slides over my skin, leaving goosebumps. "Can I sit by you?"

I gesture to the seat beside me, the same one he sat in last class, and he lets his backpack drop to the floor as he sits. He looks to me expectantly.

"What?" I say finally, an unsteady smile spreading across my face at his cheeky grin.

"I'm waiting for you to apologize."

"For?"

"Not calling me. You asked for my digits and then never called."

I think he's trying to look hurt, but the smirk on his face is too damn irresistible to feel too sorry for him. "I'm sure you managed to fill your time just the same."

He shrugs. "A guy can't wait around forever."

"Forty-eight hours is hardly forever."

His smirk turns into a full-blown panty-melting smile.

"What'd we get?" he asks, referencing the product for our project.

"A pen." I dig out the paper with the information and hand it to him, but I'm saved from any more of his charm when Professor Sanchez starts in on today's lecture.

For fifty long minutes, I do my best to take notes and absorb the material, which is a feat of Olympic proportions with Nathan beside me. He makes me feel so... aware. Aware of him and of my body reacting to him. This is ridiculous. Hot guys don't usually turn me into a distracted mess, but there's just something about him.

When Professor Sanchez dismisses us, I shoot up from my seat, ready to flee. Nathan slides his leg out in front of him before standing, blocking my exit path.

"You got plans tonight?"

I don't, of course. "Yeah, sorry."

He doesn't look like he believes me. "We're having a party tonight."

Sydney and Emily slide up behind me. We're in their way, but they look less interested in leaving than they do eavesdropping.

"Text me, you have my number." He steps into the aisle and then looks back. "Hope to see you later."

His long legs carry him out of the auditorium quickly, and I stand stupidly frozen in place until he's gone.

"I still can't believe you're dating him," Sydney says. "He's so hot."

Emily pushes in front of Sydney so she's walking beside me as we climb the stairs. "You're going tonight, right?"

"Actually, I'm pretty tired. I think I'm going to stay in."

"What?! No way," Emily says loudly and then lowers her voice. "We have to go."

"We?" I don't even try to hide the humor in my tone.

Emily's never been mean to me like Bri, but this is the most she's spoken to me directly. Still, I think we could be friends if it weren't for the weird situation we're in, so I don't call her out for trying to use me to go to my fake boyfriend's party.

"I think this could be good for all of us. Bri would never admit it, but she's dying to go. She's shyer than you'd think when it comes to socializing with people outside the team," Sydney says as we push out of the building.

Emily nods her agreement.

"So, I just invite her to the party and all will be forgiven?"

She snorts. "God, no. First, we convince her to go, then we have to show her how awesome you are, then maybe she'll ease up."

"That sounds simple enough." I roll my eyes.

"Just leave it to us." Sydney and Emily take off, smiling and laughing as I follow behind them to practice. Why do I think my fake boyfriend has already been more trouble than he's worth?

I'm lying in bed reading when Sydney storms into our room with matching neon green towels wrapped around her body and on top of her head. She's got a big smile on her face. "Get up. I talked Bri into going and I made a few calls. Practically the whole team is going." She does a little happy squeal and claps her hands.

"The whole team?" I ask, panic rising. I don't need any more witnesses to what is surely going to be an epic failure of a night. I don't know any real details about the party. I don't even know where Nathan lives.

Resigning myself, I grab my phone.

Me: Hi. It's Chloe.

I wait for a response, tapping my pinky on the back of my phone. Sydney pulls three different dresses from our closet and puts them on the bed. Her wardrobe is a rainbow of colors and the three she pulled are no exception. A yellow dress with straps that crisscross in the back, a purple strapless spandex number, and a hot pink, super short dress with thick straps and a square neck.

After five minutes of watching Sydney deliberate, pick the hot pink dress and then switch to the purple one, and then go back to the hot pink, I still haven't heard from Nathan.

Me: So, this party... where is it? The roommates wanna go so looks like I'm in.

I try not to overthink it and press send. This way, if we run into each other, it won't be like I'm admitting to being into him. I mean, I don't even *want* to go... except I kind of don't hate the thought of seeing him again. Outside of class, of course, where I can flee at any second. And it's just a party. As long as I steer clear of the Everclear and don't invite him back to my dorm, all should be fine. We're going to be partners all semester so I might as well get used to spending time with him as friends.

"You should start getting ready," Sydney says as she plugs in her blow dryer and spritzes her hair with a heat protectant spray. "Parties at The White House are packed. It's best to get there early."

The White House? I feel like that name should mean something to me, so I don't ask what the hell The White House is even though I'm dying to know.

"What happened to showing up to parties fashionably late?" I bite my tongue before I add that at Golden we never arrived at a party before eleven. I need to quit reminding them of my past.

"You can be fashionably late to parties on frat row, but parties at The White House are the kind of events you want to be there for every possible minute. You don't want to miss anything. I mean, you've seen that place, it's incredible. They've had some epic parties there."

"Mhmm." I brush past her and disappear into the closet. "How do you guys want to get there? Should we take an Uber?"

She laughs. "Did you guys seriously Uber to parties within walking distance at Golden? We'll just walk. It would take us longer to get an Uber than it would to walk there. Wear flats and carry your heels; that's what I always do. We can stop and slip on our heels before we cross over at the fieldhouse."

I store every piece of information she offers in case I need it later. It's going to be a very long night.

eight

Nathan

*D*atson is wearing a beer guzzler helmet, passing out cups for the keg, and making a point to talk to every one of the fifty or so people walking around the first floor of our house. He and Shaw moved in today, and Datson has named himself the one-man welcoming committee.

"How are the new roommates?" Gabby asks as I follow her around the party.

"Good." I shrug and step in front of her to stop someone from plowing into her. The party is just getting started, and people are already beyond drunk. First week of school parties are crazy.

"Where's your drink?" she asks, finally noticing I don't have one. Aside from the night with Chloe, I'd been doing a good job of keeping the partying under control. Before I can answer, she grabs my hand and pulls me toward the kitchen.

Datson swoops in just as we near the liquor bottles on the counter. He holds out a red cup. "Need a cup or are you drinking straight from the bottle tonight?"

I take a cup without answering him and head to the keg and pour a beer.

"Now you're ready," she says and links her arm through mine. I'm not sure if I should be insulted or not that no one has noticed how much I've cut back.

"Ready for what?" I ask, noticing the huge grin on her face that is a dead giveaway that she's up to no good.

"Operation girlfriend."

Both brows lift under the hair falling into my eyes. I brush it away and go to tuck it behind my ears. It's a habit that makes me miss my long hair. I cut it a few months ago, and I'm still not used to my once chin-length hair being cropped short.

"I don't think I'm exactly in the place right now for a girlfriend. I couldn't even buy her a drink at the bar."

I know she heard me, but Gabby ignores me and pulls me around the room. "Alright, what's your type? Blonde, brunette, redhead? Ooh, how about that girl over there with the pink hair?"

Shaking my head, I indulge her. "What if her natural color is awful, and she goes back to it a month after we're dating?"

"That is strangely insightful." Gabby stops and glances around the room. I do a quick perusal and drop my eyes. Having my best friend shop for girls for me isn't awkward at all. She huffs something about my being picky. "How about the girl in the yellow dress by the window?"

The Fake

Gabby moves toward her before I can respond. I've never seen her and she looks nervous. Yellow dress, blonde hair, tall and tan—athletic build. I can't place which sport, but I'm banking on her being a student-athlete. Ten bucks she's a freshman. Or, I guess, ten high fives because that's all I'm fucking good for.

"Hi!" Gabby startles the poor girl, and I do my best to hang back and not make this situation any more painful than it already is.

I love Gabby, I do. She's full of life and has nothing but good intentions but I don't want to be set up. I think dating and relationships should happen naturally when you least expect it. Just walking along minding your own business and BAM, hot girl drops in front of you. Sort of like how Chloe and I met, but with less alcohol and exactly zero of the shame and regret in the girl's eyes the next morning.

Speaking of, I glance around the room in hopes she came, but even before my eyes finish a once over of the room, I know she's not here. When Chloe is around, I can feel it.

Gabby pulls me closer as she introduces herself. "I'm Gabby. Are you new?"

The girl nods and looks like she's about to pass out from nerves. "Maureen."

When I don't speak up for myself, Gabby continues, "This is Nathan. So, Maureen, are you single? Do you think my friend here is cute?"

I take a sip of my beer and it goes down all wrong, making my throat burn and my eyes water. When I can speak, I say, "Excuse her, too much time sniffing glue as a kid melted her brain."

"Whaaat?" Gabby asks innocently.

"You can't ask people things like that," I mutter and offer Maureen an apologetic smile.

She giggles, and I know she's not for me. It's not a sound I can imagine hearing every day. Probably petty, but shouldn't a guy want to hear his girl laugh?

"At least she didn't eat it," Maureen says.

"I like her," Gabby proclaims, her eyes not leaving Maureen. My best girl may have visions of braiding hair and naked pillow fights, but I have no such fantasies. I mean, well, okay, that's a damn good visual regardless of my disinterest.

"And I'm single," Maureen adds, interrupting me from mentally undressing her, except the naked vision of her isn't her at all.

I can't get Chloe off the brain no matter how hard I try. But she isn't here and Maureen is, so the least I can do is be a gentleman and make a little small talk. "Where are you living?"

Before Maureen can answer, Gabby pulls away. "I'm going to get a drink." She winks at me and then turns to Maureen. "Nice to meet you."

"I live in Freddy. What about you?"

"I live here."

"Really?" Her eyes are wide, and I swear she went from sort of interested to planning our destination wedding.

I'm about to tell her I need to take a piss just to get away without being rude, when she places a hand on my forearm. The nervous and shy girl is gone and replaced by one who wants to eat me alive. "Why don't you show me around?"

I take her through the kitchen and outside. We've got a nice patio set up and a pool that several people have already jumped in.

"And this is the backyard," I say because honest to God, I just don't know what else to say. Clever, I am not.

"Oh, that pool is amazing!"

Dock another point for the high-pitched squeal that has me squeezing my eyes shut. "You like to swim?"

"I'm on the Valley swim team."

"Ah."

She slips off her shoes and then takes my hand as she heads toward the pool. She's got a death grip on me, and she drags me behind her. I manage to slip out of her clutches as she steps down into the pool. It's only a couple feet deep and her dress is plenty short enough to stay dry. I step back and watch as she twirls around and splashes in it.

I spot Shaw, who is also in the pool. He eyes Maureen with interest. She seems nice, I'm just not feeling it, so I motion with my head for him to go for it. It's two seconds too late, though. Maureen uses those long legs to run and jump from where she stands in the shallow end to me on the top step. She flings her arms around my neck and I'm crashing forward, taking us both into the pool before I know what's what.

Chloe

One step inside The White House and I understand why my roommates were so excited about coming. The house itself is huge and white... hence the name, I suppose. I try and act casual and like I've been here before as we step through the front door into a huge entryway.

The living room and kitchen are open concept and extend into one huge space. To the right is a staircase, and I'm guessing that's where the bedrooms are. We pass by a theater room and a bathroom that already has a line of girls waiting their turn.

This place is extravagant. And I know extravagant.

"Who took Zeke and Wes' spots in the house?" Sydney asks and they all look to me.

Emily and Sydney have dropped all pretenses of freezing me out now that they know my White House connection, but Bri is watching me like she's waiting for me to screw up. I wish I didn't feel like that's exactly what I'm about to do. I don't even know for sure if Nathan is here. He still hasn't responded to my texts.

"I'm not sure," I answer and keep moving. The place is packed just like Sydney said it would be. I need to find Nathan so I can... crap, what am I going to do when I find him?

"Ladies." A guy with dark hair sticking out around a red beer helmet steps in front of us with cups. "Welcome. Keg and liquor are in the kitchen."

The girls all take a cup and head in the direction of

the booze and I hang back.

"Hey, have you seen Nathan?" I ask him quietly.

"Pool," he offers as he places a cup in my hand.

"Thanks." I exhale a sigh of relief that Nathan is here, but then that starts off a whole new set of emotions—namely excitement at seeing him again. And crap, I need to reel it in. Friends... we're just going to be friends.

I slip past Bri and Emily without them noticing. Sydney and I make eye contact and I mouth, "Be right back."

The outside is as nice as the rest of the house. The yard is bigger than I expected with a large patio that is partially covered. The pool is the real showstopper, though. There are a dozen cushioned lounge chairs placed around it, all filled with people.

Quite a few people are in the pool, too, and my gaze flits over the girls lying in neon light-up floaties and snags on a couple in the shallow end coming out of the pool fully dressed. The girl is giggling at the state of them. Her dress is molded to her skin, leaving very little to the imagination, but she doesn't care. She's holding on to the guy and he's... breathtaking.

I know because I inhale sharply and forget to breathe as I take him in. Desire, panic, jealousy—I feel all of those things and nothing at all because the guy... the freaking guy is my fake boyfriend.

nine

Chloe

I watch in what feels like slow motion as Nathan pulls
himself out of the pool. The pretty blonde attached to
him is all smiles. Well, this is spectacularly awful. The
guy my friends think I'm dating is here with someone
else and my roommates are about to find out I'm a big
fat liar.

Also, I think I might be disappointed, which is
ridiculous. We're just friends. Friends who slept
together once after a drunken night of secret sharing.

"Is that Nathan?" Sydney's voice is right behind me
and the claustrophobic feeling that tightens my chest
tells me Bri and Emily are also near and watching the
foray between Nathan and his actual date for the night.

"Yep."

Sydney scoffs. "What a ho. You should go tell that

girl to get her mitts off your man."

I resist laughing at this totally messed up situation but just barely.

When Nathan turns so I can get a good look at his face, it doesn't look altogether pleased, which makes me feel a teensy bit better. He looks up and directly at me like he knew exactly where to find me. My pulse quickens, and I break eye contact first, staring at my feet and wishing I'd never agreed to come here tonight.

Did I really think I could waltz in here and he'd snap to my side and pretend to be my boyfriend while I win over my teammates?

When I look back up, he's coming my way with a sexy smirk. He's completely soaked. The white t-shirt he's wearing clings to him and if there were such a thing as a male wet t-shirt contest, he'd win. Hands down. Cut abs that I've seen, felt, licked—oh, my freaking God—are clearly visible. I'm making my way down his body, trying not to ogle and failing miserably, when he gets to us. The blonde is two steps behind, not letting my man, correction, *her man*, get away.

"Hey, Surfer Princess, you came." He briefly looks to each of my roommates and nods.

I hear Bri scoff and repeat the nickname like it annoys her.

The blonde catches up and stands next to him, wringing out her hair. "Oh, my God, I'm soaked."

Nathan stands in front of me, dripping wet but smiling like he's happy to see me and not the least bit bothered by his drenched clothes. I'm not sure how long we stand there just staring at one another before the blonde interrupts.

"Do you think I could borrow some dry clothes?" She bites at her bottom lip and looks up at Nathan innocently. I know that look and I cannot let her go with him. If he were my boyfriend, I'd be crazy jealous right now. In fact, my fake feelings are confusing the hell out of my body because I *am* jealous right now.

Sydney elbows me and I stumble forward. I'm standing so close I can see drops of water running down from his hairline. I reach out and place a hand on his hard, cold chest without thinking. "Hey."

I'm too breathless. Too scatterbrained. Too affected by him. And he freaking knows it.

"Hey," he parrots.

"Can I talk to you for a minute?"

"Mhmm." His smile is filled with innuendo.

I'm pretty sure he thinks talk means take off all our clothes, but I don't have time or the privacy to correct him. I need to get him alone and beg him not to out me.

A guy wearing hot pink swim trunks with little alligators on them slung low on his hips joins us. He looks familiar, but I can't place him. "Dude, that was hilarious. You should have seen your face when she pulled you in." He looks to me. "Hey, you're the girl from Comm class."

Nathan tips his head toward the guy. "Chloe, this is my teammate Tanner Shaw."

Tanner lifts his chin. "And roomie."

"He and John Datson moved in today," Nathan clarifies. "Shaw, can you lend Maureen some dry clothes?"

"Definitely," Shaw responds and wraps an arm around her shoulders. Maureen only looks disappointed for a second before she recovers and bats her eyelashes at Shaw.

I remove my hand from Nathan's chest, but he grabs it now, sending a possessive thrill through me.

Sydney steps toward us, takes my elbow, and whispers, "Don't disappear all night. This is a good opportunity to spend time with the team."

I nod, and then she adds, "And bring your man and his new roomie with you."

Nathan leads me back into the house. He pushes through the crowd, never dropping my hand and tugging me with him. I follow behind, watching his shoulder and back muscles work under the thin, wet material of his shirt. I'm aware that people are staring at him and saying things, but his touch—even cold and damp—makes it hard to concentrate on anything else. The way I feel when he's around makes it easy to remember how I ended up drunk and naked the first time we met.

He leads me up the stairs, past a basketball court and a couple of bedrooms before he steps inside a room and flips on the light. "This is me."

The room is a decent size, but the contrast to the rest of the house is apparent. A simple bed and desk are the only furniture and there isn't a single thing hanging on the wall. He strips off his t-shirt and holds it in his hand. "So…"

"Sooo," I mimic, and he grins.

"You said you wanted to talk to me or was that code for get naked because you're still fully clothed?"

"Oh, right." I walk around his room to avoid staring at him, taking in details about him. Detail one, his phone is on his desk so maybe he wasn't ignoring me. Detail two, there are no less than five half-empty Powerade bottles also on the desk, but no laptop or books. "Sorry to just drop in. I tried to text."

"It's a party. No need to RSVP, sweetheart."

"My roommates still think we're together."

"Yeah, I got that from the death glares they were sending me and Maureen."

"Sorry if I ruined your date for the night." I turn to face him so he can see I mean it. He's dropped his jeans and only wears a pair of wet black boxer briefs that do nothing to hide... well, everything. I quickly turn back around, heat flooding my face. "I'll go down there and tell them the truth. This whole charade has gone on long enough. You must think I'm crazy."

His phone rings, cutting off any response he might have been about to say. He picks it up and looks at the screen, his brows pulling together as he says, "Sorry, I gotta get this. Can we talk later?"

"Of course." I move to the door. "Is there a bathroom up here I could use?"

He points. "Across the hall."

"Thanks."

He nods as he puts the phone to his ear and answers.

I let myself out and find the bathroom. Inside, I splash my face and search for the words to try and explain this to my roommates, but I'm at a total loss. The little bit of ground I won tonight is going to be pulled out from under me when they find out I made the whole thing up.

Why couldn't I have just owned up to my one night with Nathan? Looking back, I don't think it's possible that my roommates could have possibly disliked me any more than they already did just because I got drunk and slept with the first person who was nice to me. I think it's because I could see it in their eyes—acceptance. They couldn't believe he was with me and dammit, why wouldn't he be? I'm pretty fantastic.

Acceptance. I sigh. Isn't that what led me to sleep with him in the first place? He looked at me like I was just me and not the girl who was shrouded in scandal. I wasn't lying when I told him I don't do that. The blackout drunk or the one-night stand.

I'm so embarrassed I threw myself at him only a few hours after we met. And yes, I *threw* myself at him. I remember that much very clearly. He kissed me and then I practically ripped my clothes off.

I stare at my reflection in the mirror above the sink. I look the same as the girl who was living in California, the girl who had very few cares in the world, but I can't tell the real from the fake anymore. Who am I if I'm not the girl who was given a full-ride scholarship to Golden to play volleyball? Did I deserve that spot or, like everything else, was it bought for me by parents who love me maybe a little too much to see how doing such a thing could be worse for me than letting me fail?

Letting out a deep breath, I shake my head and decide that it doesn't matter. All I can do now is focus on showing my new teammates that I deserve to be here. This is my chance.

Out in the hallway, I take a step toward the stairs, but Nathan's voice grabs my attention. Even in a hushed tone, I can tell he's upset.

"How could you be so fucking stupid?"

I freeze and press myself against the hallway wall. It sounds like something is thrown to the floor before he speaks again. "It's stupid and reckless. You're not Vin Diesel, bro. Quit tearing up the road like you're auditioning for the next Fast and Furious spinoff. Fuck, Heath. You gotta help me out here, I'm doing the best that I can."

I'm holding my breath, heart racing. I know I should stop listening, but I cannot make my feet move.

"Yeah, alright," his gruff voice comes once more followed by silence like he's hung up the phone. I start down the stairs when he calls out, "FUCK!"

I glance back just as he exits his room. He doesn't see me, but I can't miss the wild intensity of his blue eyes. He takes off in the opposite direction, and I follow after him. He looks like a man about to make very bad decisions.

I hurry to keep up, which is no easy task in these heels. He heads down the hall and enters another bedroom. This one is bigger and looks a lot more lived in. He doesn't touch anything in the room, though. He moves to a slider and opens it to a small balcony that overlooks the backyard and the party below.

He's pacing, running both hands through his hair. He looks like a caged animal. Finally, he lights up a cigarette and closes his eyes as he inhales. When he opens them, he glances over to me like he knew I'd be standing there, though I don't think he saw me follow him.

"Wanna talk about it?"

"It's fine." He blows out a cloud of smoke and shakes his head. He doesn't look like he's going to be sharing his troubles anytime soon so I lean my hip against the railing and we stand like that in our own quiet bubble away from the noise and chaos below. We've got a bird's eye view of the party, but Nathan stares straight ahead into the night. I don't know what I expected by following him out here, but he looks like he could use a friend.

I'm starting to get cold and wondering how much longer we're going to stand out here when he says, "I don't think you're crazy."

It takes me a minute to realize he's referring to our talk earlier. "That makes one of us. I don't recognize myself anymore. Crazy is probably the nicest way to describe sleeping with you, freaking out, and then conning my roommates into thinking you're my boyfriend."

"I think it's the first time anyone has ever used me to get ahead." He chuckles. "I kinda liked it. I'm usually the guy girls use to piss off their nice conservative fathers or boyfriends."

"Well, if I'm ever looking to piss off my dad, I'll keep you in mind." He's smiling and I feel good about that. "Alright. I should get down there and see if I can get my teammates drunk enough that they like me after they find out I made up a boyfriend to win them over. You're good?"

He nods, and I turn to leave. I'm only a step away when he says my name quietly—rough like sandpaper. "Chloe."

"Yeah?"

"It was fun being your fake boyfriend. Just be yourself. They'll come around. And if you ever wanna go out again for real…" He trails off with a shrug.

"Thank you, I'm just not in a place to date for real right now." He nods in understanding, puts his cigarette out, and we walk back into the house, passing through the bedroom and into the hallway. "And you? Everything going to be okay with you? It was hard not to overhear."

He lets out a small chuckle. "Little brother." He shakes his head. "God, he makes me so mad sometimes. The idiot got two speeding tickets in the same fucking week."

"I didn't peg you as such a responsible big brother."

"Yeah, well, when I gotta figure out how to pay for it... it makes me a helluva lot more responsible."

My mouth forms an O and I start to ask why he has to pay for it but stop myself because it's really none of my business. Nathan reads the questions on my face, though.

"My family back in Michigan is struggling a bit. My dad passed away, Mom lost her job..." He checks himself and smiles stiffly like he's afraid he's overshared. "Anyway, my problem."

I try to hide the pity I feel, but I know he sees it when he adds, "It's fine. Really. I'm not usually such a downer. Let's get you a drink."

My phone buzzes and I pull it from my purse to check as we walk.

Sydney: Where are you? We're all out on the patio. Come get to know everyone! You can make out with your hot man later.

"Wait," I say as Nathan starts to descend the stairs.

The Fake

"What if we could help each other?"

He cocks a brow. "What do you mean?"

ten

Nathan

"No way. Now I do think you're crazy."

Chloe looks deflated by my resistance. Her full red lips fall into a frowny pout. This girl isn't used to hearing no, and I can see why. She's fucking adorable and sexy when things aren't going her way.

"I told you, it's fine. I'll figure it out."

"I just figured it out for you," she insists. "Seriously. We pretend to keep dating for a little while longer, and I'll pay you for your time." That last bit has her looking unsure for the first time since she told me her idea.

"I can't take your money when I'm trying to date you for real."

She quirks a brow. "Date or fuck?"

Not gonna lie, my dick twitches at her use of the word.

She doesn't wait for my response. "Look, I've got a lot riding on this season. I need my teammates to like and respect me or I might as well give up and head back to California now. For some reason, my dating you makes them like me more." She rolls her eyes, but she's smiling.

"So that's a hard no to dating for real?"

She laughs, and the sound makes my entire body feel lighter. *This* is how I want my girlfriend's laugh to make me feel.

She doesn't respond but her face tells me she's already made up her mind.

"I get it, and I respect it. And I appreciate the offer, but I don't need a quick hundred dollars. I need a grand, at least."

The blank stare she gives me has me feeling uneasy about the hope spreading inside me. Fuck. Could it really be this easy? Fake date a girl I actually like—talk about a dream job.

"No," I say again, mostly for my own benefit.

Bending down, Chloe unbuckles the delicate straps of her silver heels. They wrap around her ankles in the sexiest way but turns out her taking them off—also sexy. She steps out of them and picks both shoes up in one hand, stands, and extends them toward me.

"Not really my style."

She rolls her eyes. "These shoes are worth over nine hundred dollars. You could probably sell them for close to that. I've only worn them once."

"Nine hundred dollars? For shoes?!" I shake my head. "I'm not taking your shoes."

"The point is I have the money." She shrugs one

shoulder. "You're used to people using you to piss people off, I'm used to people using money for all the wrong reasons."

"And I'm a good reason? Spare me the pity. Heath can rot in jail for unpaid tickets." Though as I say it, my stomach twists. Fucking Heath.

"It's not pity."

I give her a hard look.

"Okay, not entirely."

I start to blow by her before I do something stupid like agree to take money from her, but she steps in front of me. "Let me do this. Please? Let me do something good with my money for a change. And it isn't like I'm getting nothing out of this. My teammates think you're hot and awesome. Two of them have already started speaking to me just because they think I'm dating you. A few more weeks and I think I can get them to truly accept me." She places a hand on my chest and warmth spreads through me. "Volleyball is everything to me. It's all I've lived for, for as long as I can remember. It's my last year, and I want to prove to myself and everyone else that I deserve to be here. And I need them to like me at least a little bit for that."

"I don't know," I say, but I already feel like the weight of the world has been lifted off my shoulders just entertaining the offer. I run a hand through my hair. "Hot and awesome, huh?"

She rolls her eyes. "Their words, not mine." She puts her shoes back on the floor and holds on to my shoulder as she steps into them. I watch, fascinated, as she buckles five-hundred-dollar bills onto each foot. She stands when she's done, nearly eye-level to my six-foot-three height. "So, we have a deal?"

My throat is thick, so I nod my agreement.

We head down the stairs and back to the party. Am I really doing this?

"Should we set some sort of terms?" she asks.

I shrug. "Never done this before. Not really sure. Let's just roll with it."

This whole thing is bizarre. I don't say that though because this bizarre thing is saving my ass. Best not to think through the details too hard right now.

Her confidence deflates a bit when we find her teammates outside, and that makes me ready to do anything for her. Pretending to be her boyfriend is low level when I think of the things I'd probably be willing to do to win her over.

"Okay, you ready?" she asks as we stand a few feet away.

"Just one thing."

"What?" A tiny crease forms between her eyes as if she's deeply concentrating on some minor detail she's forgotten in the fake boyfriend user guide.

"No sex."

The crease disappears, and her brows raise. "Okay, no sex."

"You agreed way too easily."

She smiles and responds dryly, "I'm hurting on the inside."

I chuckle, and I can sense her relax a bit.

"Alright. I'm ready."

She hesitates. "Wait, why don't you want to have sex with *me*?"

I grin and step closer. The wind blows her hair into

her face, and I lightly brush my fingers across her forehead and tuck it behind her ear. Her breaths come quick and shallow as I lean in. "Because when we sleep together again, I want to know it wasn't for any other reason than how hot and awesome I am."

She laughs—that sweet, perfect sound.

She doesn't move and neither do I. I want to kiss her and make her remember how good we were together, but this is her show now. I'm just expensive arm candy. Maybe I should feel shitty about the whole situation, but I'm too relieved at the moment to feel anything else. Not to mention, jacked about spending more time with Chloe.

She takes a step back and then pauses and comes forward two and presses herself flush against me. Both hands rest on my chest as her lips touch mine, hesitant and unsure. My surprise at her actions makes me slow to respond, but when I taste summer, my body is frantic for more. Deepening the kiss, my hands go to her hips and then around her back. I press her tighter against me, forgetting all about the party, her roommates, my money troubles—it's just me and her.

"What was that about?" I ask when she pulls back, far too quickly.

We're both out of breath, and her cheeks have dots of pink. "Thought we should get it out of the way so it isn't awkward between us." Her eyes dart to my lips.

My dick has serious questions about what the fuck we just got ourselves into. Awkward is the last thing I feel as I pull her toward her teammates before I break my own rule on night one.

Chloe

Nathan and I sit side by side on a lounge chair facing Sydney and Emily. Bri and two of my other teammates have also joined us, and I mentioned to Nathan that Sydney thought Shaw was cute and now he's wandered over, too.

Nathan is the picture of comfort beside me. He has one hand on my thigh and continues to field questions as Sydney drills him about the basketball team and what it was like winning the NCAA tournament last year. My roommate is either overdoing it to include me and Nathan or she's a closet hardcore basketball fan.

I, on the other hand, am a nervous wreck. Our agreement has fully sunk in and the fact I agreed to pay him to pretend to be my boyfriend is making me spiral a bit. I know it's not the same as buying, say a place on the volleyball team or admission to a top university, but using money to solve problems still feels icky. Though, I meant what I said to him. It's nice to give money to someone who actually needs it instead of to people who just need to buy a third vacation home.

Nathan's big hand rests on my bare leg. He's got these big, powerful, long fingers that really work for me.

"Anybody need another drink. Nathan?" Shaw asks and takes one step toward the house.

Nathan shakes his head.

Shaw gives him a confused look. "You've been milking that same beer for the last hour."

"Keeping tabs on me?" he asks and then follows it up with, "I'm not drinking much anymore."

Shaw laughs. "Riiight."

"Really?" I can't keep the surprise out of my tone. The way he drank the night we met, the tolerance, the fact he was carrying a freaking flask, I had him pegged for a total party guy.

"It's a recent development," he admits, looking a little embarrassed. Then, with a sexy smirk, he leans in. "One too many mornings waking up naked to some crazy girl kicking me out of her place."

He'd said it just to me, but Shaw must have been listening because he pipes in, "Beer goggles. I so get that, my man. I've woken up next to some real dogs. You too, huh?"

Without taking his eyes from me, Nathan shakes his head. "Nah, my beer goggles have just as perfect vision as I do."

"Awww," Sydney squeals with delight. I don't glance around but I know everyone is watching us.

I crowd his space, my chest pressed against his shoulder and my lips at his ear so to everyone else it looks like a sweet, private moment. "Laying it on a little thick, aren't we?"

He turns his head and brushes his lips against mine. "Learn to take a compliment, Chloe. I'm the type of fake boyfriend who likes to give them."

I let out a shaky breath once he turns back to face the group. This fake dating thing is going to be tricky.

Shaw leaves and comes back juggling seven cups of beer, which he hands out. Everyone takes one despite no one speaking up when he asked.

"How did you two meet?" Bri asks when Shaw is seated next to her.

All eyes are on me.

"Oh, it's a boring story." I wave them off.

"What?" Nathan mocks, offended. "Don't be like that, sweetheart. Tell them how I won you over with a single glance."

I do some quick thinking to plausible places we could have happened into each other before the athletic mixer. "We met at the fieldhouse."

"And?" Sydney sits forward with wide eyes.

"And he asked me out."

"Worst re-telling of the story ever." Nathan's eyes twinkle as he plays along. He squeezes my leg with that big hand that hasn't moved from where it splays out over my left thigh. "What Chloe failed to mention is that she walked into our locker room."

"What?" A collective gasp. My teammates are really eating this up.

"Yep," Nathan continues. "She walked in early one morning and caught me as God intended."

Emily stares blankly.

"Naked."

Sydney giggles. "How did you get the locker rooms confused? They're on two different sides of the building!"

"Yeah, how did you get them mixed up?" Nathan asks, giving me an amused smile.

"Like you said, it was early, and I was still figuring out

the layout of the fieldhouse."

"So what happened after you walked in on him?" Mallory, a junior teammate, asks.

"Well..." I start and take a drink of my fresh beer to give me a second to think. "I was mortified and ran out of there as fast as I could, of course."

Nathan nods. "But I took one look at her and knew I had to ask her out so I threw on my gym shorts as fast as I could and took off after her."

Their eyes dart from him to me, so totally enraptured with this ridiculous story. What the heck, I'm in this deep.

"Inside out," I say, and the attention is back on me. "His shorts were on inside out when he came running after me."

Nathan's lips twitch. "Inside out," he repeats.

We stare at each other for a long moment. He's grinning wide and so am I. As fake dates go, I think we're nailing this one.

The rest of the night goes by without any more questions about our relationship that require us to make up wild stories. I yawn and Sydney scolds me as she tries to stop herself from doing the same. "Stop that. It's contagious."

The party has died down. No one is in the pool anymore. The music is still going, but the few people who are still hanging outside are standing around talking.

"I should probably go. Sydney and I have an eight o'clock class in the morning," I tell Nathan.

Sydney groans in protest of me leaving and surprisingly, I feel the same way. Somehow, I had fun tonight.

My teammates and I stand. Nathan and Shaw follow suit.

"I'll walk you guys out," Nathan offers.

Sydney stops. "You aren't sleeping over?" she asks me.

"Oh." I look to Nathan for help.

He wraps an arm around my waist and pulls me to him. "I've got early morning practice. How about I come by your dorm before class and we'll grab coffee?"

I nuzzle against him awkwardly and nod. "Sounds great."

God, he's good.

The walk back is uneventful and quiet. Well, except Sydney. She's been recapping the whole night for us, but by the silence from everyone else, I think it's safe to say we've all tuned her and her constant chatter out.

"And, wow, Chloe. Damn girl." My name out of Sydney's mouth grabs my attention. "The way Nathan looks at you." She looks up toward the sky and holds a hand to her heart.

"How does he look at me?"

"Totally smitten. He fell hard and fast." I stare at her in confusion, and she rolls her eyes. "He's in love with you. Which is crazy, since you've only been dating for such a short time."

"That is crazy."

Emily nods. "Crazy but true. It's pretty obvious."

I look to Bri for her take, knowing she won't bullshit me, but she stays quiet. She doesn't dispute my fake boyfriend's fake love though so I'm calling that a win.

eleven

Nathan

"We suck." Joel sits next to me on the sidelines, watching the team do a passing drill. His words are the nice version of what I'd been thinking as Datson and a freshman we've not so cleverly nicknamed Fresh, somehow collide. It's a disaster.

He looks to me when he speaks again, "We've gotta do something before Coach sees just how bad it is."

It's a captain's practice, which means Coach Daniels and the rest of the coaching staff aren't here. Regular season practices don't start for another week, but Joel is right. If Coach sees this, we'll spend the first week of real practice doing sprints until we get our shit together.

Joel stands after another bad pass goes flying out of bounds. "Come on, guys. It's passing the damn ball. Not that fucking hard."

The Fake

He walks out on the court firing instructions. Joel is a natural leader. The guys respect him, and they listen. He's a good captain. I haven't provided a lot of value to this point. I'm more like the silent partner who nods in agreement so we're a united front. I hardly feel qualified to hand out advice when I'm one mistake from being tossed myself.

After our morning practice, I shower and head to Freddy. I call Heath on my way to campus. With the time difference, he'll be up. And if he's not, well, he should be.

It's not Heath who answers though.

"Hi, Nathan."

"Mom, hi." I slow my walk. "Where's Heath?"

"School started back today."

"And he didn't take his phone?" I thought the thing was attached to his right hand.

"We're sharing a phone now. Having two was really a waste of money. Especially when I'm still paying for you to be on our plan."

I don't think she means to make me feel like a burden, but the fact that I might be somehow responsible for taking resources that they need has me feeling awful twenty seconds into the conversation.

"Nine more months and you can remove me forever," I say with a little more frustration than intended.

"Well, don't get all moody with me. I get enough of that from your brother." Her voice softens. "How's school?"

"It's fine. Listen, Mom, I just called to check in. Will you have Heath call me when he gets home?" I'm

91

probably a shitty son for not wanting to chat but talks with my mom never leave me feeling better.

"Sure, but I'm not expecting him until late. He's working at the country club after school today."

My feet turn to lead, and I pause in the middle of the sidewalk. "What about hockey?"

"He quit the team last night."

I don't ask why. I know he did it to try and help out financially, but if he quits then everything I've done to this point will have been for nothing. I shouldn't have been so hard on him last night. He's a kid, making kid mistakes.

"He can't quit, Mom. He's got a real shot at college."

She sighs. "I know. I tried to tell him, but he said he needed to start carrying his weight. I couldn't talk him out of it."

"I told him I'd figure something out."

"Even so, we're struggling to cover all the other expenses. It adds up. He understands. Maybe once I get a job…" Her words trail off. I'm not sure she even believes it enough to finish the sentence.

Waiting for my mom to get a job and then keep said job for more than a month is like wishing on a star. She sighs and the guilt I feel about Dad claws at my throat.

My mom was a teacher before my dad died. She worked at a private school teaching science. She was the mom who, despite working long hours grading papers and putting together lesson plans, still volunteered and still found time to be there for Heath and me. She never missed a high school game.

But now? Depression makes it hard for her to function. I've read all about it and I'm trying to be understanding, but it's hard not to take it personal sometimes. She hasn't made one single game since I've been at Valley, and I have my suspicions that she's not made a lot of Heath's games either. I don't know this woman and as awful as it might be, I don't really want to know her. I want to remember how she was before. It's almost as if I lost both parents four years ago.

"How much does he need?"

She's quiet for a few minutes. "Eight hundred. I have an interview today so I might be able to help in a couple of weeks."

I run a hand over my jaw. It's on the tip of my tongue to tell her she should consider maybe talking to someone, but it's not like I'm in any condition to dole out advice on a happy, healthy life. So instead, I say, "I don't have that much right now, but I'll do what I can."

Somehow. Some way.

She doesn't respond. No thank you, just dead air. I think she's embarrassed, but so am I. It's not cool to be the poor kid at any age.

"Make sure Heath is at practice today. If he misses too many days, the coach will cut him." Hockey is his dream, and he should get a chance to see it through. As much as I know my mom loves Heath and me, she can't see beyond herself right now and Heath needs someone to set an example and be there when he screws up. Because he's gonna keep doing stupid shit—it's part of being eighteen.

It's quarter 'til when I get to Freddy dorm and hustle up to the fourth floor.

Chloe answers with wet hair and a half-eaten apple in one hand. "Hey. What are you doing here?" she asks, holding her free hand in front of her lips as she chews and talks.

"We're having coffee before class."

"Oh, you were serious about that." She leaves the door open and walks over to a chair where she picks up her backpack. "Everyone's gone so we don't really have to do this."

Taking her bag and putting it over my shoulder with mine, I head out to the hallway and wait for her to join me. Maybe this is all fake to her, but I like spending time with her, and I'll take as much of it as she'll give me. Beats sitting around thinking about all the other shitfucked things going on. As long as I don't think about the circumstances too hard, all I feel about hanging out with Chloe is excitement.

"Wait," she says and goes for her bag.

"I got it."

She shakes her head and unzips one of the pockets and retrieves her phone. "Venmo okay?"

I nod and give her my email. My phone is in my pocket, but I feel the vibration from the notification when she's done.

"All good?" She walks past me toward the stairs.

I don't pull out my phone to check. "Yep."

That weight I'd been feeling is back. I brush it off so she can't see my misgivings. She's not paying me for my time, just for a façade, or that's how I rationalize it. Feels like salvation and destruction all at once.

"How are things with the roommates?" I ask as we exit the dorm.

"Sydney fell asleep still talking about the party last night, and it's been almost twenty-four hours since Bri glared at me."

"Progress."

She nods and takes another bite of her apple, then tosses it in a trash can outside of Freddy.

"What classes did you have this morning?"

"Applied Comm and Ethics."

"Business Ethics with Professor Penn?"

When she confirms it, I laugh. "She's nuts, but at least you won't fall asleep in her class."

"She brought a bundle of tacos to class this morning and ate every single one while lecturing. Lettuce and beef were spewing as she talked. I may never eat tacos again."

I nod and lead us to University Hall, holding the door for her to go first. "At least it wasn't fish tacos."

Her eyes go wide. "Nooo?"

"Oh, yes. I had her last year." I shudder at the memory.

There's a short line at the café, but I sigh in relief when I spot Katrina working behind the counter. She always gives me her employee discount. Joel's girlfriend greets me and Chloe with a big smile when it's our turn.

"Hey, what are you doing here?" she asks me and then her eyes move over to Chloe.

"Katrina, this is Chloe. Chloe, this is my buddy Joel's girlfriend."

"Nice to meet you."

"Same," Katrina says. "What can I get you guys?"

Chloe looks over the menu, which isn't all that extensive. Coffee, muffins, and the usual breakfast pastries. "Can I get a bran muffin and a small coffee?"

"Cream or sugar?"

Chloe shakes her head and then Katrina looks to me. "I'm good. Just the muffin and coffee."

I pull out my wallet.

"You're not eating?" Chloe asks, confusion marring her features.

"I don't do breakfast." Which is true but mostly out of necessity. When Wes and Zeke were living at The White House, we took turns making breakfast before early practices, but now Joel spends more nights than not at Katrina's and the routine has sort of faded away. Cooking isn't really my jam. Even toast is a fire hazard.

"I got it." Chloe moves to open her bag, presumably to grab her money.

I wave her off with the cash in my hand. "It's on me."

This is one of those awkward things that I wish didn't stress me out. I want to buy the girl a muffin and coffee and still be able to afford to have dinner tonight. But I'll gladly eat Ramen for the third night in a row for her.

Katrina rings us up, and I pay. She hands Chloe the coffee and a to-go bag with the muffin and then hands me a much heavier bag. "It's for later," she says casually. "I know you boys never eat unless it's hand-delivered by Joel's mom."

I force a chuckle and mumble my thanks, embarrassed at the handout, but thankful nonetheless, and shove the bag in my backpack.

At an unhurried pace, Chloe and I walk toward Moreno Hall. Her hair has mostly dried now and the blonde strands are wavy, framing her face and falling down her back. She's a beautiful girl. Casual suits her, I think. Those silver strappy shoes that cost more than I can fathom were hot as fuck, but she seems so much more accessible now. The Chloe of last night is squarely out of my league. This Chloe, however, I might stand a chance with.

"What's your schedule like this afternoon?"

She swallows a bite of her muffin before she responds, "This is my last class of the day, then practice and studying in the library. You?"

"Econ at one. Lifting at two."

She repeats it like she's trying to memorize my details in case she's quizzed. "I just realized I don't know anything about your classes or practice schedule... What do I say if someone asks me where you are?"

Her vulnerability makes my chest tighten. I highly doubt someone is going to ask her my whereabouts at any given moment, but I take her hand and squeeze reassuringly. "Tell them you're not my keeper." She rolls her eyes. "I have my phone on me, text if you need anything. And if all else fails, do what I do."

"What's that?"

"Bullshit 'em."

The next day before class, I wait outside class for Chloe. She slows when she sees me.

"Hey."

"Hey, there." I hold out the paper bag in my right hand.

She takes a hesitant look inside and then smiles. "Thank you."

Inside the lecture hall, I take the chair next to Shaw and pull Chloe into the seat on the other side of me. She takes a bite out of her muffin and then places it on the desk and grabs a notepad and pen from her backpack.

"Bran, really?" I ask, without hiding my dislike.

She shrugs, smiles, and takes another bite.

Professor Sanchez starts in on the lecture about knowing your target audience, but I watch Chloe. When she's down to the last bite, she holds it out and whispers, "If you're gonna hate on it, at least try it."

I don't really want it, especially because I bet there's a blueberry one—my favorite—in the bag Katrina forced into my backpack, again, for later, but I lean over and take the bite directly from her hand. Green eyes swirl with heat as my tongue and lips connect with her fingers.

She covers her reaction quickly, rolls her eyes, and sits back in her seat like she's paying attention to the lecture.

I grab her pen and angle the notebook so I can write her a note.

Things I've learned about Chloe:
  1. Likes bran muffins (yuck)
  2. Likes my mouth on her fingers

Then I draw a line through *on her fingers*. She likes my mouth. Period. She takes the pen from me and starts her own list.

Things I've learned about Nathan:
  1.

She looks up and frowns, pen poised to write, but she obviously can't come up with anything. I take the pen again and fill in number one for her.

The Fake

1. Likes blueberry muffins

We hand off the pen and she writes a number two and then looks to me.

Likes your mouth. Period, I scrawl after pulling a pen from the side pocket of my backpack.

She smiles. A real honest to God grin that makes her look like the laidback, fun surfer princess I like to imagine she is. I realize I don't actually know all that much about her. And I want to.

What are we doing this weekend?

Her brows furrow before she responds, *I didn't know we were hanging out this weekend.*

I think it would seem weird if we didn't hang out.

She seems to mull that over before nodding.

Pushing my luck and not giving one single fuck, I add, *We should probably hang out a few times a week so it seems legit.*

That look of trepidation is back. *That's a lot and totally not necessary.*

As if I care.

I disagree. It's totally necessary. Plus, we have the class project to work on anyway.

She stares at the paper a moment, pen between her teeth, before she begins to write and write and write... a freaking novel from the looks of it. I can't read it because her hand is in the way. My surfer princess is a leftie. When she's done, she sits back, expels a breath, and focuses entirely too hard on Professor Sanchez.

We should come up with some terms. Duration: one month. Times we need to hang out per week: 2—we can use those to work on the project. We can split those hangouts between our places, although I'd prefer that my teammates are included as much as possible since they're the whole reason for this. Should probably keep the hanging out to public places so people see us together and we use the most of our time. We've already said, no sex. PDA is okay when it feels appropriate to the situation. Anything you want to add?

Jesus. A list of dos and don'ts is a real mood killer. Seems like she needs this, though, so I roll with it. Mostly.

A month is too short. How about two? And I want at least one night a week that isn't spent studying.

Maybe I'm crazy for wanting to extend this out longer, but I don't exactly think it's going to be a burden.

Two months is overkill. If they don't like me in a month, I doubt another month is going to make a difference.

Right, I keep forgetting this is about her teammates.

Six weeks and all bets are off on PDA.

I move up to the list above where she started to list things she knows about me and add a third.

3. Likes PDA.

To emphasize my point, I drop the pen and lace our fingers together. Her hand fits perfectly in mine, and we both sit back and listen to Professor Sanchez for the rest of the class. When he finishes, I realize I have no idea what we discussed in class, but I had a damn good time while he yapped for an hour.

"What time you wanna hang?"

"Oh." She busies herself with her backpack as she searches for words… probably to blow me off.

"We can do whatever you want," I offer.

She straightens. "Whatever I want?"

twelve

Nathan

*C*hloe told me to meet her at Ray Fieldhouse at eight.

It's Friday night, so the place is quiet as a morgue. She's waiting for me just inside the side entrance for athletes. Leaning on the wall with her phone in hand, she's slow to raise her head from the screen, which gives me a couple seconds to take her in.

Tight black shorts that are... well, they can hardly be called shorts they're so short—and I'm in no way complaining about that—and a white off-the-shoulder t-shirt that comes just to the top of her not-shorts.

"Hey." She pushes off the wall. Her eyes do a slow perusal of me and she smirks. "Ready?"

"Depends. Gotta say, I'm intrigued. I've never had a chick tell me to meet her at the gym on a Friday night."

We head down the hall toward the weight rooms. She

stops outside of the basketball team's private gym. After last year's national championship win, they did some renovations on an unused indoor tennis court area to give us our own workout room. The other teams share so it's a definite perk.

"I see. I'm just the key to the good weight room. We're working out, for real?"

She nods and flashes an innocent smile. "Well, we could go to the other workout room if you want to slum it with me."

A rough chuckle fills my chest, and I press my thumb to the keypad entry.

"Fancy," she mocks when it beeps us in.

No one else is here, as I expected, but I doubt they'd balk at Chloe being here anyway.

"Wow," she says as she walks into the center of the room.

"Don't walk over Ray," I tell her as her feet get dangerously close to stepping on our beloved mascot in the center of the floor. "It's four years of bad luck."

She smirks. "Superstitious much?"

"Just not willing to risk it. We've got one in the locker room, too. You step on him and it's seven seasons of shit."

The way we're looking in practice right now, I'm not convinced someone hasn't been stomping on him every chance they get.

"So, now what?"

She turns to face me, hands on hips. "It's leg day."

I quirk a brow, but she's all business as she steps onto the treadmill and presses go. She takes the speed to a light jog. I watch as she warms up. She invited me along so I'm guessing she isn't opposed to that. And damn, it'd be hard to look away.

She looks over her shoulder. "You gonna work out with me or just stare at my ass the whole time?"

I take the treadmill beside her. "Both. I'm good at multi-tasking."

After five minutes of jogging, she takes off doing walking lunges across the room. I step in behind her, keeping my promise and working out while I continue to check her out.

She seems to have a whole routine because she goes right into each one with barely a second to let me catch my breath: bear crawl, side shuffle, high skips, wall sits.

I'm in good shape. When I can't sleep, I exercise to pass the hours, so my endurance is awesome, but Chloe is making me sweat to keep up with her.

Thirty minutes have passed before she finally looks to me, face red with exertion and eyes ablaze with excitement, and says, "Ready to work out?"

Dafuq we been doing? That's what I think, but instead, I just wave my hand in front of me for her to lead the way.

Chloe heads to the squat rack. She places the barbell on her upper back and steps back and does a quick warm up set. When she racks it, I snap out of it and move to help her add weight. "Don't you guys do this as a team?"

She nods as she follows the weight with a clip to hold it in place and then moves right back under the bar to go again. I stand behind her as a spot, just in case, as she busts out a set of ten.

"Bonus workouts, I dig it." She's in the zone, and my

words take a minute to register.

"I need to be stronger and quicker on my feet. I'm not as tall as some of my competition so I need to make up for it any way I can. No weaknesses I can control."

"Alright." Her words poke at some insecurity inside me. I had to bust my ass to get where I am so I understand the basic logic behind her desire to outwork the competition. "Let's put some real weight on there then."

Her green eyes flash with competition.

I add what I think is a challenging but doable weight to both sides.

"I've never squatted that much before."

"No weaknesses you can control." I throw her words back at her, which does the trick. She lets out a breath and gets in position. Determination radiates off her, but I stay close to grab the bar if she needs to bail.

She doesn't need me, though.

"Atta girl." I help re-rack the bar after her third rep, and she turns and throws her arms around me.

"I did it!"

Sweat mixed with ocean and sunshine fills my nostrils, and I contemplate kissing her for all of two seconds before she seems to read my thoughts and steps back.

"What's next?"

For the next forty minutes, we workout side by side. We take turns picking the exercises. I push her to add more weight, and she pushes me to move quicker between sets. Her competitive spirit and my desire to flat out not be shown up by a girl makes me work harder. She has this effect on me, I'm finding—she makes me want to be better at a lot of things.

It's nearly nine o'clock when we sit on the floor catching our breaths and giving our shaky legs a break.

"Payne." Coach's deep voice catches me by surprise, and my head snaps up to find him standing just inside the weight room. He's dressed in workout clothes with his headphones in hand. Note to self, Coach comes to work out late on the weekends. "What are you doing here?"

I jump to my feet and then proceed to wobble because damn my legs hurt. He takes in me and then Chloe while I find my words. "We were just finishing up."

Chloe moves behind me. "Sorry. You've got the good equipment in here."

Coach smiles at her. "That we do." He looks to me and that smile falls a little. He nods with his head to the door. "Get out of here before I've got the whole team bringing their girlfriends in here."

We shuffle past him into the hallway, and Chloe busts up laughing. "Sorry," she says between giggles. "I hope I didn't get you in trouble."

"Nah, I'm already on his shit list."

She looks to me for an explanation, and I shake my head. "It's a long story."

"I'm at the gym on a Friday night... I've clearly got time."

We make our way out to the parking lot and pause where our paths split and we'll be forced to go in opposite directions.

"I did something dumb, got caught." I shrug.

"Something dumb?"

The truth is on the tip of my tongue, but I like the way Chloe looks at me now and if she knows the truth... well, it's a risk I'm not willing to take. Good things haven't come my way too often lately, and I'm not ready to gamble giving her up.

"I showed up to practice pretty hungover... in fact, I might have still been drunk."

"So that's why you've stopped drinking so much?" she says as if it's all clicked in place. "And then you met me." She bats her eyelashes.

I nod, unable to force another lie. "And then I met you."

Chloe

Sunday night, Nathan and I are sprawled out on the floor in the common area of my dorm, working on our communications class project. Bri is at a study group, Emily's in her room with the door closed, and Sydney's in our room but has the door open just enough we can hear the music she's playing.

"A pen?" Nathan asks, his pencil tucked behind his ear. He flips through my notes, long legs propped up on the coffee table.

"Not just a pen. A retractable roller pen with extra ink cartridges. It retails for over seventy dollars."

His eyebrows lift up toward his hairline. "A seventy-dollar pen? That's crazy."

"Which is the point of the project," I remind him. "We need to figure out how to market it to our classmates. What would make you spend that much on a pen?"

"Winning the lotto."

I tilt my head. "We have to come up with something."

"Yeah, I know. I'm gonna have to think on it. We can pull together the current marketing details and customer profile and come back to it."

"Yeah, alright."

"Or we could blow this off and grab dinner at my place? Joel's mom brought over enchiladas."

"Joel's mom really feeds you guys?"

"Hell yes." He grins. "I'm not even embarrassed about it because it's so good. So much better than that cafeteria shit."

I stare down at my notes. He's right, we need time to process, but I want Nathan to be here when Bri comes home. "How about we order takeout, finish up the outline, and then watch a movie or something here?"

He nods slowly. "Yeah, alright. We could do that."

Unlike the eager guy I've gotten used to, he doesn't seem very excited about my plan. And then it hits me. Of course, he doesn't want to spend money on takeout when he can get a free meal at his place.

"My treat for…" I gesture in front of us. "Well, everything. I owe you."

Laughing, he shakes his head. "I'm good, holding out for enchiladas. I've got a granola bar in my backpack if I get desperate."

He goes back to studying my notes and I order takeout—three times as much as I would for just myself. It arrives just as we're finishing up the outline. I grab two plates, setting one in front of him even as he says, "I'm good, seriously. I'll eat later."

"Have you had Lotus House?"

He shakes his head.

"Oh, my God, you have to at least try it." I hold out my fork full of Chow Mein and one side of his mouth pulls up in an amused grin before he opens wide and leans forward.

I wait while he chews and nods his head.

"Amazing, right?"

"Really good."

I hand him the container of food, and he takes it from me with a shy smile but then shovels in two more big bites. I wave him off when he tries to hand it back and grab for the sesame beef.

Sydney pops her head out of our room. "Did I hear something about a movie?"

"Yeah, you wanna watch something with us?"

She rushes into the room and takes a seat on the couch. "Can we watch *New Girl*? We just started season two."

It stings a bit to know they have another thing together that I've been missing out on.

"Yeah, *New Girl* sounds great. I haven't seen it. You?" I look to Nathan.

"Saw a few episodes but never from beginning to end. Sunday night used to be movie night at the house. I miss it."

I'm having a hard time picturing him and his

roommates all sitting around watching a movie together. I've seen their theater room, but still.

Sydney knocks on the wall behind the couch in what I can only assume is some sort of bat signal for Bri to come out because not five seconds later, she pops out. Her footsteps slow as she glances around the room. Nathan nudges my elbow with his.

"Wanna watch with us?" I ask, fully prepared for her to say no or maybe even kick me out.

"I don't want to interrupt date night."

"It's fine," I say at the same time Nathan says, "As long as you're cool with me feeling up my girl during the show."

My mouth falls open, and I expect Bri to scoff and go back to her room. Instead, she laughs. Like *laughs* laughs. I didn't know she was capable of making the sound. She takes a seat on the couch. I give Nathan, aka Mr. Miracle Worker, a playful slap.

"I'm kidding," he says, grabbing the remote from the TV stand. "What episode are we on? Season two, episode one?"

Sydney tucks her feet under her on the couch. "Season two, episode three. Emily is on her way."

Our door flies open as if it were scripted. "I'm here," Emily says, out of breath. "Season two, episode three," she repeats. "Jess tried dating two guys at once and met the hot doctor. Except we don't know he's a doctor yet. Sorry, Sydney." She collapses on the couch between Bri and Sydney.

Standing, I place an unopened carton of food on the coffee table. "General Tsao's chicken?"

Emily dives for it. "Thanks, Chloe. Hey, Nathan."

He waves to her, and I give Nathan an OMG, we're hanging out and no one forced them look. He moves to my chair and pulls me onto his lap. It's big enough that we'd just about fit side by side, but I'm more on his lap than not. I turn to face him and mouth, "Thank you."

He responds by leaning forward and kissing me lightly on the lips.

"Mmmm, you taste spicy."

He doesn't pull away immediately. Our mouths linger, barely not touching, eyes locked. My heart races with the desire I see reflected back at me. I make the first move this time, hesitantly pressing our lips together. He lets out a little growl as he takes over the kiss. I part my lips just as his tongue sweeps in.

A pillow hits the side of my face.

"That's enough, you two," Sydney says.

Nathan chuckles and pulls away, but he keeps an arm around me, one hand on my thigh the entire show. A detail that no one else in the room can see, but I like it anyway. And that's not good.

I can't fall for my fake boyfriend. What if in a week or two, it blows up and we can't stand to be around one another? All of this will have been for nothing. I close my eyes and try to ignore the tingles and desire I feel being this close to him.

"Is there a weird song that turns you on that really shouldn't?" I ask as we're cleaning up.

He takes the empty Chinese containers from the coffee table. "You mean like Nick and the 'Humpty Dance?'"

I nod.

He thinks for a minute and then shakes his head. "I can't think of one. Why?"

"Just curious." I bite down on my lip.

"Uh-uh. You have one, don't you? What is it?"

I bite my lip and his face lights up. "Oh, this is fun. Let me guess. 'Genie in a Bottle?'"

I shake my head no.

"'The Pony?'"

I scrunch up my face. "Seriously? Ginuwine should turn everyone on."

He tosses the trash and then crosses his arms in front of him, studying me carefully.

"'Ice Ice Baby,'" I admit quietly and watch his face transform into a huge smile. "Don't laugh. It's my jam."

"I wouldn't dream of it." He presses his lips together tightly and goes back to helping me pick up. Under his breath, he begins to lightly hum the song.

"You said you wouldn't laugh," I say as he breaks out singing for real. He spits out the first verse as he walks to me.

When he finishes, we're standing chest to chest, smiling at one another.

"Jerk," I tease.

Our gazes lock, and I swear he's going to kiss me. No witnesses, just us caught up in this happy fake relationship we've created. I have to admit, we're good at pretending. So good that I think we're both lost wondering what's real and what's not.

I can survive another year without a boyfriend, I remind myself. It's my final shot to prove I belong—that I always belonged. No weaknesses I can control, and Nathan's definitely starting to feel like a weakness.

"I'm tired," I say and step back. There's a note of disappointment in his body language as he watches me put distance between us.

"Yeah, I should go." He walks to the door and doesn't glance back as he leaves.

And now I've got "Ice Ice Baby" on the brain and no fake boyfriend to make out with.

thirteen

Nathan

*M*onday, late morning between classes, I drop onto the couch in the living room. Shaw tosses me a remote without asking and restarts Tecmo Super Bowl.

"Where were you last night?"

"With Chloe."

He nods. "You missed a crazy night at the baseball house. Jefferson bought four boxes of wine." Shaw shakes his head. "I had the mother of all headaches this morning. Cheap wine hangover is rough."

"Yeah," I agree, feigning interest, but in truth, a night out getting wasted with my buddies doesn't have quite the same appeal anymore.

I side-eye him as I select the Raiders, and he picks the 49ers.

"Get the fuck out of here, you can't play the 49ers."

The old video game was made with a clear bias. 49ers are unbeatable.

He grumbles but picks the Giants. "You and Chloe, huh? She seems cool."

"She is."

"Think she'd put in a good word for me with Sydney?"

I chuckle. I'm just as likely to need him to put in a good word for me, but obviously, I can't tell him that so I keep my mouth shut as we play three games only opening it to trash talk him when I kick his ass all three times.

I glance up at the clock in the living room, and Shaw catches me and stands up quickly. "Shit, we're gonna be late to Comm."

"I'm thinking of skipping."

Alright, so I'm a pussy. I don't want to face Chloe. I'm not embarrassed about wanting her... I mean, who wouldn't? But it's hard to keep my brain... and my dick... in check when we go from rubbing up on each other in front of her roommates to her running away from me when we're alone. After our time at the gym together and then last night... I guess I thought there were some real feelings there. Guess just on my part.

I know it seems like it'd be easy to remember she's paying me to pretend to like her, but I try and block that detail out as much as possible.

She doesn't like you like that, asswipe. Or maybe she does, but the way she catapulted herself out of reach last night just as I was about to kiss her—she's not giving in to any baser-level instincts.

"Yeah?" Shaw nods and stands there thoughtfully.

"Maybe I'll blow off my afternoon classes, too. I mean, if the captain of the basketball team can...." He shrugs with an annoying smirk.

"Fuck," I say, but I stand and grab my backpack to head out.

We get to class a couple of minutes late, and I slip into the seat next to Chloe with a small smile in place. She scribbles onto her notepad and then angles it toward me.

Slacker

I take out a pen from the side pocket of my backpack.

Surfer Princess

Her face lights up and all that coaching I did on the way over about remembering my place and not getting in too deep goes right out the window. I proceed to draw an exaggerated sketch of her catching a wave.

She lifts a brow at the finished piece and writes, *That's not anatomically correct.*

Okay, so I made her boobs a little—a lot—bigger. It's art; a guy can dream.

You wanna work on the project tonight?

I hesitate with my answer, but I guess I'm a glutton for punishment. *Sounds good.*

After weightlifting, I head back to the house to shower and get ready for my study sesh with Chloe. I strip off my sweaty clothes and turn the shower on to let it warm up. While I wait, I scroll through my phone then say fuck it and pull up porn.

I'm not usually picky and will click on whatever the top trending videos are. Sex in just about any format does it for me. Today I'm looking for something specific. Or rather I'm excluding something specific. No blondes. No green eyes. Nothing that reminds me of Chloe.

That's a lot of somethings it turns out because I scroll past video after video until I finally find one with a brunette with blue eyes framed behind dark-rimmed glasses. She wears a short skirt and a button-down white shirt that can barely contain her large boobs. The busty brunette leans over a large desk where some porn dude wearing only a tie tells her she's been a very good secretary. I mute the sound as he comes around the desk and then bends her over it.

I wrap a hand around my semi. The steam from the shower starts to fog up the window in the bathroom and I put my phone on the counter and get more serious about this quickie release.

I glide my hand up and down my growing erection as I watch the CEO secretary fantasy play out. It's pretty cliché and uninventive as far as porn goes, but my underutilized dick only cares about finally getting some action. And all I care about is getting off without thinking about the surfer princess driving me to bad porn.

Getting caught hooking up with other people would blow up our fake relationship façade, but even if I could get away with it, would I? Doubtful. My dick and I only seem to want her. Confirmed when I eventually close my eyes and step into the shower to play out my own cliché fantasy. The one that has a blonde goddess kneeling in front of me and taking me into her hot mouth as she looks up at me with those green eyes that own me.

All three of Chloe's roommates sit in the living area with us while we work on the project. I feel like I'm a pretty good gauge of their acceptance of her and I'd give it a solid five. They aren't including her, but they aren't excluding her either, so it's a start. The exception is Sydney. I don't think Sydney dislikes anyone. She chatters non-stop while the five of us work, but she's a nice buffer to what might otherwise be an awkward tension.

"I came up with a couple ideas on how to sell it to the class, but none of them are great," Chloe says with a disappointed scowl.

Chloe and I sit on the floor again tonight. We're side by side looking over her ideas. She leans over into my space and reaches for the current marketing plan notes on the floor beside me. I hold stock still and try not to notice how she always seems to smell like sunshine and the ocean or how her boobs brush against my arm. Aaaand fail. There's no way not to notice her or the way my body responds to her.

She glances up, green eyes dark. I stand abruptly. "I gotta make a call." Everyone in the room turns to look at me and I add, "Be right back." I add in a wink for good measure before I slip into the hallway.

My damn palms are sweaty. I feel all strung out on hormones like some fucking kid finding daddy's porn magazine stash. Except all she did was brush against me. For fuck's sake.

I grip the phone tightly as I wait for Heath to answer.

"Hey." He sounds like I woke him, and I have to check the time before I respond.

"Shit, sorry. Did I wake you?"

"How long have you been at Valley and you still forget you're three hours behind."

"Yeah, well, let this be your warning—don't do drugs, fucks up your brain," I joke.

He doesn't laugh. "Thanks for taking care of the tickets."

"You can repay me by not getting any more. Two in one week? That's fucked up, Heath."

"I know, I know. I feel awful, but I can't take it back," he mutters.

"I'm serious. I can't bail you out again. Last chance."

He grumbles out another sullen apology, and I feel like I've sufficiently made my point.

"Now that I went all Dad on you, tell me about hockey."

Heath gives me a rundown on the team this year, and he sounds excited and determined, which makes me feel good about all I've done. I just want to give the kid everything I had and more. He finishes with a yawn.

"Send me your schedule. I'm gonna do my best to make it to at least one."

"Alright."

We're both quiet, and I know I need to let him go

and get back inside to Chloe. "Proud of you. Stay out of trouble, and I'll call ya later."

"Right-o, daddy-o."

"Fucker."

That gets a laugh out of him and makes me feel less like an old man.

I pocket my phone and head back into Chloe's dorm. The girls barely look up at my re-entry. Chloe looks me over like she's trying to determine my mood. *Frustrated as hell, baby doll.*

My shower time earlier didn't do jack to stop me from wanting her. In fact, I think it did the opposite. I let my mind go crazy with possibilities and now I can't stop picturing her doing every dirty thing she did in my fantasies.

"We were going to watch an episode of *New Girl.* You wanna stay?"

I glance at our half-finished marketing plan, and she follows my gaze. "I'll finish it later."

I know this concession is for her roommates—putting off homework so she can do what they want, and it pisses me off a little for her.

"I should go. I have some other things to do." I nod to her laptop. "Email me what you have so far."

"Oh, sure." Her brows furrow in confusion. Probably because I haven't questioned a thing she's done on the project. I've let her take the lead and, to be honest, do most of the work. Aware that the roommates are watching now, I lean down and lift her chin so I can place a kiss on her lips. "Later."

I'm buried in demographics and sales numbers for this stupid pen that I can't imagine anyone wanting when my phone pings with a text notification. I rub at my eyes and close Joel's laptop.

Chloe: You missed a great episode.

Fuck, I've been at it for two hours. Which means...

Me: Admit it, you watched more than one. Traitor.

Chloe: I didn't exactly have control of the remote. They're going to watch one more. Want me to wait and watch with you?

Me: Nah, go ahead.

Only a few minutes pass before she sends me another.

Chloe: What are you doing?

Me: Thinking about going to bed. Might go for a run first.

Chloe: A run before bed??

Me: Relaxes me, helps me fall asleep.

I leave out the fact it sometimes helps *keep* me asleep all night.

Me: What do you do when you can't fall asleep?

Chloe: The usual. Count sheep, read a book, watch porn, listen to music.

Me: Whoa, whoa, whoa. You watch porn to help you sleep?

Chloe: Just checking to see if you were paying attention.

Me: To you? Always.

Me: Now back to my question.

Chloe: Having a roommate makes watching porn a little awkward.

Me: Bummer, I hadn't thought of that. I myself enjoyed some erotica earlier today.

I'm afraid I've overshared when she hasn't responded two minutes later. I'm about to turn my phone on silent for the night when a text finally appears on screen.

Chloe: Let me guess, lesbian porn?

Me: Nope.

Chloe: Gang bang?

Jesus Christ, I'm getting worked up just thinking about her sitting in her dorm tapping out those words.

Me: Nah, standard dude with chick porn. Sorry to disappoint, you freak.

Chloe: To each their own, I suppose.

A part of me, a very large, throbbing, hard part of me wants to push the conversation further. We're only a few texts away from sexting. But this isn't how I want to do this. I like Chloe, and I don't want to be relegated to sexting and kisses when her roommates are watching.

Me: Night, freak. Talk to you tomorrow.

Chloe: Okay, well happy running and sweet dreams.

I hold my breath as I re-read it a dozen times. She's hit a nerve and has no idea. Such an innocent sign off, but for me, it's filled with all types of hope and promise. When I snap out of my shock, I respond in kind.

Me: Sweet dreams, Surfer Princess.

I push away from my desk and stare at my bed. Sweet

dreams? Nah, that's not likely.

fourteen

Chloe

I'm studying in the library Friday night when Camila FaceTimes.

"Hey, stranger," she says when I answer.

"I know, I'm sorry things have been crazy."

"You'll be forgiven if you promise to come visit for my birthday next month."

I stare at her hopeful face and feel guilty for hesitating.

"Please, Chlo. I miss you. JT's throwing a party for me, and I need my best girl there."

"Of course, I'll come."

"Yay!" she squeals, and I turn the volume down on my headphones. "I can't wait to see you."

"Me, too."

"Where are you anyway?"

"Oh." I glance around and give her a sheepish smile. "The library."

"On a Friday night? Are the roommates still being bitches?"

"No, actually that's gotten better. I'm just catching up on some school stuff."

I'm staring at the screen and listening to Camila tell me about her plans for the night so I don't notice as he approaches, but when Nathan takes the seat in front of me, I almost drop my phone.

He's in his standard solid-colored t-shirt and jeans, but his hair isn't in its usual disarray. In fact, I think there might be gel in it.

"Hey, Cam," I interrupt her. "I gotta go. Can I call you tomorrow?"

"Yep, I'm heading out anyway. Love ya."

"Love you, too."

I take my earbuds out slowly. "Hi."

"What's up?" The man doesn't have any books with him—not even a backpack to give the impression he might be here to study. We didn't make any plans for the night so to say I'm surprised he found me without so much as a text to ask where I was or what I was doing is an understatement.

"I'm studying. What are you doing here? How did you find me?"

A pleased smirk plays on his face, and his blue eyes twinkle with mischief. "I figured you were one of three places. Just happened to get lucky on my first stop. And I'm here to save you from spending a Friday night at the library." He leans in. "Doesn't look good for your image."

I snort, lean back in my chair, and cross my arms. "And whatever you have in mind will be good for my image?"

He stands. "I thought we already established being seen with me was good for you." He points a thumb toward his chest. "Hot and awesome."

He's one hundred percent accurate there, but I still don't move.

"Come on, princess. It'll be fun."

With a quick look around the library, I realize I don't want or need to be here. School has never been particularly hard for me, and the library is really more of a hideout. Plus, spending time with Nathan sounds better than just about anything else I can think of.

"Alright."

He takes my backpack after I've loaded it up with my laptop and books. His long legs hurry down the stairs and across campus at a clip. My stomach is a little uneasy when I realize we're headed to my dorm room. Things have been better with the roommates, but I still tense up every time I walk through the door until I gauge their mood toward me.

"Are we hanging here tonight?" I ask as I unlock my dorm room.

"Nope," he says, sounding very proud of himself. "Just wanted to drop your stuff and pick up something."

"What?" His excitement is contagious, and I'm smiling while I try and figure out the plan.

"A roommate or two."

I flash him a confused look that is more than a little jealous at the prospect he might be interested in one of my roommates. Maybe I'm not ready to date him for real, but I don't like the idea of him dating anyone else either. Hypocrite much?

He shakes his head. "I can only handle one girlfriend, don't worry. Shaw likes Sydney, so I thought we could bring her along."

"What if she says no?"

"She won't."

I take my backpack from him and open the door, walking into the living room where Sydney and Emily are watching TV.

"Hey, guys," I say.

"Hey," they respond in unison, staring past me to Nathan.

He breezes past me like he owns the place and takes a seat in my chair. This continues to please me.

"I think I've seen this one," he says by way of greeting. "Is this the episode where—"

"Don't give it away," Emily interrupts. "Sydney hasn't seen it yet."

"Ooooh, right." He pretends to zip his lips, and they all fall silent watching the show.

Shaking my head at how easy it is for him to win people over with little to no effort, I walk toward my room. "I'm gonna get changed."

"Where are you going?" Sydney calls after me.

Nathan answers, "The Hideout. You guys wanna come?"

I can't hear their response, but not a minute later, Sydney rushes into our room pulling out her ponytail and grabbing the dry shampoo from the top of her dresser.

"Coming with us, I presume?" I smile but a small part

of me is annoyed at how Nathan was able to march into my dorm and make plans with my roommates. I know he's doing it for me, but it still rankles that they like him better than me. I'm their teammate after all.

She nods. "Are any of his friends going to be there?" I keep my back to her as I pull on fresh clothes and examine myself in the mirror. "I think Shaw is going."

"Really?!" She squeals in obvious delight.

"Is Emily coming, too?"

"No, she's waiting for Bri to get back. They're going to Mallory's apartment to hang tonight."

There's a knock on my door. "You guys about ready?" Nathan calls from the other side. "Shaw's swinging by to pick us up."

Sydney has already transformed herself for a night out and flings open the door. She passes Nathan, and he steps into my room, glancing around before his eyes lock on me.

"How did you pull this off so well?"

"Wasn't really that hard. Shaw's got game apparently."

"She didn't even know he was going. I think *you're* the one with game."

He shakes his head and runs a hand over his jaw. Now that I'm studying him closer, I think he cleaned up his facial hair, too. He still has the scruff, but it looks cleaner... like he put some effort into this fake date.

I glance down at what I'm wearing. Jeans and a black midriff tank top. I suddenly wish I'd put on a dress and added some eye makeup. "Am I dressed okay?"

"You look great," he says, giving me a once over that makes my stomach flip and motions with his head.

"Come on. They're waiting for us."

The Hideout is busy when we arrive. We grab a booth and Sydney and Shaw slide in opposite us without any prompting. I can't help but notice they look more like a real couple than Nathan and I do—turned toward each other, laughing and talking—all smiles for one another.

Tanner Shaw is a good-looking guy. He's not as tall or built as Nathan, but that's true of basically every other guy I know. They've both got blue eyes and light hair, but nothing about Shaw makes me look twice. And everything about Nathan makes me want to never stop looking.

"Gabby working tonight?" Shaw asks, looking around. Families and couples are seated at booths in the dining area, but the bar space is almost entirely Valley U students. Some I recognize and others give it away with their frat letters across their chests.

"Nah, she's out of town visiting Zeke," Nathan answers and places a hand on my leg under the table.

I want to ask him who Gabby is, but Shaw asked so casually I think I should know so I pretend I do and stay silent.

"What are we drinking?" Sydney asks, smiling so big I think her face might start to hurt. I love that about her—she wears her heart on her sleeve while I keep mine buried under layers of sweaters like Joey in that *Friends* episode where the girl he's dating repeatedly punches him. Except my layers are metaphorical and so are the punches to my heart I'm trying to avoid.

"I'm gonna grab a pitcher. Be right back." Shaw stands. "Want anything else, babe?" he asks Sydney.

Babe. The endearment rolls off Shaw's tongue so

easily. I steal a glance at Nathan, and he rolls his eyes playfully at how quickly they've slipped into couple mode.

"I'll come with you." Sydney follows behind Shaw, leaving Nathan and me by ourselves.

He smiles, straight white teeth contrasting with the hard angles and scruff on his jaw. "You want something to drink besides beer?"

"Beer's fine," I say. "I'm not a big drinker. My tolerance is shit."

"I may have noticed that," he says and places his arm around the back of the booth. His fingers brush against my shoulder, and I lean into his touch and angle myself like Sydney did with Shaw.

Instead of outright asking about Gabby, I decide to vaguely inquire about his dating history. "Have you and Shaw gone on a lot of double dates?"

He laughs. "Nah, definitely not. I think this might be my first double date ever, come to think of it."

"But you've dated a lot?" I avert my eyes and pretend to be very interested in looking around the bar while I wait for his answer.

"Not really. My life was a bit of a mess before I met you."

Something about coinciding with a positive change in his life makes me happy. Really happy.

Shaw and Sydney return with a pitcher and glasses. Taking a glass and pouring a beer, Nathan slides it in front of me with a wink. He pours one for himself, too, but doesn't immediately take a drink.

Sydney carries the conversation through my first beer. She and Shaw are getting to know each other, too, so it's easy and natural for Nathan and me to add input without it seeming like we don't know the other like someone in a relationship would. But surprisingly I know, or have deduced, more than I thought. Surface level stuff, but it's something.

We finish the pitcher and then take an Uber back to their place. Datson is playing video games in the living room, and Shaw heads straight for him. "I demand a rematch from this afternoon. You want winner, Payne?"

Nathan shakes his head. "Gonna hang with my girl."

Sydney has already parked herself next to Shaw on the couch.

"It's fine," I insist and take a seat in an oversized chair.

"Want something to drink?" he asks, looking at me.

I nod, and he disappears into the kitchen. He returns a minute later and squeezes into the chair with me. He positions us so I'm basically on his lap. One arm is around my waist and the other holds his beer.

Every word, every laugh, every movement from him amps up my awareness of him in new ways. Yes, I know we've already slept together, but it's a blur—a tangle of moments. Good moments, if I'm honest, but they're still just pieces of him through Everclear glasses. And let's be real, Everclear glasses are foggy as fuck.

"Damn. I've never seen anyone lose so fast." Datson punches Shaw in the arm and then looks to Nathan. "You're up."

I start to move, but Nathan tightens his hold. "Shaw, toss me the controller."

"You think you're going to win with one arm?" Datson raises a brow.

"Nah, two arms and Bo Jackson." He leans over the arm of the chair and places his beer on the floor and then sits up and wraps both of his long arms around me so that he can get both hands on the controller.

"I could move," I say quietly, turning my head and finding his mouth so close I can smell the faint scent of beer and the mint gum he chewed on the ride back from The Hideout.

He keeps his eyes on the screen, but his arms squeeze tighter. "Don't you dare. I've got you right where I want you."

I'm not sure if the last part is meant for me or Datson as I hear the latter groan, "Fucking Bo Jackson."

I sit forward suddenly, breaking his hold. He raises a brow in question.

"I've gotta pee," I announce, not so eloquently before fleeing and putting some much-needed space between us.

Sydney is two steps behind me and when I get to the bathroom and go to close the door, she calls out, "Wait up."

She follows and locks the door behind us.

"I don't really have to pee," I say when she looks at me like she's waiting for me to use the toilet.

She moves past me and pulls up her dress. I turn and give her some privacy, staring into the mirror at my flushed cheeks. When she's done, she joins me at the sink.

"You're staying over with Nathan tonight, right?" she asks as she adds another coat of gloss to her lips.

"I don't know. Nathan and I haven't talked about it. I'm not sure what he has going on tomorrow."

Which is all mostly true.

"The thing is, if you leave then I have to leave, too, but if you stay then it's just assumed I will."

"You really like Shaw that much?"

"Oh, I'm not going to sleep with him tonight."

"No judgment." I hold my hands up and smile.

"I'm a fifth date kind of girl," she says and smacks her lips in the mirror.

"Won't he assume differently if you stay tonight?" I ask with light laughter.

"I always tell them ahead of time there will be no sex. It makes them work harder, swear to God. Take sex off the table and suddenly, you're a goddess."

Maybe that's why things feel so intense with Nathan. We took sex out of the equation and it made both of us want it that much more. Except, it's not just sex I crave from him. Being in his arms while he plays video games and going out on double dates... I want those things too even if I know the reality is it's not the right time to get involved.

Nathan and Datson are still playing video games when we emerge. Shaw meets Sydney in the hallway, and I slip past them.

"Damn." Datson tosses the remote on the coffee table. "I thought I had you that time."

"Bo knows." Nathan spots me, stands, and lobs his remote next to Datson's. "Thanks for the game."

He reaches me in three long strides, crowding my space as he brushes my hair behind my ear. "Whatcha wanna do?"

I look back where Sydney and Shaw are still standing. She's leaning against the wall and he's got one arm on the wall beside her, leaning in close. Nathan follows my gaze and nods.

"Yo, Shaw, water ball?"

Shaw takes his time before turning his head and answering, like he can't bear to look away, "Hell yeah."

"You in, princess?"

"Do I even want to know what water ball is?"

He smirks. "You'll see. First, let's get you in a suit."

The four of us head upstairs to change for the pool.

"I don't have a suit." This seems like an obvious problem, but no one else seems concerned.

"Got ya covered." In his room, Nathan pulls out a white one-piece swimsuit from his top-dresser drawer and throws it to me. I catch it by instinct but feel totally weirded out by the fact he has some random girl's suit in his room that he loans out to whoever might stop by for a dip in the pool.

I hold it out from me by my pinky finger. "I don't think so. No offense, but sharing suits with your jersey chasers isn't happening. It's weird and highly unsanitary."

He rolls his eyes. "It's Gabby's."

I stay quiet as I stare at the suit with narrowed eyes. A suit that has a name.

"She's always forgetting to bring her suit when she comes over, so she just leaves it here."

"Oh." I still don't move, and we're in some weird standoff over a swimsuit.

"It's clean and, far as I know, no one else has worn it. Gabby and I are just friends so you're safe from whatever cooties you think I have."

"I didn't mean it like that."

He levels me with his stunning blue eyes.

"Okay, I did. Sorry."

A slow smile tips up the corners of his mouth. "You'll be forgiven when you get changed and meet me in the pool. We've got a game to win."

"So, water ball is just basketball in the pool?" Sydney pushes at Shaw's chest and then takes the small Nerf ball from him.

Shaw must not have had a loaner suit on hand because she wears a t-shirt tied up tightly just below her boobs and a pair of shorts rolled at the waist to make them shorter.

"Rules are simple," Nathan says with a cocky glint in his eye that makes my breaths come quicker. "Two on two. First to ten wins. And, I apologize in advance that I'm gonna make your man look bad."

"Impossible," Sydney says at the same time Shaw splashes Nathan with water and comes at him like he's going to dunk him. Nathan grabs me and holds me in front of him to protect himself.

Our bare legs tangle in the water and my butt is pushed back into his crotch.

"Save me, babe," he says, ducking behind me.

So casual and easy the whole thing seems for him. Save him? Yeah, right. I need someone to save me from falling for my fake boyfriend.

fifteen

Nathan

I toss a pillow on the floor while Chloe watches me with guilty eyes.

"I'm so sorry about this."

"It's fine. This way, I get to spend the night with you again. Not exactly how I pictured it, but at least this time, you won't kick me out in the morning, being it's my house and all."

Her mouth drops open.

"Relax. I'm teasing." I settle onto the floor and then realize I haven't turned out the light so I jump up. Pausing at the switch, I glance at her. "Ready for bed?"

I don't miss the way she takes me in; her lips are her giveaway. They quiver just the tiniest bit when she's turned on. A fun little fact I plan on keeping in my pocket for later.

I flick off the light at her slight nod, and we're enveloped in darkness. Neither of us says a word as I lie back on the floor and stare up at the ceiling.

We may be six feet away from one another, mostly clothed with zero chance of anything happening between us, but my body is blind to the situation and one hundred percent ready to go.

I contemplate jerking off to her snoring, but it doesn't come. She's as wide awake as I am.

"Well, this is awkward," she says finally.

We both break out into laughter that helps break some of the tension. My dick and I make an executive decision to put me out of my misery, and I jump to my feet. "I'm gonna crash in Joel's room. He's at Katrina's tonight."

Jerking off in your buddy's room... so not cool, but this situation calls for unconventional solutions.

"Wait, don't go. This is stupid. Get in the bed. I trust you."

I pause with my pillow tucked under my arm. Chloe has her reasons for keeping this thing platonic, which I respect, but our agreement is starting to feel like the longest foreplay ever. We've only hung outside of class a few times, and I'm positive I'm using some sort of *Guinness*-level super strength to remind myself why we're not really dating.

Chloe pulls back the covers in invitation. I try not to look at her bare legs, I really do. I slide onto the opposite side of the bed and lay back. Aaaand I'm never falling asleep. She smells like chlorine and the sun and hot summer days.

She rolls on her side facing me. "Tell me about your

brother."

Nothing deflates a penis like the mention of another dude—especially one related to you.

"What do you want to know?"

"Anything."

"He's a senior in high school. Plays hockey, pretty good, too. I think he has a chance to play college level and maybe beyond if he sticks with it."

"That's cool. You guys are close?"

"We were. Our dad passed right after my senior year of high school. I came to Valley and sort of left him and my mom to deal with shit on their own. I know that's awful. I was just trying to deal in my own way and being at Valley partying and playing basketball gave me something to focus on."

"That had to have been hard."

"Yeah, but Heath had it way worse. My mom fell apart, got fired from a job she'd had for twenty years. She hasn't been able to move on." I swallow down the guilt for not being there when they needed me. "When I eventually pulled my head out of my ass, I had to switch from big brother to father figure, and that isn't fun for either of us."

"It sounds like he's lucky to have you."

I snort. "I doubt he feels that way." I notice I've angled toward her without even realizing it. "What about you? Do you have siblings?"

"No, only child. I always wanted an older brother with hot friends."

"If you were my little sister…" I stop and shake my head. "Not even going there."

Her eyes light up, but she scrunches her face like

she's disgusted at the idea. "Ewww, I'd be your sister."

"We could have a whole Cersei and Jamie Lannister thing going on." I shrug. "No kids though, Joffrey was a monster."

We laugh and then she yawns. My cue to let her get some sleep and also for me to stop thinking about sleeping with her before the lower half of me starts to get ideas again.

"'Night, Chloe."

We're facing one another. She's got both hands pulled together by her face, and I've got one arm draped on the pillow behind her. Her eyes are locked on mine for three long seconds while I hold my breath and wait for her to make a play. I can't be the asshole who makes her feel uncomfortable by making the first move, but I'm dying to kiss her again.

"'Night, Nathan," she says finally and her lids close.

I don't go to sleep. Never really planned to. Sleep and I aren't friends anyway, so it's really not an inconvenience. I'm lying on my back, counting blondes instead of sheep. Her breathing has slowed and evened out, so I get up quietly and head downstairs.

Everyone has gone to bed, so I've got the downstairs to myself. I put in my earbuds and crank up the music. My nighttime workout playlist is loud and angry, drowning out everything but the beat.

Chloe

When I wake up, it takes me a minute to remember where I am. The bed is cold and empty, but the room is still dark. A glance at my phone confirms it's the middle of the night. I sit up and look around, but there's no sign of Nathan. Not on the floor or at his desk. Weird as it sounds, I can feel he's not here.

Once I'm out of bed, I find my shoes, slip them on, and then open the door just a crack. I'm like a runaway trying to sneak out in the middle of the night. The house is silent, so I tiptoe down the hall and stairs. I'm only a few steps from the front door—so close to getting out of here unseen.

I'll send Sydney a text when I get home and tell her I left because I wasn't feeling well. I'm not feeling great, so technically it's true. I feel embarrassed and disappointed and confused—definitely not well.

Leaving in the middle of the night is maybe a little dramatic, but I don't want to deal with the whole awkward next morning routine. Ironically, I think it might be more humiliating to wake up alone than it was naked and only remembering pieces of the night before.

I'm trying not to be offended that he found it so awful to sleep in the same bed as me that he actually got up and went to sleep somewhere else. Trying and failing.

I take one last glance over my shoulder to make sure I'm not seen and freeze. The living room is dark with only the light from the TV that's out of view casting a soft glow in the room. Nathan has his back to me, raising and lowering a set of dumbbells, alternating curls with each arm. I'm frozen, trying to decide if I should tiptoe back upstairs or risk him hearing the door when I leave, that it takes me a moment to really take in the scene before me.

He's shirtless and only wearing the gray sweatpants he put on for bed. He turns his head slightly and I hold my breath and press against the wall. He's got earbuds in so I'm probably safe to sneak out, but I don't do that. No, I walk toward the hot guy lifting weights at two o'clock in the morning.

When I get closer, I can see *New Girl* is on the TV. It's silent, but the subtitles are on. My heart does a funny flutter thing in my chest when I realize he's catching up on the episodes I watched without him.

I come around behind him at an angle, waiting for him to see me and hoping I don't scare him into dropping a weight on his foot or something. I swear the man has been curling for a solid three minutes and doesn't look like he's even breaking a sweat... oh, nope, there's the sweat. Sweet, delicious sweat.

I'm unabashedly giving his abs and chest a thrice over when I finally make it back to his face and catch his dark blue eyes on mine. His mouth is pulled into a smirk. He sets the weights on the floor in front of him and then takes out his earbuds.

"Hey, everything okay?"

"I feel like I should be asking you that."

"I couldn't sleep."

"Me either."

He drops onto the couch and wipes his forehead with his bicep. Eyeing my shoes and phone in hand, he asks,

"Sneaking out?"

"I thought maybe I was keeping you from sleeping. Looks like I was right."

He shakes his head. "It's not you. I just don't sleep well."

"So you work out instead? Like the running before bed."

A small shrug accompanies his answer. "Passes the time."

I turn my attention to the TV, easily getting lost in the episode. He turns the volume on, and the sound reminds me of my mission. "I should go."

"Let me grab a shirt, and I'll walk you."

"That's really not necessary." I step to the door quickly to emphasize the point.

"I'm not letting you walk home alone in the middle of the night." He starts for the stairs. "Give me just a minute."

Once we're outside, I'm glad he's with me. I'd like to think I'm pretty tough, but it wouldn't have been the smartest move to walk home by myself.

Our pace is slow, and we walk side by side, so close our arms brush, even though there's no one around to see us. It's like our bodies seek each other, bridging the gap the daylight and our brains won't allow.

There's a puddle on the sidewalk from the sprinklers that run twice a day, and I angle my next step to avoid it and, in the process, break our connection. Goosebumps dot my arms from the chill of the night and the withdrawal of his heat. My body is quite literally protesting the separation.

Dear Brain,

The Fake

This isn't real. Get your shit together.
Signed,
Me

His beautiful blue eyes flash to me and I step in closer. This time, when our arms touch, he grabs my hand and intertwines our fingers. My heart hammers in my chest.

"Tonight was fun."

He nods.

The dorm is in sight, and I announce it like he can't see it for himself. I comment on the full moon. Another nod. This whole silent thing he has going on is making me too tense, too hyperaware.

"There are so many stars out."

Silence.

"Did you live in Freddy before you—"

He pulls me to him, and the end of that sentence is cut off by the hard smack of my free hand against his chest.

"Wha—"

He chuckles and lightly places his hand at my mouth, not covering it exactly but making it clear he wants me to be quiet. "I really want to kiss you, and you're making it damn near impossible to find a moment your lips aren't otherwise occupied."

He drops his hand, and I keep my lips firmly shut. He waits, maybe for me to protest or maybe because he thinks I'm dumb enough to speak after that speech— hello? I'm not speaking. Kiss me already—but finally, his lips drop to mine.

His arms wrap around my waist, and I press into him. I open my mouth and he takes over. Not unlike the first time, our kiss is full of want and desire that makes me lose myself. When his hands slide down to my ass and he pulls me into him, I moan into his mouth. He feels so good. *This* feels so good.

We're roaming hands and sloppy kisses. He dips his chin and presses his forehead to mine. Our chests both rise and fall as we catch our breath.

"We should probably take this inside before the campus police stumble on us going at it in front of your dorm."

He takes my silence as agreement and steps toward the door. When I don't move, he turns to see why I'm planted in my spot. I'm rooted in place by all the reasons I know this is a bad idea and maybe by my own insecurities, too.

"I don't... I mean, we shouldn't."

Understanding dawns on him, and he drops my hand.

"It's just that we said we wouldn't, and I think if we do, then things will get complicated."

He nods slowly and places his hands in the pockets of his sweats. "Got it."

He doesn't though. I don't even have it. We've blurred the lines between real and fake and it's messy— all of which I was trying to avoid.

"I'll talk to ya later." He takes off with a little two-finger salute, and I head inside Freddy.

As I'm setting my alarm for only a few hours from now so I can work out before the fieldhouse gets busy with the usual Saturday crowd, I can't push Nathan out of my mind.

I like him, I like the way he sees me and the way I feel when I'm around him, and I have to hope that if what we have is real and not just some weird mixed signals from all of our faking, that after I've found my place at Valley and cemented my spot on the team, he'll still want to kiss me.

sixteen

Nathan

"Dude, get up, tell Chloe to put some clothes on—or not, and come out to the pool. I invited a bunch of people over." Datson's voice doesn't wake me but rouses me from the half-asleep state I've been in since early this morning when I got back from walking Chloe to her dorm.

The fucker keeps knocking until I get up and open the door. "Fuck off, John."

He hates being called by his first name. I really need to remember to bust it out more often.

"Low blow, sleeping beauty. Not my fault you stayed up half the night banging your smoking-hot girlfriend."

Oh, how I wish.

"Get your suits on and come hang." Datson's black hair falls into his face. He's got some sort of long in the front short in the back situation going on that makes him look like a backup singer in some cheesy boy band that I can't name because I don't know their names. And you can't prove otherwise.

"Chloe's not here. Now piss off."

He shoves his massive shoulder in front of the door before I can close it. "Don't be such an old man. Call Chloe and tell her to come back. Even Joel's hanging."

I manage to get him out of my room and close the door. I pull on my swim trunks and shoot Chloe a text to see if she wants to come hang by the pool with the team. I'm salty, but I still want to see her. If that's not pathetic, I don't know what is.

Her response comes an hour later when I've assumed she's ghosted me and I'm four beers in.

Chloe: Hanging by the pool actually sounds great. On my way.

Well, that's surprising. I figured that kiss scared her away for good, but I guess she's still determined to win over her teammates no matter the inconvenience. I never thought I'd be such a pussy about being used as a fake boyfriend. All the perks, well, except sex, and none of the downsides, well, except... no sex.

I head inside for the liquor and fill a plastic cup with Jack. Joel still buys the shit even though he hardly partakes anymore. In fact... I fill two and decide today we're doing this up right.

The entire team shows as well as the usual girls who come to hang. I'm parked next to Joel on a lounger while we make freshmen wait on us when Chloe shows up.

"Who's that?" Joel asks as Chloe tentatively steps outside. Cut-off jean shorts and a baggy white shirt that falls just below her boobs and hangs off one shoulder. She's stunning, per the usual.

"That is my girlfriend."

Joel laughs but then checks my expression. "You're serious. When? And *how?*"

"It's hard to explain."

Chloe looks around the party. She doesn't see me, and I can take her in without having to pretend that I'm not.

I take another drink and find my cup empty again. "Yo, Fresh."

The three freshmen all look to me at once. "Get me another Jack." I hold up my cup. "And whatever my girl wants." I point toward Chloe but seems they already know my business because they don't look to see who I mean.

She's spotted me now and lifts her hand in greeting. I give the smallest of waves with a single pinky finger. The freshmen approach her and there's some back and forth before one of them leaves carrying my cup and hopefully going inside to fill it. Chloe starts toward me, and I've got a weird mixture of excitement and dread coursing through me.

"I feel like I don't understand what's happening here. First off, I have no idea how you convinced that gorgeous girl to go out with you, and second—if she really is your girlfriend you should look a lot happier right now. Like get down on your knees and kiss the ground happy."

When she's right in front of me, staring down at me

with confusion, my chest tightens.

"Can I talk to you for a minute?" she asks, looking between me and Joel.

I don't budge or speak, but Joel is a gentleman and gets to his feet. "Hi, I'm Joel, nice to meet you."

"Chloe. Same."

"Ah, you're the new volleyball chick. Heard about you."

Her face looks a little panicked until Joel adds, "You had a good season at Golden last year."

She nods.

"Well, welcome. Can I get you something to drink?" He takes a step toward the house.

"I got it covered," I say as I spot Fresh coming out with two cups.

"Alright then. Have fun. Play nice, you two."

Chloe doesn't wait for an invitation to take Joel's seat. "Everything okay?"

I nod and Fresh hands Chloe her drink and then me mine and hurries off. I take another long drink, reveling in the burn.

There's a perfect amount of alcohol that does two things. One, it gives me blinders so that the only thing on my mind is the present. Not my dead dad, my depressed mother, or my brother who is basically raising himself. And two, it allows me to sleep dreamlessly.

Too little and I lie in bed with a thousand thoughts racing through my head and too much and I wake up in a cold sweat reliving the worst day of my life.

I don't understand psychology and the brain, but I know there's a perfect amount of Jack that will get that bitch drunk enough to just settle in for a good time without slapping me in the face later.

I'm staring straight ahead at the party going on in front of me when Chloe climbs on to my chair. She parks herself on top of me, sitting on the chair between my legs so we're sitting face to face. Her long legs fall over the side of the chair, and I rest my drink on her knee without thinking. Touching her has become automatic.

"You look nice."

The green ties of her suit top are pulled in a perfect bow behind her neck. The same dark green as her eyes.

"What's going on?" she asks.

Being near her reminds me how much I want her and how stupid it was to agree to this fake dating nonsense. Though, I'd do it again in a heartbeat. I don't want her to go back to being isolated and the punching bag for her teammates.

"If this is about last night, I'm really sorry."

"I get it. We had an arrangement, and I fucked with it."

She looks pained. "We're friends. I like hanging out with you. Let's keep it at that for now, okay?"

"Except when your teammates are around?" I don't mean for it to come out in such a bitter tone, but it does. I rub a hand over my unshaven jaw. "I'm a dick right now. Give me a few more and I'll be the life of the party." I lift the cup and take another swallow.

Chloe takes my cup mid drink, puts it on the ground, and then stands and takes my hand, tugging me forward. I stand and follow as she walks away from the pool.

"Where are we going?" I ask when she leads us inside.

She doesn't answer and I keep on following along like

a chump through the house and out the front door. A silver Mercedes is parked on the curb. California plates C MAC.

"Nice ride," I say, but she doesn't get in.

We cross the street past the fieldhouse and the baseball field until I'm sure she's just fucking with me when the sand courts come into view.

Wordlessly, she unlocks a cage of balls and takes out six of them. She lines them all up in a row, save one she rolls in her hand. She kicks off her sandals and stands just behind the boundary tape. Tucking the ball between her elbow and hip, she leans down and grabs a hand full of sand. As she rises, she lets it fall through her fingers. Then, standing tall, she serves the ball. A mean hit that lands just in bounds on the opposite far corner.

She hits all six balls before she switches sides and does the same thing. I watch her work out her frustrations on the ball. She's badass. Surfer Princess is tougher than I've been giving her credit for.

After the third switch, she lines up the balls and then looks to me. "Your turn."

I've never been one to back down from a challenge, so I kick off my shoes and go to her.

I toss the ball and jump, mimicking her movement and hitting it so hard it flies two feet out of bounds on the opposite side.

The alcohol makes me feel invincible, and I hit the next five in steady succession, each one harder than the last.

I collapse to the ground when I'm done. "I should have picked a sport where you can hit things."

Chloe lies beside me in the sand. "Right? It's the best

therapy."

My breaths come quickly, the buzz I had wearing off.
I should apologize for being an asshole, but that opens
a door I'm not walking through. She doesn't press,
though, just lies beside me in the sand, not taking my
shit but helping me work through it without
internalizing it or giving me a pass.

I want to stay mad, feel anything but what I do, which
is like I'm falling for a girl who doesn't feel the same way
I do.

seventeen

Chloe

*W*hen we get back to The White House, the number
of people out back has tripled. Nathan's still quiet, but
he seems more relaxed now.

"I'm gonna change my shirt real quick. You need
anything?" Nathan asks as we stand in the kitchen,
staring at the party outside. His black t-shirt is covered
in sand.

"I'm good."

"Be right back." He races off to his room, and I fill a
cup with vodka and Sprite Zero.

I hesitate, trying to decide if I should make him a
drink. Is that blurring the lines too much? Too
girlfriend-y? It has to be some sort of record for
overthinking a drink when I'm still undecided after a
solid minute. I finally say screw it and fill a cup with the

Jack he was drinking earlier.

"Double fisting it. Nice."

I jump and turn to find a pretty blonde smiling. She must have come through the front.

"Sorry," she says with a laugh. "I didn't mean to startle you."

"I was in my own little world." I motion upstairs. "I'm waiting for my... Nathan."

This excites her, and her glossy lips pull into a big smile. "Oh, me, too."

Oh, no. I wonder if this is going to be another Maureen incident. Trying to get ahead of another situation, I extend my hand. "I'm Nathan's girlfriend. Chloe."

She doesn't take my hand, though I don't think she's trying to be rude. She just sort of stares blankly at me. I pull my hand back and wave.

"Nathan? Nathan Payne?" She searches my face with wide eyes.

I nod.

"Since when?" The smile on her face is my first indication that I've screwed up. She doesn't look jealous. She looks happy. Really, insanely happy.

"Oh, it's recent." The big smile she's giving me is unnerving. "I'm sorry, what did you say your name was?"

She shakes her head. "Oh, God, right. I'm Gabby."

"Gabs, what are you doing here?" Nathan comes into the kitchen pulling a navy t-shirt over his head. Monochrome t-shirts are all I've seen him wear, but he pulls it off like they were Burberry instead of Hanes.

"Zeke's in Vegas for the weekend, so I came back

early."

Nathan looks between us.

"I just met Chloe. Your *girlfriend*."

I glance from Nathan to Gabby. I can't tell if she's buying the story or not, but I'm ready to fall on my sword.

"I can explain."

Nathan sweeps in beside me and wraps an arm around me. "Chloe's a transfer. We met a few weeks ago, but I wasn't sure if she was interested so I didn't say anything."

"I'm really happy for you," Gabby says to Nathan and makes a sweet face at him. Something about the way she says it and how I can feel how much she actually means it makes me feel awful for lying to her.

Gabby shocks me by taking my hand and turning a mischievous smile to Nathan. "I need to hear the details from your girl. I'm stealing her so she can tell me how you made an adorable ass of yourself asking her out." She looks at me. "He did, didn't he? I can just picture it."

I laugh uneasily, and Nathan offers me a reassuring smile.

"Relax. Gabby's good people," he murmurs in my ear, and I hand him his drink before Gabby pulls me outside.

She's a fiery little ball of energy. Short and petite, big blonde hair and green-blue eyes. She has some scarring on one side of her face, but she's stunning. I wish I could dislike her, I mean, the girl keeps a swimsuit in my boyfriend's bedroom, but she's just too damn nice.

After I've given her the quick version of the crazy

how-we-met story Nathan and I concocted, she changes her focus to getting to know me.

"Where'd you transfer from?" We're seated on two lounge chairs facing one another and she rests both elbows on her knees, totally hanging on every word. I thought she had been putting on a show for Nathan's sake, but the longer we sit here, the more I'm convinced she's truly interested in getting to know me.

"Golden in California."

"That's awesome. I'm a transfer, too. Well, sort of. I was an online student, so this is my first semester on campus." Gabby smiles a little shyly. "Are you a sophomore?"

"Senior actually."

She looks appropriately surprised. "You transferred your senior year?"

"It's a long story." Gabby looks like she's ready to settle in and hear every sordid detail of my life. "Tell me about *you* and Nathan, he says you two are close."

It's then that I notice the gigantic engagement ring on her finger. She holds her hand up proudly.

"I'm engaged to his former roommate, Zeke. He graduated last year and moved to Phoenix to play for the Suns, which is why I haven't been around as much. I'm splitting my time between Valley and Phoenix. But actually, it's Blair I have to thank for introducing me to Nathan. Blair, my best friend, is dating the other former roommate Wes. She's not here because Wes is an assistant coach now, so I doubt they'll be around much. He wants to let the guys relax and have fun without the coach killing their fun. Anyway, when I moved to Valley, Wes and Zeke were living here and so we spent a lot of time here. Nathan and I became close. He's the best. Joel, too. Have you met him?"

She doesn't wait for my nod. Gabby goes on to fill me in on people I haven't met or even heard of, but I'm smiling at her animated descriptions and updates for each of them. Also, I'm slightly concerned she hasn't taken a breath.

Nathan slides in behind me. "All right, you've stolen her for long enough," he says as he bear hugs me. His mouth brushes my ear. "Whatever she told you about me is all lies."

"As if we were talking about you. Big head, much?" I flash Gabby a conspiratorial smile. It's fun to have someone to joke with, I realize.

Gabby watches us interact, and I can't shake the unease of this whole situation. Lying to her makes me feel super guilty. She's the first person I've met, besides Nathan who's welcomed me with open arms. Maybe it's silly to want her to like me, but I do. I like her, and I don't want to screw up Nathan's world while trying to fix mine.

As the night wears on, people begin to trickle out until it's just the roommates, me, and Gabby. The guys want to play Tecmo Bowl so we head inside.

"We're having a girl's night Monday to celebrate my engagement. You should come."

I glance at Nathan for help, but his eyes are glued to the TV screen where little football men run down the field.

"That sounds fun, but I have volleyball practice every day throughout the week."

"So come after." She lifts a shoulder and lets it fall.

Taking out her phone, she says, "Give me your number and we can text to figure out the details."

My mother calls just as I pull into the Prickly Pear Monday night. I've been dodging her calls for the past few weeks, but I know I can't avoid her forever.

"Hi, Mom," I answer, killing the engine.

"Well, it's about time. Your father was prepared to borrow the Johnson's jet to come see you if you didn't answer."

"Sorry, Mom. I've been busy."

She knows it's a cop-out, but she doesn't call me on it. "I have news."

"Oh, yeah?"

"We talked to the university, and they've agreed to reverse your expulsion. Isn't that great?"

"How?"

"Your father told you he'd take care of it; he took care of it. Do you want us to fly out to help you move or we could hire a moving company and you could drive back this weekend?" She continues making plans for my assumed return to California.

"Mom, wait. I don't understand. How did this happen?" A little thrill runs through me at the prospect of going back to my old life, but just as quickly it vanishes, knowing there's no going back. That life is gone for good.

"Chloe, the details aren't important."

A heavy weight settles in the pit of my stomach. "Mom?"

"We made a donation to the school to add a covered parking lot on—"

"I don't believe you."

"Well, I'm quite serious."

"No, I mean, I am flabbergasted that after everything that went down, you two would think buying my way back in would make me happy. Did you learn nothing?"

A fine and a slap on the wrist is all the repercussions my parents faced for buying my way in, and I can't help but wonder if they realize how much more I was impacted since they got off basically scot-free.

"Stop being melodramatic. Chancellor Tomason understands that your father and I only want what's best for you. The gift was not contingent on your re-acceptance."

"Oh, well, then it's perfectly fine." I roll my eyes even though she can't see me. "Mom, I appreciate the gesture, but I'm not coming back."

"Chloe—"

"No, Mom. I need to deal with this my way. It's important to me to do this on my own. You can't buy me back."

She starts to speak again, but my mother knows just when to turn on the doting mother switch and I can't handle it today. "I love you, and I forgive you. I know you were doing what you thought was best, but I'm not coming home like this."

I hang up and let my shoulders droop. Unsurprisingly, she can't let me get the last word. I open the text message and hold my breath.

Mom: Just think about it. We miss you.

Me: I'm not going to change my mind. I miss you too.

And because I feel guilty for going against them when they've always tried to give me the world, I send one more text.

Me: I love you. I'll call soon.

I walk inside the bar, a bundle of nerves. I'm anxious about making friends with my fake boyfriend's best friend. Attaching myself to anyone associated with Nathan feels risky, but I miss having friends.

Camila and I text almost every day, but it's not the same as having friends to do things with. Nights watching TV, weekends getting dressed up and going out, hanging out on campus and re-telling stories from drunken nights… I miss having all of that.

At Golden, I had a variety of friends. Being part of a team gives you an instant set of friends—well, assuming they don't resent everything about you and wish you had never come to their college—but it's nice to have people outside of that world too. Sometimes a girl needs to vent and let loose.

Being on a team is a delicate balance of friendship and respect. Camila was the best of both worlds. Outside of volleyball we still have a lot in common. We were paired together right off freshman year and were inseparable on and off the sand until I left.

Gabby spots me from the table she's sitting at. She waves and stands and starts walking to greet me. Three more heads turn to look at me from her table.

"I'm so glad you came," she says, hugging me and pulling me toward the group. "This is Blair, Vanessa, and Katrina." She points to each of them individually. "Guys, this is Chloe. I was just telling the girls that Nathan finally settled down."

Smiling awkwardly, I take a seat at the fifth chair they've pulled up to the end of the table.

"You need a drink?" the girl to my right asks and I nod. "I was just about to get a refill. Come on." The bartender is busy, so we take a seat on the stools to wait. "I'm Blair," she reintroduces herself. Long brown hair falls over her shoulders and brown eyes nearly the same shade take me in with a friendly glint.

"Wes' girlfriend, right?"

Her smile could light up the neon signs hung all around. "That's right. How long have you been dating Nathan? I haven't seen him much since Wes moved out."

"Not long." I can't bear to tell any more lies so I decide I'm going to keep it as vague as possible tonight.

Blair fills me in on much of the same details Gabby did when I first met her about the dynamic between the group as the bartender gets our drinks. When we return to the table, Vanessa leans forward, her elbows resting on the hard wood, and her shoulder-length brown hair falling into her face. "I need some serious details on what Nathan is like as a boyfriend. I pictured him all caveman, not letting his woman out of his sight, but here you are with no obvious ball and chain."

The other girls are nodding and grinning.

"He's…" I search for adjectives. "Sweet."

Vanessa purses full lips that are coated in a bold purple shade and her big eyes narrow skeptically. Her facial expression says far more than her words. Or word, in this case. "Sweet?"

Nodding, I take a sip of my drink.

Gabby saves me, her blonde hair falling forward. "You should see how he looks at her. It's swoon city."

"Have you guys said I love you yet?" Blair asks at the same time Gabby asks, "Does he have a cute nickname for you? I love those."

And Vanessa. "Is he good in bed?"

Gabby covers her ears. "No, I can't hear about Nathan's penis." She looks at me. "Nathan is gorgeous, and I love him, but these three have already traumatized me enough with vivid details about their boyfriends' penises. I hope his dick is long, thick, and beautiful, but it's hard to unlearn those sorts of details."

We all laugh at the same time, which saves me from answering. Instead, I say, "It's still new, but I like him a lot."

That much at least is totally true.

Nathan

I'm on the couch playing video games when my phone starts blowing up with texts.

Gabs: I LOVE Chloe. Good work.

Joel: Finishing up with a late workout. Wanna crash girls' night?

Frank: Need to talk to you. Give me a call.

Heath: <picture attached>

I open the meme Heath has sent and chuckle. It's our main form of communication, sending them back and forth every day when we don't have anything else to talk about. I respond with one of my own, and I'm getting ready to text Joel back about going out when the phone rings in my hand. Frank.

"What's up?" I answer. "I was just about to hit you back."

"Got something for you."

"Told you I was done, man."

"Yeah, I know, and I get it, but this is a one-time run. Five hundred, free and clear."

I hate the way him dangling cash in front of me makes me so eager and excited. Money may very well be the root of all evil, but being without it fucking sucks.

Thanks to Joel and Wes dropping their used books from last semester in my room—neither would admit it, but it isn't like I don't know their class schedule—I was able to pay Frank back, but since I stopped dealing, there isn't any new cash coming in. Everything Chloe gave me went straight to my mom, save a couple hundred to live on until I find a new income stream.

"No can do. Gonna have to get someone else."

"This drop requires a certain finesse. I want someone I can trust."

Finesse equals sketchy as fuck. "No way, man."

He's quiet for a beat. "A grand."

Chloe

When the guys show up, I'm buzzed.

"Where's Nathan?" Gabby asks them, saving me from having to admit I don't know where he is. We had class together today, but I haven't seen or talked to him since.

"Said he'd meet us here." Joel's dark hair frames a face that's almost too handsome to be real. He slides in next to Katrina and pulls her close.

Blair introduces me to Wes, and Vanessa introduces me to Mario. I watch in adoration as the couples get lost in one another. I wonder if Nathan and I look that convincing. Gabby seems to believe we're legit, anyway.

"Zeke's in Phoenix?" I ask Gabby, pulling that bit of information from what she told me when we met.

She nods. "I should Facetime him once we're all here. Speaking of, there's your guy now."

Nathan's already spotted us and walks through the bar to our table with an easy smile, but his eyes are a stormy blue. He's trying hard not to show his agitation, but I see it. He's probably not all that pumped about having to spend an extra night with his fake girlfriend.

Since the kiss and our talk on Saturday, we've both been treading a little more carefully around each other. Our touches and interactions feel more intentional and less intimate.

He's a loyal friend, even a loyal fake boyfriend, and I doubt he likes lying to his friends any more than I do. It doesn't stop me from being excited to see him.

He grabs a chair from a vacant table and pulls it up between me and Wes.

"What's up?" He and Wes give each other a nod before Nathan turns to me. "Hey, babe."

"Hey, *babe*." As soon as I use the endearment, I laugh. He leans in to cover my amusement at the pet name. He's so not a babe. "Promise never to use that one again," I say. "Too weird."

"You can call me whatever you want." He winks as he extends an arm around the back of my chair.

"I'm gonna grab a pitcher," Wes says to Nathan. "Need a glass?"

"Not drinking tonight." Nathan rubs his thumb along my shoulder.

I don't miss the raised eyebrow Wes shoots in Nathan's direction.

"I'll help you." Joel stands and goes with Wes to the bar.

"Nathan Payne, I'm so mad at you," Gabby yells across the table, smiling.

"Uh-oh, what'd I do this time?" His tone is down despite the playful way I know Gabby meant the jab.

"You've been keeping Chloe all to yourself. We love her."

I fidget nervously at her kind words. Nathan plays the doting boyfriend well, looking down at me with a smile on his lips, his eyes still troubled.

I glance at my cell, eyeing the time.

"You have early class tomorrow?" he asks quietly.

"No, early morning workout."

"You ready to go?"

I nod, partly because of the guilt I feel for sliding into

their group under false pretenses and in part, I want to give him an easy out. "Yeah, I should get to bed early tonight."

"Gotta cut and run, guys," Nathan announces. "Need some time with my girl." He drops a kiss to my temple.

"What? You just got here!" Gabby protests.

Joel and Wes come back with the pitcher and cups.

"Catch you guys in the morning," Nathan says without meeting anyone's gaze.

We stand, and I give Gabby a genuine smile. "Thank you for inviting me out. I had a really good time."

"Of course. Consider yourself invited for every future girls' night. I'll text you."

When we get outside, Nathan asks, "Need a ride?"

I glance at my car but know I've had too many to get behind the wheel. "Yeah. I was going to call an Uber though if you want to stay."

He shakes his head. "Nah, I don't really wanna be here."

He leads me to his car and opens the passenger door for me. I give him a rueful smile at the unnecessary gesture until he adds, "Handle sticks."

He closes me in and rounds the car to hop in the driver's seat.

"This isn't what I pictured you driving," I tell him, glancing around the car and noting the hot pink flower-shaped air freshener hanging from the rear-view mirror. I tap the flower and I catch a whiff of the fruity smell—strawberries, I think.

"Are you suggesting a handsome, rugged guy like myself can't also enjoy a pale red hue?"

"Pale red?" My lips turn up at his description. "That is Barbie-vomit pink."

"Don't play Barbie like that."

"Like what?"

"Like you didn't have the dream house, the convertible, and the portable closet."

"Did you?" I ask, amused at his knowledge of Barbie accessories.

"Nah, this was Gabby's car. She wrecked mine last semester and then Zeke bought her a new one, soooo she gave me this."

"Wow."

He nods, and we fall silent for the rest of the ride.

"Do you want to come in?" I ask when he pulls into the parking lot behind Freddy.

He searches my face before responding, "I don't think so."

I'm slow to move, delaying leaving him. Despite not wanting to get too involved, I really enjoy being with him. "I'm sorry if it was weird to have me hanging with your friends. Gabby is…"

He smiles. "I know. Gabby is unrelenting. She wouldn't have taken no for an answer. And it's fine. More than fine. I'm glad you're getting to know them."

I open the door. "See you tomorrow?"

"Busy day tomorrow, but definitely Wednesday in class."

Another car pulls up behind us, forcing me out. "See you then."

nineteen

Chloe

The weeks pass in a blur of school and practices.

"We're going to The Hideout for dinner if you want to come," Emily says as we're leaving the locker room on Friday night.

"I gotta pass. I need to pack. Heading to California early tomorrow for the long weekend."

"Oh," she says. "That sounds fun. Well, maybe next time."

"Definitely," I add, hoping there's an offer next time.

I head back to the dorm, not stopping to shower first. Nathan and Shaw are exiting Freddy as I walk up.

"What are you doing here?" I ask. With the exception of class, which he mostly sleeps through these days, we haven't hung out much. Once or twice to work on the project, but that's been it. I've been legitimately busy enough that even the roommates haven't questioned his absence.

"Shaw needed to get the last of his stuff from the dorm." Nathan's got a small box tucked under one arm.

I glance at Shaw, who is holding a much larger box labeled *Porn*.

"Nice."

"Wouldn't want to make it awkward." He smirks.

"What are you doing?" Nathan asks me. He glances at Shaw before adding, "Want to come over?"

"Actually, I need to pack."

He tilts his head and stares at me with confusion.

"I'm heading to California for the weekend."

"You are?"

Shaw laughs. "Do you two ever talk or just bang?" He shrugs his shoulders which lifts the box. "No judgment. My kind of relationship."

I might need to let Sydney in on that tidbit. She hasn't said a lot, but any time I mention Shaw, The White House, or the basketball team, she gets hearts in her eyes.

"Yeah, sorry, I was going to tell you. It's Camila's birthday. We made the plans a while back." Is it weird that I feel guilty for not actually telling him?

"You're gonna miss a hell of a party tomorrow night," Shaw says. "We've got the entire weekend basketball free, and I am making the most of it."

"You don't have practice this weekend?" I ask, acknowledging that Shaw is right, and it looks like we never talk… because we're in a fake relationship. I bet Shaw would find that hilarious.

Nathan shakes his head. "Last free weekend for a

while."

"So, go with her," Shaw states like that's the logical conclusion to our situation.

Nathan is shaking his head again before I can respond. "It's a little early to be meeting the family. It's cool."

"Actually, I'm not staying with my parents." I mull over the idea of Nathan coming with me and I have to say I don't hate it. In fact, I've missed spending time with him. "Come. It'll be fun. I can introduce you to my friends, and we can hang on the beach."

Shaw shifts the box. "Good, it's settled. Now, can we get these boxes to the car? Mine isn't light."

"Call ya later," Nathan calls over his shoulder.

Inside, I shower, field texts from Camila about the weekend, and then start to pack. Nathan texts as I'm trying to zip up my overflowing suitcase.

Nathan: Have a good weekend. Don't worry, I'll tell the guys I stayed so you could have time with your friends.

Disappointment creeps in making me realize just how much I liked the idea of him coming along. I've missed spending time with him outside of class and our project.

Me: Offer stands to come with. Could be fun.

He doesn't respond right away, and I decide to further plead my case.

Me: Ocean is great this time of year. There's lots of cheesy, touristy stuff or we can just hang at the beach, surf, whatever. My friends are dying to meet you.

I don't know why I add the last part, but I know once I tell Camila, the statement will be true.

I drop my phone on my bed and scroll through videos on my laptop to kill the time. The longer it takes him to respond, the more I'm convinced he's wording a very nice letdown text. When my phone pings, I brace myself for the disappointment.

Nathan: Alright. I'm in. Let's do this.

"What year is this?" Nathan asks from the passenger seat of my car. We've been driving for a little over an hour and already blown through small talk on the weather and school.

"Uhhh…"

He lifts a brow. "You don't even know, do you?"

"It's new. This year or last, I think." I shrug. "I got it for my twenty-first."

"When's your birthday?" he asks, side-stepping the conversation. That's the thing about Nathan, he never makes me feel weird about having nice things or money even though I know he probably thinks it's over the top.

"December twentieth. Yours?"

"December first."

"Fellow Sagittarius." I glance over. The freeway is quiet this early, something I love about Arizona. Traffic in Southern California never seems to let up. "Tell me about your twenty-first."

He gives me a look that says it's too early for storytime.

"We've got five more hours to kill. Entertain me. What did you do? Did you do the obligatory twenty-one shots?"

"It was actually quite the night, from what I hear."

"Ominous."

"We went to The Hideout. I didn't do twenty-one shots, but I did a lot. About the time I passed out, Wes got in a brawl with Blair's ex over some naked photos."

"Wes got in a *brawl?*"

Nathan smirks. "You've never said that word in a sentence before, have you?"

"Sure, I have," I say with a laugh. "I've been in all sorts of *brawls.*" Rolling my eyes, I try out the word again. "Brawl, brawl, brawl."

He claps. "Very convincing, Surfer Princess."

"Well, I spent mine mostly sober. I had an early flight the next morning, so Camila took me to the bar and we ordered two shots of tequila and then went home."

"Well, we'll have a do-over for your twenty-second."

I nod. By the time my birthday rolls around, I don't even know if we'll be speaking. I don't mention that, though. We haven't talked about what happens when this whole thing is over.

We switch seats after another hour, and Nathan drives while I flip through the radio. I prefer it over a playlist. Randoming onto a song you haven't thought about, but it's just perfect for the moment… I love that about scanning through the radio.

I sit back after settling on a classic rock station, Stevie Nicks croons about love. I look over at Nathan behind the wheel, looking too good for words the way he rests his left hand at the top of the wheel.

"You look good driving my car. I could get used to being chauffeured around."

He looks me over carefully, blue eyes scanning me from head to toe. My pulse quickens, but I don't dare move a muscle as he stares at me like he's really seeing me. Like he always does. "I think I could get used to this, too."

Nathan

Chloe hadn't really told me anything about Camila other than she's like a sister to her so when a girl with dark brown skin and black hair with short bangs comes running out to the car to greet us, I can't help but note all the ways they look nothing alike.

They're about the same height, but that's where the similarity ends. Camila is dark where my surfer princess is light and where Chloe is more reserved, Camila fills every second of silence with her excited chatter about our arrival.

Camila's vibe actually reminds me of Gabby, and that makes me smile to think Chloe might have someone like my best friend looking out for her.

Camila ushers us inside her apartment.

"I still haven't found a new roommate," she whines and gives Chloe a pouty lip.

"You lived here?" I ask.

"Yep." She looks around the place like she's missed it.

I didn't ask Chloe what she told Camila about me or our weird situation, but when she leads us to the guest room, or Chloe's old room, and disappears to give us a chance to settle in, I finally question my role for the weekend.

"Does Camila know we're not really together?"

She shakes her head. "I told her we're dating, but that it was new. I thought it would be easier until I could explain in person."

I mull that over. Is it easier or is she just really going the extra mile to sell this to everyone in her life?

"If you want me to tell her now, say the word. If anyone would understand, it's Cam. She's always had my back. She's one of the few friends who didn't magically disappear when things went down."

"Up to you, princess. I'm glad you have her though. Friends like that are hard to come by."

"Speaking of friends, I was thinking maybe we should tell yours, too. At least Gabby and Joel."

"Definitely not Joel, he's got a big ass mouth."

She laughs. "Okay, but Gabby. I felt really awful lying to her. I can tell how much she cares about you."

"Yeah." The reasons I haven't told Gabby have more to do with me than Chloe. I guess I'm still hoping this thing will turn into something real before our fake relationship is over. I can't shake her. Even distancing myself and loads of porn hasn't helped. "I'll think on it."

We hang out at Camila's place for the evening, and she invites over a hand full of people—most of which know Chloe. I stand by her side and am introduced as the boyfriend. Not a bad gig, really, and it feels awesome to be out of Valley. I rarely get to leave with the team schedule and the expense of flying.

"I'm gonna grab another drink," I say when I notice her cup is empty. "Want something?"

"Thank you." I know she means for more than the drink.

Wandering inside, I fill our cups and linger a moment before heading back to the deck where everyone is hanging out. I think I expected it to be lavish and over the top, but it looks like any other college apartment—mismatched furniture, minimal wall hangings, and more plastic cups than dishes. The location is pretty sick, though—only a mile or so from the beach.

Camila enters and slaps her empty cup on the counter, grabs the rum and Diet Coke, and fills it up. "It's good to see Chloe so happy. I've been worried about her."

I smile and nod, my go-to when I don't know what the fuck to say. Chloe is happier than I've seen her, but I'm almost certain that's due to Camila, not me.

"Guess I have you to thank for that." Camila lifts her cup, and I clink mine against hers.

We cheers and drink before I say, "I didn't do

anything. She's a tough chick."

Camila lets out a long breath. "You didn't see her two months ago."

"That bad?" I equal parts want to know and don't. The latter feels like an invasion of her privacy on some level.

"She couldn't go anywhere. Team turned their backs on her, some of our friends. And don't get me started on her parents. They're completely clueless about who Chloe is and what she wants. They threw more money at the problem to convince Golden to take her back."

"Chloe's coming back to California?" I don't like the tight feeling in my chest at the thought of her leaving Valley to come back to a place where she was made to feel unwanted. Or the idea of her leaving me.

"She didn't tell you?" She nods at my blank stare. "I'm not surprised. She still worries everyone is going to blame her for things she has no control over."

"But she's not coming back, right?"

She shrugs. "I doubt it. We've filled her spot on the team, so she'd have to give up volleyball—the one thing that keeps her sane." She smiles. "Well, one of the two things that keep her sane, now that she has you."

The next morning, I'm up with the sun. Sleeping next to Chloe all night, or not sleeping as it was, has me agitated and nervous. There's no winning when it comes to sleep. I can't even entertain the possibility that I might have a nightmare in front of her. Talk about a fucking ten on the humiliating scale.

"Morning." Chloe slips out onto the deck, looking rumpled and mussed and exactly what I wish my girl looked like in the morning. Except she's not mine—at least not in any way that matters. "Coffee inside."

"Don't like coffee," I say, my voice too deep and hoarse. I clear my throat and turn to rest a hip on the side railing. "What are you doing up so early?"

"I can never sleep in here. Even in high school, I'd wake up early every morning to run on the beach, listen to the waves, or surf. The ocean is my happy place."

"Surfer Princess," I say with a grin.

"I was planning on going for a run this morning if you want to come."

Chloe

*W*e drop onto the sand, both panting from the last sprint. Nathan pulled his t-shirt off somewhere around the one-mile mark and tucked it in his waistband. His chest lifts and rises with his breaths, sweat sliding down the cut muscles of his abs.

"Good God, woman. You can go forever."

Five miles has never felt better. Running next to Nathan... yeah, that'd inspire anyone to push a little harder.

Sitting ten feet from the water, we both stare out into the ocean. The sun is still rising in the sky behind us.

"I love it out here," I admit. "Reminds me how small and insignificant we all are by comparison."

When I turn to him, he's staring at me with stormy blue eyes.

"What?"

He shakes his head. "You just surprise me sometimes is all."

I stand and brush the sand off my shorts. I'm sweaty and dirty and need a shower in the worst way. "Ready to head back?"

He doesn't budge but holds his hand up like he wants me to help him up. I grab ahold of him, except when I pull, so does he and I fall to the ground—half on him and half sprawled in the sand.

"Is that a no?" I chuckle and move off him so fast I wonder if I dreamt the burn on my skin from the contact.

Wrapping his arm around me and pulling me back close, his voice reverberates against my back. "May never be ready."

Nope, definitely didn't dream the scalding feeling of his skin touching mine because it's back and lighting my insides on fire.

I stay quiet then, sinking into his hard chest, listening to the ocean and enjoying the gentle lull of his steady breathing. I feel so safe and untouchable like this. I don't need Nathan to protect me, not here, but the idea that he might want to makes everything else as insignificant as we are to the ocean.

An older couple walks by hand in hand. I've seen them before, though it's been a few months now. They walk the beach together every morning.

Today I notice how they're smiling at one another and looking more in love than I would have guessed possible at that age. Funny, I never noticed that before. I'd always assumed they were married, but I'd never been able to see the love surrounding them.

"Alright, I guess I'm ready," Nathan says, sounding like he'd rather eat sand than leave.

"No." I push harder against his chest to prevent him from moving. "Just a few more minutes."

"You're on my team," Camila says to our friend Jill, who joined us for a day at the beach. Jill is one of the few who didn't turn on me after the shit last year, but we're not as close as I am with Cam.

"Seems only fair since I got the best player out here." Nathan hugs me from behind and kisses the top of my head. Without my teammates, I don't feel the need to pretend to be anything we're not so every touch and glance between us makes my heart flutter.

Camila makes a retching sound. "Ugh, you two are going to make my lunch come up."

She and Jill take their positions on the other side of the net, and Nathan reluctantly lets me go. Or at least that's what I'd like to think since he inches away slowly, not dropping his fingertips from me until he can't reach.

Jill serves to my right, and I lunge to save it. Nathan takes his time setting it and I spike it over right between Cam and Jill.

We take the point and I move to serve. It's my favorite part of volleyball, I think because it's one thing I can control. Once a serve is over the net, it's all reactionary. Sharp senses and repetition training until the movements happen almost on instinct are key. But serving is all about power and control.

Nathan is a natural and his height is a definite help. We win the first game, and he lifts me up to celebrate. I'm screaming, babbling nonsense mostly, as he runs a lap around the beach. When he can't carry me any longer, he sets me down and falls to the ground beside me. I lay back, letting the sun kiss my skin, and Nathan's eyes scan the full length of me.

He takes me by surprise when he covers my body with his and kisses me on the mouth. It's just a quick, chaste kiss, but I wrap my arms around his neck and demand more.

It's not until I hear Camila and Jill drop down close to us and he pulls back that I realize him devouring me was for show. At least I think it was. He's sporting that smirk that does me in every single time, and his eyes are a dark blue that makes me wonder if he's as keyed up as I am.

I know this is fake, but my libido doesn't and even if she did, I think she'd tell me to pipe the fuck down and let her have her moment.

"You guys want to go back and get showered and changed for tonight?" Camila asks when Nathan has removed his fabulous body from mine and sits in the sand in front of me.

Nathan looks at me as he answers and his deep voice rakes over me. "Yeah, let's shower."

When we get inside our room for the weekend—my old room—I glance at all our stuff tossed around and the mess makes me smile. Sharing space with him makes me insanely happy.

"Today was fun. I'm glad you came," I say as I pull out the dress I want to wear tonight.

"Me too."

"I'm going to tell her." I motion with my head to the door and the general direction of Camila's room. "I thought about it, and I don't want to leave here with anything hanging over my head. When I moved to Valley, I was still carrying so much pain from everything, but I'm not anymore. I'm happy." He shoots me a questioning glance. "I am. I mean, the situation with the team isn't perfect, but it has nothing to do with Camila and lying to her... well, it just doesn't feel right. She deserves the truth. She's stuck with me this long."

Nathan takes my hand and squeezes. "I'll be here. Whatever you need." He clears his throat. "That reminds me. Cam mentioned you might be moving back to California."

I shake my head. "My parents worked out a deal with the university so I could finish my degree here, but too much has happened. Valley is the clean start I need. My chance to prove that I can make it on my own."

"I get that," he says. "That's how I felt my freshman year when I got to college, but don't confuse clean start with avoidance."

I tense at his words.

"Not saying you are," he adds when I shoot him an insulted look. "But I know what it's like to try and start with a clean slate… it's messy and not all that clean."

I nod, but I can't seem to shake his words as we get ready for a night out to celebrate Camila's birthday. I'm still thinking about it as we head to JT's house. He graduated last year and has an apartment that's basically on the beach. His parents are better off than mine— both of them doctors with their own medical TV talk show—so he gets my situation more than most.

The party is still small when we arrive and I decide to talk to Cam before more people show up. I introduce Nathan to JT and a few others I vaguely know and then make excuses so I can talk to my bestie.

"I'm going to chat with Cam and then get us drinks. You good?"

Nathan smiles as he nods and falls back into conversation with JT.

I link my arm through Camila's. "Take a walk on the beach with me, birthday girl."

She eyes me suspiciously but smiles. "Okay."

Neither of us speaks as we walk arm in arm. We kick off our shoes and hold them in our free hands.

When my feet hit the wet sand, I breathe in the salty air. "I missed this."

"You could come back. I've always got a room for you."

I smile at her and lean my head against hers.

"Something tells me you'd miss that fine hunk of male. Nathan's really great. I'm glad you have him."

"Actually, that's why I wanted to talk to you."

Her brows pull together in confusion.

"I don't have him. Not how you think." Saying it out loud makes me realize how much I like him. I want to have him.

I give her the short version of the story. The bullet points. One-night stand, my big mouth claiming him as my boyfriend, and his real reason for helping me… money.

"Do you think I'm just as bad as my parents?" I ask, unlinking our arms so I can look her in the eye.

"Of course not." Her tone is sincere but something in her expression tells me she's holding back.

"But?"

"I don't know if I believe that's all this is. I've seen you two together. You can't fake that kind of chemistry. Why not just date him for real?"

"I don't want to get swept up in some guy so soon into the school year. I have to prove to myself that I deserved to be at Golden. I know it probably sounds dumb, but I need to know I could have done it on my own. And that I still can. But the more time I spend with him, the harder it is to not get carried away. And there's the whole setup. I never know when we're pretending or when it's real. He might not even be interested in me if it weren't for me paying him." I groan.

"You said he asked for your number after your one night… I'd say he's interested."

"He was then, but that was weeks ago, and I've shown him a whole lot of crazy since then."

"Talk to him. Tell him how you feel."

"What if he doesn't feel the same and then this whole thing would have been for nothing?"

"That's another thing. You have to stop trying to win over your teammates by using Nathan."

"You think I should come clean with them too?" My

stomach churns at the thought of Bri's smug face.

"I do. I get why you did it, but it's not solely on you to fit in there. You're an incredible player and a pretty kick-ass person, too. Don't play their games. You're too good for that. You've never let people push you around, not even when they came down hard on you for your parents' bullshit. Stand up to them, Chloe. You belong there. Don't let them make you feel otherwise."

Her words hit on something I'd been thinking but hadn't verbalized, and I know she's right.

"You're right. I know you're right. It's been harder than I expected to start over."

She nods and hugs me, making me miss her and adding a new sense of determination to be as tough as she thinks I am. "I've got your back. If you need me to come to Valley and kick some ass, just say the word."

"You'd brawl for me?" I ask, thinking of Nathan and stealing his word.

"Hell yes, I would."

Nathan

"Everything okay? You've been quiet tonight."

Chloe walks just ahead of me to the cross streets where the Uber is supposed to meet us to take us back to Camila's, her arms wrapped around her waist. "I just forgot how much I loved it here. I miss it and I'm already a little sad about leaving."

She's silent again for a minute before she adds, "I told Cam."

I glance over and raise a brow. "And?"

"She was understanding. Felt good to tell her the truth." She drops her hands in front of her and fidgets with her fingers. "Speaking of truth, I need to tell you something."

"What's that?" I ask, trying to prepare myself for the worst.

She glances back at me, her blonde hair blowing into her face and the blue dress making her body blend in with the darkness. "I like you."

I chuckle out my relief, and my heart skips a fucking beat. "I like you, too."

Stopping in front of me, she blocks my path. "No, I mean, I *like* you. The flirting, the touches, the kisses, spending time together—I wanted all of it. And not just because it's helped with my roommate situation. Volleyball and proving myself is my number one priority, but I'm done pretending this is all for show. At least for me."

It's always been easy to be with Chloe. I've had to fake very little of our time together. I thought she knew that. I mean, she's the one who keeps pushing me away. But the thing is, I've learned not to question the good. Grab it, swallow it up before the bad crashes in again. So I don't question it, I just go for it.

I frame her face with both hands and bring my lips to hers. "It was never for show, princess."

twenty-one

Chloe

The next morning, I wake up with a smile on my face.

Stretching my arms over my head, I sit up and then jump out of bed to go find Nathan. After a lot of kissing, he pushed me into my room and insisted he sleep on the couch. I'm sure it was supposed to be some gentlemanly move, but I missed him beside me.

He's on the couch, his long legs over one end and his head propped up on a pillow at the other. He's got one arm over his eyes and a Golden throw blanket covering his lower half.

My mouth waters at his bare chest, and I press my fingertips to my lips. They're tender from his bruising kisses and scruffy face, but I'm ready to do it again.

I make coffee and pour myself a cup and him some Gatorade into a mug with the intent of taking them into the living room and maybe snuggling in next to him on the couch, but his gruff voice comes just as I pick up the mugs to take them to the other room.

"Morning."

I hand him one of the mugs. He glances down at the orange liquid and laughs. "Morning."

I watch him over my mug as I take a sip. He does the same.

"What's the plan for today?"

"I thought, if you were game, we could go surfing."

"Hell yeah." He nods. His eyes widen, and his smile is ridiculously adorable. "Can we go now?"

I laugh. "Yeah, just let me change."

We get ready for another day at the beach, and Camila wakes up and decides to come too. I'd left my boards here when I moved so we take my hybrid and longboard. Nathan is a natural, and the waves are pretty calm out this morning so I'm able to coach him up onto the board for a couple rides.

Camila stops us as we're coming in. "I'm gonna head back. I told Jill I'd meet her for lunch. You guys want to come?"

I look to Nathan, and he shakes his head.

"I think we're gonna stay here. Meet you back at the apartment later?"

She smiles. "Sounds good."

We take our boards to Camila's SUV and then head back down to the beach. We drop onto the sand, wet shoulders and knees touching.

"You wanna stay out on the beach or..." I let the sentence trail off with my mind going to all sorts of places.

"I wanna take you out on a date." He's sitting with his arms hugging his knees so he has to lean over his arm to kiss me.

"A date?" I ask when he pulls away.

"Mhmm. Thought we could check out the cheesy, touristy stuff you mentioned. Up for it?"

The wind blows my hair into my face, and the wet strands stick to my lips. Nathan brushes them away and tucks the hair behind my ear. I lean into his touch and nod. "Definitely."

I throw on a dress over my suit, and Nathan pulls on his gray t-shirt.

"Ready?"

Hand in hand, we make our way to the pier at a slow pace. I've been here a million times, but seeing Nathan take it in for the first time makes it worth it. There's a steady line of people, and it's as busy as I've ever seen it with the beautiful weekend. The late summer days are still providing stellar weather, and everyone wants to soak up as much of it as they can before it turns cool.

Nathan insists on stopping and seeing everything, and I don't mind at all with the goofy smile he wears. We watch a couple getting a caricature done, wander through the arcade, and to the park. I let him set the pace and the itinerary.

He wins me a stuffed bear shooting baskets, and I buy him a Japadog for lunch. When our feet hurt from walking and we need a break, we head down by the water.

"Have fun?" I ask, even though it's clear he did with the big grin that hasn't left his face.

"Yeah, I really did. Thanks for humoring me. You've

probably been here a million times."

"I can honestly say today was the most fun I've ever had at the pier."

He holds his hand out and opens his palm to me. "I got you a little something to remember it."

I reach for the keychain. "Oh, my God, when did you get this?"

It's bright pink and has an outline of a girl on a surfboard.

"Saw it while you were getting lunch. Thought it was perfect for my surfer princess."

"Thank you. I love it." I reach in my pocket. "I got you something, too."

"You did?"

I nod and hand him the tickets I got while I told him I needed to use the restroom. "You can't come to the pier and leave without riding the Pacific Wheel."

Up on top of the wheel, Nathan places his hand on my thigh and squeezes. "Is this a bad time to admit I don't love heights?"

"Are you serious?"

He plays like he's going to bury his head in my chest but then rubs the side of his face against my boobs. "Ah, much better. I feel safe now."

I laugh, and he pulls his head up to smile gleefully at me. The hand on my thigh moves up under the hem of my dress and my heart rate increases.

"Today was without a doubt the best date I've ever had. I'm sorry I couldn't take you on every single ride and buy you something better than a cheap keychain."

I wish I could wave away his money problems and whatever misplaced guilt he has for not having it to spend on me. Doesn't he know I don't need it? I've had more than I've needed my whole life and never been happier than I am just hanging out with Nathan. "Money doesn't buy everything, Nathan Payne. I'd rather walk around and do nothing with you than have all the stuff you can buy on this pier."

"You mean that?" He threads his hand through my hair and holds the back of my neck. "Because there were some pretty kick-ass trinkets back there. I think you might be getting the short end."

"Not even close."

I kiss him with the sun setting over the Pacific Ocean and the pier lights buzzing as they come to life. The wind whips around us and I press against his warm sun-kissed skin. The weeks of wanting him and holding back make our kisses frantic and sloppy.

We stumble off the wheel and down the pier, laughing and stopping every few feet to kiss and stare at each other. I feel like we're finally seeing each other without any pretenses or expectations, and us like this—as a real couple—we're even better than I ever imagined when we'd been faking.

Camila sent a text to tell us she went to a bar down the street from her apartment and to stop by if we wanted, but when the Uber drops us off, it's a race to be alone. Inside my old room, he kicks the door closed and presses me against it.

Soft lips caress while the scruff on his face scratches. Gentle and hard. Tender and demanding.

We're both sober, so tomorrow morning there'll be no regrets and no excuses. I want him and he wants me. Period. End of discussion.

Nathan slides the straps of my dress down and his mouth follows, trailing kisses from my shoulder to the top of my breasts. I arch into him, wanting more even as his erection presses into my hip.

I hook my leg around him, which causes my dress to slide up. His fingers find my ass, and he lifts me up so I can wrap both legs around him. The new positioning has him just where I need him, and I grind against him at a pace that has us both breathless and panting.

"Condom," I rasp.

He curses under his breath. "I didn't bring any."

"Bathroom."

He seems to understand and tightens his grip on my right side. His left hand opens the door and then steadies me as he carries me down the hall toward the bathroom.

"Where?" he asks when he steps over the threshold.

Neither of us bothers to turn on the light as I reach around him to the top right drawer where Camila and I have always stored the condoms. I grab three. Better to be prepared than not. "Got 'em."

He places me on the counter and pushes himself between my legs. Both hands frame my face as he kisses me, deeply owning my mouth. Savoring and exploring all at once.

We have the entire place to ourselves. Which makes my screaming out as Nathan's mouth moves lower and bites down on my sensitive nipple awkward only for the neighbors.

His hands press into my thighs and move up until both thumbs brush against my pussy through my bikini bottoms. He alternates torturing me. Left then right. His touch is too soft even when I push against his hand. It started just like this last time. I make a little sound like a whine and he chuckles.

"You remember." He adds pressure. "You remember how I tortured you until you begged me. I thought you didn't remember, but you do, don't you?"

"Yes."

"Let's test your memory, shall we? What did I do next, princess?"

"Mouth." My one-word answers are bordering unintelligible, but Nathan understands.

"Hmmm. Sure it wasn't this?" He slips one long finger under the material.

It feels good, and I don't want him to stop, but it's not what he did last time.

"I'm sure," I say finally when he stops and withdraws his finger. "You said you wanted to taste me and then…"

He smirks and lowers his head. Softly, he kisses my inner thigh and glances up, waiting for me to say it.

"And then you licked me through my panties."

Just saying it makes my sex clench. No amount of alcohol could keep me from remembering the feel of his wet tongue lapping at me through the satin barrier, though I'm insanely happy for the repeat I think is about to happen.

When his tongue flattens against me, I groan, and my

hands go to his hair. I thread my fingers through the thick strands and pull, showing my appreciation and urging him along.

He doesn't seem to need any help, despite my attempts. His mouth covers me completely. My bottoms are soaked from him and from me. He alternates swiping his tongue along my seam and pushing it inside so the material wedges, creating a whole new sensation.

By the time he hooks a finger under my wet bikini and slides it inside of me, I'm already writhing on the counter. I'm ninety-nine percent sure his mouth and index finger are the only things keeping me from tumbling onto the floor.

The first orgasm lasts so long I can't be sure it isn't two. And before I gain full control of my body, he's got my bikini bottoms on the floor, covers himself, and pushes in.

"This... Oh, God, do I remember this." I grip his shoulders as he fills me completely and pauses. His eyes close, and his chest shakes like he's as overwhelmed as I am.

When he starts to move, it's slow. An unhurried pace that contradicts the strain on his face telling me he's holding back until I'm close.

Draping my arms around his neck, I kiss him with everything in me. Emotions and promises and desires. My feelings for this man run the gamut. I like him.

I *really* like him.

I like how he wanted me that first night. I like that he wanted my number the next day despite my throwing him out of my dorm. I like that he's never made me feel unwelcome.

His climax comes on the cusp of mine, and we hold on as our bodies shudder.

I let my back fall against the mirror as Nathan gets rid of the condom and cleans me with a washcloth.

Both our heads snap up at the jingle of keys, and we run from the bathroom to my bedroom. He shuts the door just as Camila calls out, "Anyone home?"

"Welcome back," I yell and collapse onto the bed in a fit of laughter. My dress is bunched up around my waist and my bikini bottoms are missing.

Nathan's deep chuckle echoes mine, and he walks from the door to the bed. His shorts are untied and he's sporting some serious just-sexed hair but other than that, he looks as good as before he fucked me in the bathroom.

He plops down beside me and rolls on his side so he's facing me. "You almost got me caught."

"Me? That was all you. You and that hot as sin mouth."

"Why didn't you tell me you remembered?"

"It's foggy. I remember parts of it. I don't remember finishing or passing out after."

"We drank a lot that night." He grimaces. "Sorry about that. I should have looked out for you more. I'd had a shitty day and then there you were standing by yourself in red looking like you were trying to decide between fighting the world or hiding from it."

I sit up so I can adjust my dress to cover my bare vag and boobs.

"Let me help." He pulls from the hem and lifts it over my head, taking my bikini top with it so I'm completely naked. "Much better."

"Not fair." I pull at his shirt, and he raises his arms so I can get it over his head. I toss it to the floor and nod to his shorts. He smirks as he strips naked and throws his trunks toward his shirt.

He's comfortable in his skin. And he should be. His body is a work of art. Most athletes have bodies built for their sport, but Nathan's body is chiseled beyond anything necessary for basketball.

"I should have gotten a glass of water before I let you get me naked," he says. "Think Camila will mind if I walk through her house like this?"

"I don't think anyone would mind if you walked around naked all the time."

He smirks and winks. "I'm gonna grab some water. Want something?"

He stands and grabs a pair of boxers from his bag.

"I'll come with you." I grab his t-shirt and put it on while he watches me with amusement.

"I don't know why that's so sexy, but fuck." His heated gaze sweeps over me. "Come on."

We walk quietly down the hallway like we're sneaking, which makes me feel like a kid. If Camila saw us, she'd probably high five Nathan and pat me on the ass and tell me to get back in there.

In the kitchen, I rummage through the junk spot. In the tallest cabinet above the refrigerator. We used to buy chips and cookies and stash them there for late nights, and I'm happy to see it still contains my favorites.

I pull down a bag of Tostitos as he fills two glasses with ice water from the fridge.

Sitting on the counter with my chips and him leaning back against the counter with a glass... it all feels so natural. Since we both have roommates, our time together never feels like this... like it's just the two of us. And sure, Camila is just down the hall, but right now... right now, it's just us.

I don't know what we are or what tonight means to him, and I'm trying not to go there. This... tonight... means everything. I know even as I'm in the moment that it's going to be a day I never forget.

twenty-two

Nathan

"No way, I don't believe you," Chloe says. "How long?"

"Above my shoulders. I could get it in a little man bun and everything. God, the guys gave me shit for it."

"I can't picture it." She narrows her gaze. We're sitting on the bed totally naked talking. Speaking of the guys giving me shit... I'm pretty sure they'd kick me off man island if they knew we'd been doing nothing but talking for the past few hours. Totally naked. My dick stayed hard for the first two, but the poor guy has given up the fight.

"I've got some pictures from when it was long." I walk over to grab my phone out of the front left pocket of my shorts. Her eyes sweep over my body from head to toe and... there he goes... my dick stands back at attention.

Sitting on the bed together with our legs crossed, knees touching, I pull up my photos and scroll back to last spring. I stop on one of me and Gabby and hand it to her.

"Wow." She looks from the picture to me and back again. "You've got a whole thing going on here… and I am *here* for it. Why did you cut it?" She holds the phone up. "Do you mind?"

I nod my permission, and she flips through the pictures while I try to figure out how to answer her. I did it so my best friend would date me isn't exactly the truth, but it isn't a total lie either. Gabby had all but told our friends she didn't like my hair, and Gabby represented everything I thought I wanted—sweet, beautiful, and fun.

"It was indirectly Gabby's idea," I say. "She made a comment about liking short hair. I miss the long, but I don't have to steal hair ties from chicks anymore, so there's that."

Chloe's eyes snap to me. "Did you have a thing with Gabby?"

"No." I shake my head. The sting of rejection is still there. "I did like her for a while, or maybe I just liked the idea of her." I shrug. "She didn't feel the same way."

I wince at my honesty and how it sounds when I say it out loud.

"Her loss." She puts the phone on the bed and crawls into my lap. I've never been so happy to have been rejected. I don't have feelings for Gabby anymore, not like that, but if Chloe wants to take pity on me and try and prove how happy she is that things didn't work out with my best friend... well, I'm not about to stop her.

The next morning, I stand back while Chloe and Camila hug and tear up saying their goodbyes. I look at my phone while they talk, trying to let them have their time. I glance up as Camila looks over Chloe's shoulder. She smiles and waves me over.

"I'm so glad you came. Thanks for looking out for my girl. You've got my number now if I need to come down and cut a bitch."

"Easy, killer." Chloe laughs and hugs her again. "But thank you. Love you."

"Love you, too, Chlo."

The ride back starts out cheerful. Loud, very bad singing, on my part, to songs on the radio. Chloe knows exactly zero song lyrics despite claiming to know them all. I don't care, though. Off-key, wrong words, her voice makes my chest feel like it's cracked wide open.

About seventy miles out, the singing stops and Chloe goes to staring out the window. Pressing and talking about feelings isn't really my bag, but I know I have to say something.

"Missing California already?"

"Yeah and thinking about how crazy our schedules are going to be now with your games starting soon."

For the next seven months, basketball runs my life. I look forward to it and dread it equally every year. Sounds like she does, too, but it seems like she's in more than a *life's about to get crazy* funk.

"Worried about seeing your roommates again?"

"No, not really. I mean, we still have a long way to go, but I'm not worried they tossed my stuff out into the hallway while I was gone. They're probably not waiting by the door anxious for my arrival either." She shrugs. "Cam thinks I should come clean with them. Tell them that you and I aren't really together. Except…" Hands resting in her lap, she twists the rose gold ring on her thumb. "Now I don't know what we are."

She doesn't give me time to answer. Her face scrunches up, and she visibly cringes. "Oh, God, sorry. I'm totally that girl."

"What girl?" I glance from the road to her face. I bite back a laugh at her panicked expression.

She gives me a look that says she's not saying any more, so I put her out of her misery. "You're not that girl. We're hanging out."

The words don't quite describe us, I know, but we've only been dating for real for two days.

"*Hanging* out?"

Desire to claim her, tell her I want her to be my girlfriend, and that we'll figure out the rest later courses through me, but I can't do that. Who knows what she'll want in another few weeks after her teammates come around? And they will.

I don't want to be the guy who saved her, I want to be the guy she chooses. I'd like to believe this is one of those good things in my life I'm going to be able to hang on to, but the pessimist in me isn't ready to forge ahead so blindly.

"Listen, we've got a couple weeks left in our fake relationship to figure it out. By then, you may be sick of me. Until then, let's just roll with it."

Tuesday afternoon practice is shit and the team looks sloppy. Coach is on the floor demonstrating an inbound play that should be so easy middle schoolers could get it done. Sitting on the sidelines getting water and taking a break after almost an hour of non-stop play, Joel and I share the same worried expression. After winning the NCAA tourney last year, all eyes are going to be on us and we fucking suck.

"We gotta do something," he says and drapes the towel over his head. "I don't wanna go out like this. Last year and we're going to be laughed off the court."

I'd been thinking the same thing and I think of Chloe so willing to do anything to fit in with her team. Maybe it's not the rookies. Maybe it's us.

"What about having the team over tonight? Just the guys."

He nods. "Like a team intervention? We could go over all the shit they're fucking up."

"Nah, man. No basketball talk, just hanging, relaxing, getting to know them."

"You wanna make friends with the rookies?" He quirks one dark eyebrow.

I shrug. "What we're doing now isn't working. You got a better idea?"

Joel doesn't answer right away. Coach yells out for us to sub back in, and we get to our feet quickly.

"Let's do it," he says. "I'm willing to try anything."

After practice, Joel and I each tell a few guys about the plan for the night and then he takes off to get supplies while I go back to the house and survey our stock. I text him a list of things and then jump in the shower.

When I walk back into my room naked except the towel I'm currently using to dry off my hair, Chloe's there on my bed. Books and laptop sprawled out, she smiles up at me, heat in her gaze. "You just walk around naked on a Tuesday afternoon?"

"Not usually hot girls sitting on my bed when I get out of the shower. Did I conjure you up because the Chloe I was thinking about while I soaped up was naked too and you're fully clothed?"

"We're supposed to work on our Comms project. You forgot, didn't you?"

"Shit. Yeah, sorry. Team is coming over in an hour."

She nods and looks me over. I still haven't bothered to cover myself. "But you have an hour?"

Pretending I don't know what she's angling at, I sit on the bed and pick up a textbook. It's upside down, but she doesn't notice. "Sure. We could probably get the first section done in an hour. You think?"

I run my fingers through my still damp hair and then run a hand over my chest to wipe away some water drops. She watches every movement I make; her pretty lips part and quiver. She's so still I can't be sure she's breathing.

"Chloe?"

Her gaze snaps to mine. "Sorry, yeah, let's do that."
She tries to recover, fumbling with a notebook and pen.

"Chlo?"

She looks up, hesitant this time.

"I'm totally fucking with you. I've got an hour and you think I want to do schoolwork?" I drop the textbook on the bed and then sweep my hand across the comforter to send it all to the floor. Didn't quite think it through because her laptop hits the floor with a thud.

"Fuck." I wince. "There's a good chance I just killed your laptop." I lean over the bed to retrieve it and check it for damage, but Chloe stops me and pulls me on top of her.

By the time I make it downstairs, fully clothed, the team's all here.

"Good luck," Chloe says, looking past me to the team hanging out in the living room and kitchen. "Wanna hang out tomorrow after class?"

"Can't. We've got a late workout. Tomorrow night?"

"Team dinner."

We both nod, knowing it's going to be hard to mesh our schedules for a while.

"Well, I'll see you in class at least," she says, tilting up on her toes like she's going to kiss me and then dropping as if she's unsure.

"Definitely." I lean down, cup her face, and press my lips to hers. I don't waste any time sweeping my tongue past her lips so we're full-on sucking face. Damn, this girl gets me all worked up.

"Hey, hey, no girls allowed," Joel yells from somewhere. I raise a middle finger above my head and keep right on kissing my girl.

Chloe smiles, her lips curling up at the corners and the sweet sound of her laughter pouring into my mouth. She pulls back slowly. "I should go. Have fun with the team."

She turns on her heel, and I smack her ass because… well, I just want an excuse to touch it. Looking over her shoulder at me, she smiles and then disappears out the front door.

Joel wraps an arm around me while I'm still staring at the door. "You're so fucked."

I wriggle out of his hold. "You're one to talk." He and Katrina are practically inseparable. If he could bring her to practice, I'm pretty sure he would.

"I'm happily fucked," he says like that explains it.

"What the hell does that mean?"

I walk to the kitchen for food, and Joel follows behind me. "Kitty and I are the real deal—in it for the long haul. Soul mates and all that shit."

"So poetic," I joke.

"You and Chloe are still in the beginning stages, so whether you're going to be happily fucked or just fucked remains to be seen."

"I can't argue with that logic."

I fill a plate with food. I have no idea how Joel was able to get a full meal catered on the fly, but my stomach growls in appreciation.

"I invited Wes," Joel says after we've both got a plate

and are headed to the living room.

"Why? The guys—"

"Know we're tight so it makes sense he'd be here. Plus, you two need to work your shit out. With everything else fucking with the team mojo, we can't handle your shit on top of it."

I grumble but know he's right. Sitting off to the side, I watch the team interact. Joel and I are the only seniors. Aside from one lone junior, the team is made up of sophomores and freshmen. They're good guys, good players, even, but young and inexperienced.

Most of them are only a year or two older than Heath. God willing, next year he'll be off at college trying to fit in with a team just like this. That makes me pay a little closer attention and think a little harder on how I can help.

But first, I fire off a text to check in.

Me: What's up, little bro? Haven't heard from ya. How's hockey?

I've learned not to come out of the gate asking about Mom or he shuts down and I don't get any information.

Heath: Good. Uncle Doug is taking me to NMU next week to visit. Coach Frazier is gonna let me skate with the team.

Me: That's awesome. Congrats.

I hesitate.

Me: Mom going?

Heath: Doubt it.

I pocket my phone with plans to call my mom later and talk to her. Not going with him is… well, it's shitty. And I'm tired of her flaking and making excuses. I know that her pain is different. I lost a dad, but she lost a husband… not the same, I get it, but Heath still needs her.

When Wes shows up, most the guys don't even bat an eye. He's a likable coach. God knows why he's such a grumpy bastard.

He grabs a beer from the kitchen and takes a seat next to me. "Hey. How's it going?"

"Fine." I take a drink from my beer and watch the TV. Shaw and Fresh are playing NBA 2K20. "How are you?"

"Fine," he says in a mocking tone and shakes his head. "Seriously, how are you? Blair tells me you and the volleyball chick are serious."

"You wanna have girl talk?"

"Or I could just come right out and ask about the rest of the shit going on?"

"Chloe and I are just dating, but I like her. She's cool." I might be downplaying my feelings, but a few obstacles still stand in the way. Most importantly, I need to return the money she paid me. It feels all wrong now that I know how she feels, but it puts me back at square one—needing paper.

Wes chuckles. "Dodging like a pro. Nice."

I lower my voice. "I'm not using. You've seen my

piss tests."

"And dealing?"

I shoot him a death glare and start to stand.

"Stop. Sit. I'm sorry, man. I'm just worried. You totally blindsided me. I knew you were struggling, but I had no idea it was that bad." He sounds sincere so I sit back down.

"Things back home are shit. It was stupid, I know. I made a mistake. You gonna hold it over me for the rest of the season? Because if so, I need to invest in earplugs to tune you out."

"I know all about shitty parent situations. That shit's not your fault. The rest... well, that's on you."

Anger rises faster than I can control and my tone is hard. "I don't have shitty parents. My parents are awesome." But as quick as it came, it falls with the realization I'm living in the past. "Well, they were. Ever since my dad died, my mom is..." I choose my words carefully. "Having a hard time. And my brother is still there dealing with it."

"Your dad died?" Genuine shock shows on Wes' face and the reality that yeah, my dad is gone smacks me hard. It's one thing to say the words, but every once in a while, the full weight of it hits me all over. *He's gone... really gone.*

I nod. "Month before my freshman year."

"Fuck." He takes another drink from his beer. "I had no idea. I'm sorry."

"Thanks."

"My parents don't give a fuck most the time, but at least they're alive."

I'd sort of gathered that from his grumblings in the

past and the fact I've never met them, but it breaks down something between us to admit our shit to one another. "I'm sorry, too."

"Talk to Coach Daniels. If there's anything he can do to help, he will. And if not, you know the guys and I got your back."

I hate asking for help, but in this instance, I think Wes might be right. It might be time to admit I can't figure this out on my own. "Alright."

He gives me a wry smile. "Okay, can we stop having a heart to heart now and play some 2K20?"

"Whatever you want, Couch Dubya."

twenty-three

Chloe

Our team dinner is at an Italian place with a large outdoor seating area and views of the mountains. We have the entire patio, and they've pulled the tables together into one long table for us.

Coach gave us a two-drink max, but Emily waves me over to the opposite side of the patio where a firepit is lit. It's unseasonably cool tonight so I'm thankful for the warmth.

"Shots?"

"What?"

"At the bar. Come on, Coach is so busy talking she'll never notice."

I look through the open French doors to the restaurant. She's right. With the angle of the bar, it's unlikely she'll see us.

Emily smiles, clearly seeing my hesitation waver, and grabs my hand. We shuffle quickly to the corner of the bar and erupt into giggles.

"Think she saw us?" I ask.

"Nah. We're good."

The bartender eyes us as he sets a martini down in front of the guy beside us. "What can I get you?"

"Two shots of Fireball."

We have to flash our IDs before he goes off to get our drinks, but when he's gone, I turn to her. "Fireball? Are you trying to get me drunk?"

"Definitely," she says through a smile. "There's a party at Mallory's tonight."

"Oh, I dunno. I don't really know Mallory."

She rolls her eyes. "No excuses. Everyone on the team is going and that includes you."

Our shots come, and I clink my glass to hers. It does include me, and Camila was right. I need to start acting like I belong.

The dinner takes a long time—the restaurant clearly not expecting a team of girls to order as much food as we do. By the time we eat, the two glasses of wine combined with the three shots Emily and I snuck off to take at the bar have already hit me hard.

After, we pile into Bri's SUV. She didn't drink tonight. In fact, she's been the DD at all of our team outings and I gotta say I respect that she looks out for everyone. She's not a bad captain, just a little too heavy with the iron fist.

Mallory's apartment is far enough away that we decide on leaving Bri's car here tonight and getting an Uber back to the dorm later. Bri's no drinking doesn't apply to parties thankfully, and I'm hoping if she gets liquored up enough maybe I can corner her in the bathroom and force her to talk, to be friends with me.

Clearly, the alcohol has gone to my head. Emily is talking to some guy I don't know in the front room, so I go off in search of Sydney. She's always down for fun.

"Hey, Chloe," Liv, a freshman, says as I approach the kitchen. I realize I haven't really done a good job of trying to get to know any of them besides my roommates. In practices, I keep my head down and I'd thought Bri had gotten to everyone but maybe not. Liv seems happy to see me anyway.

"Hey." I stop next to her. "How's it going?"

"Good." She bobs her head, tucks her long red hair behind both ears, and glances around awkwardly.

"Not really your scene?"

"I just don't really know anyone yet. I got put in a dorm room with soccer players, so practices and team outings are the only chance I have."

I grab her hand and pull her behind me like Emily did me earlier. "Come on, tonight that all changes." I pick up a bottle of Rumchata. "Drink?"

I stop drinking to ensure Liv has a good time and I introduce her, and in some cases myself, to anyone who will listen. We dance and laugh with our teammates and if anyone minds my being here, I can't tell because I'm not focusing on that.

After two in the morning, Emily pushes me into the back of an Uber with the rest of my roommates. I slide in between Bri and Emily. Tonight was fun. The first fun night I've had that didn't involve Nathan since I got to Valley.

I decide to text him. I'm well aware that he's probably asleep, but I miss him, and I want to hear his voice... or see his words, whatever.

Me: Hey! What are you doing?

Bri glances at my phone. "Booty call?"

"Is it still a booty call if I love him?" Love might be a bit strong, but at this hour, my very strong like feels a lot like love.

I lie my head on Bri's shoulder. I never did get a chance to talk to her tonight, but the back of an Uber seems like the wrong place. Eh, when will it be the right place? "Why don't you like me?"

Emily busts out laughing and I yawn. I'm suddenly so tired and the exhaustion of weeks of stress and holding it all in finally catches up to me. Bri stays quiet and I pull my head from her shoulder. "I just want to play volleyball and I'm good. I'm really good. So why don't you like me?"

"Because I had to work my ass off to be here. My mom worked three jobs, and I still had to take out student loans and here you are, buying your way into not one but two colleges."

"I didn't buy my way into Valley."

She raises a brow.

"I didn't."

"Are you sure about that?"

"Yes. My coach at Golden put me in touch with—"

"I know. Your coach from the school you *bought* your way into made a call."

She looks at me like she's waiting for me to connect

the dots.

"It's not the same thing."

"Isn't it?"

I mull it over for the rest of our drive. Is my time at Valley just an extension of all the perks my parents gained for me? I can't believe that.

We get out of the Uber and slowly make our way up to our dorm. Instead of going to my room, I head to Bri's. She's changing in the closet, and I plop down on her bed.

"I'm sorry. I don't think it's the same thing, but I can see how it feels unfair to you. I just want to play volleyball. No bullshit."

She comes out of her closet as she pulls a baggy t-shirt over her head. Emily is already asleep in her bed on the opposite side of the room still fully dressed.

Bri lies down on the bed next to me, and I make no move to leave. She lets her head fall to the side and looks me in the eye. "Thank you. I guess that's all I wanted to hear. After graduation, I want to play professionally."

"You do?" I ask, surprised I didn't already know.

She nods. "It's been my dream forever."

I look up at her ceiling and think about my own dreams. Getting through the year and proving myself has become all I can see of the future.

"I'm sorry I ruined your dress."

"My dress?" I glance down until I realize she means the pink one. "It's okay."

"No, it's not. That thing probably cost more than my entire closet. I've been sick about it ever since. I'll pay you back someday."

"Not necessary, just promise you'll tone down the

queen bee bitch routine?"

She snorts. "Yeah, okay."

We fall silent again, and she nudges me with her elbow. "I'm sorry I've been a royal bitch to you but, Chloe?"

"Hmm?"

"I'm still gonna kick your ass in the sand."

The next morning, I wake up in Bri's bed. My phone is dead, but even without knowing the time I have a feeling I've overslept. When I sit up, nausea hits me. I'm hungover and hungry and my stomach is confused because it wants to eat but also acknowledges I may very well puke if I do.

Sydney is gone from our room, so I gingerly sit on my bed in the dark and plug in my phone and wait for it to get enough of a charge to turn on.

When the screen finally illuminates a series of texts pops up.

Nathan: Lying in bed. What are you doing? You know it's 2:13, right?

Nathan: Everything okay?

And thirty minutes later.

Nathan: Be careful, princess.

The Fake

I send him a text before I force myself to get up and get my shower stuff together. I need to wash off last night and nap before practice.

Me: I don't think I'm going to make it to class today. Can you take notes for me? Pretty please with a blow job on top?

Nathan: Morning. Rough night? Sure. No need to bribe me with sex, princess.

Nathan: Ignore that. You can absolutely bribe me with sex.

Me: Hang tonight?

Nathan: Can't. I promised Datson I'd help him with some footwork drills. Tomorrow?

Me: I don't think I'll be done 'til late on Thursday. We have a tournament this weekend.

Nathan: Tournament where? Valley?

Me: Yes, it's here.

Nathan: Sweet. Can you get me front row tickets?

I roll my eyes, but I'm smiling.

Me: Smartass, it's general admission.

The rest of the week is busy. Classes are starting to get more intense, so keeping up with homework and assigned reading on top of the long practices and extra workouts is a bit grueling. I see Nathan in class, but we both have to blow off our project.

The tournament is a small fall exhibition with only a few other schools. Even so, I'm so nervous I can't eat breakfast.

Coach pairs me with Emily and moves Bri with Sydney. It's a switch from last year and from how we've been practicing. Emily and Bri have been partners most of their collegiate careers. I expect all the progress we've made being civilized to one another to come to a screeching halt, but Bri just nods and goes about her warmups.

I think she feels a little victorious when Coach dubs them the number one pairing. During the fall season, it doesn't mean much. I know that and she knows that, but if it keeps the truce going, she can keep it... for now, anyway.

We warm up as a team first. Coach calls out the exercises from the sideline. Side lunges, shuffles, crossover, lateral bear crawl. Then we do ball drills—serving, passing, and hitting.

Finally, we break off into our pairs, and Emily and I jog to the fieldhouse. Once we're there, we do some light stretches and then turn around and head back. We're on court two so we head there for the official warmup. We work on peppering and serving warmups until I've blocked everything out.

"Work together. Quick transitions." Coach Carter gives us a last-minute pep talk. She claps her hands and Emily and I walk to our starting side.

We're up against Monte State first. I've played them before. They're tough, but I'm confident in Emily and I working together. Her height and my athleticism is a good combo.

Before I take the first serve, I look to the side where a few spectators have crowded under a blue awning. Nathan smiles and lifts his chin in acknowledgment. Shaw is here, too, but I barely afford him a second glance. My stomach flutters at Nathan showing up for me.

My parents, who used to make every game, won't be able to make as many now that I'm farther away, but it feels decidedly awesome to know I'm going to have Nathan here for me instead.

twenty-four

Chloe

"If you tell Sydney that I watched the season two final episode without her, she'll kill me."

"I won't say a word," Nathan promises from his seat next to me in the theater room. I hate to move from my big leather chair.

The end credits for the *New Girl* episode roll on the gigantic screen. The lights are dimmed, and my eyes are heavy. A party at the baseball house has Shaw and Datson gone, and Nathan said Joel was spending the night at Katrina's house. The White House is quiet, which is weird, but it feels nice to be alone with Nathan.

Valley won every match today. Even Bri was in good spirits. I promised them I'd be back to the dorm in two hours to go out and celebrate. Nathan and I spent the first hour in the shower. And the bathroom counter.

And the bed. After watching two episodes of *New Girl*, my time is up.

"Alright, I gotta go meet the girls," I say but don't move.

He chuckles, stands, and pulls me to my feet. "Wait. I need to give you something first."

I let him drag me even as I say, "I don't have time to make out again."

He stops in the middle of the staircase and crowds into me until my back hits the wall. He kisses me hard until I forget what we were talking about. All too quickly, he's pulling back and continuing up the stairs. "Come on."

"Okay, so maybe a quickie. In fact, it's fine if I'm fifteen minutes late."

He laughs as I follow him to his room. He walks over to his desk and grabs his phone. His thumbs tap over the screen and looks up just as my phone pings.

I glance down at the money transfer notification.

"I never should have taken it knowing how I felt about you. And now..." He rubs a hand over his jaw. "I can't accept it."

"What about—"

"I'll take care of it. It's my problem. Besides, I would have agreed to be your fake boyfriend even without the money."

I don't need it, and I know he does, but I can't think of how to say that without it coming across like pity.

He smiles wryly. "Okay, probably. Either way, it was the best fake out of my life. I got you."

"Nathan, it's not a big deal. Plus, you spent a lot of time helping me. It's the least I can do to repay you."

I want to ask what he'll do without it and what it means for his family, but he wraps his arms around me and pulls me close. "I can think of other ways you can repay me."

When Bri pulls up along the street of a residential area later that night, I scan the homes and the street signs. I don't recognize either. I'd been buried in my phone texting Camila and updating her on the Nathan situation and hadn't paid attention to where we were going. "Where are we?"

"One of the local football guys lives here. I think it's his parents' house," Emily says.

Cars are lined up and down the street of the cozy residential area. The houses are big and the yards bigger, giving each one its privacy. Even still, I can hear the music from somewhere inside as we make our way up the street to the house.

When Emily opens the front door, I take a deep breath like it might be the last gulp of free air I get. There are so many people inside. I follow behind them, sticking close. Sydney is already here, but unless we run right into her, I don't think I'll be able to spot her.

It's a little less crowded in the living room where a TV is on a Golden vs UCLA football game. There really is no escaping my past life. A year ago, I might have been there cheering in the student section with Camila. She has a thing for football guys. I glance around with her in mind. She'd be in heaven right now. There are so many big, burly guys I feel tiny by comparison.

UCLA scores and the room erupts in cheers. By some unspoken agreement, we move away from the noise and to the kitchen. We stand in line to get beer from the keg. Bri turns around and leans in, holding her phone up. "Sydney is upstairs in the library. She says to come up there after we get our drinks."

"The library?" Emily snorts and then looks to me. She must read it on my face. "Your parents totally have a library, don't they?"

"Where else do they store their first editions?" I mock.

Foamy beer in hand, the three of us make our way up the stairs. No easy feat with the steady traffic going up and down. The first room on the right opens up into a library with floor-to-ceiling bookshelves covering the entirety of two walls. On the other main wall, there's a huge gas-burning fireplace, lit for the night.

Sydney sits on the couch in between Liv and a guy I don't recognize sporting a hipster beard. Sydney waves us over with a big smile.

Emily and Bri take an empty love chair and Sydney scooches over closer to Liv to make room for me.

"Hey," I say awkwardly to the guy I all but sit on top of trying to take my seat.

Sydney leans forward and turns to make more room for me. "Chloe, this is Frank."

"Nice to meet you." His brown eyes assess me.

I can't tell if it's interest or friendliness in his tone, but I do my best to keep mine polite with a clear signal I'm not looking for a random hookup just in case. "You, too."

I look to Sydney and Liv, but they're in a conversation about one of today's matches and it feels weird to just butt in.

"You play volleyball, too?" Frank's tone seems light, like he's just making conversation to be nice.

"I do." I nod. "Are you on the football team?"

He tilts his head back, and his mouth curls up around his black beard with laughter. "No."

"Do you play any sport?"

He shakes his head this time. "Not for me. I like setting my own schedule. Sports are a little too time-intensive for me."

I don't know what to say to that. He's not wrong, but I wouldn't trade it for the world. I mean, obviously. I came all the way to Valley just so I could keep playing.

My phone lights up with a text from Camila. I clear it from the screen, but Frank's eyes stare down at my phone. "That the boyfriend?"

I'm not sure about the title boyfriend, but I don't correct Frank as he looks at the picture of Nathan and me on the beach laying in the sand. Our heads are tilted toward one another, and I'm smiling at the camera while he looks at me. I hold it up so Frank can get a better look. "Yep."

He takes the phone and smiles wide. "No way, you're dating Nathan Payne?"

I laugh at his reaction. It sends me back to when my roommates found out. The man has a reputation by name alone and everyone seems to know and like him, judging by Frank's smile. "Yeah."

"I know Payne," Frank says. "I haven't seen him

around in a while. Now I know why."

I take my phone back and place it screen down on my thigh. "He's busy with practice, start of the season and all that."

"Yo, Frank," a deep voice calls from the doorway and I look up in time to see a large guy—definitely a football player, motion with his head for Frank.

"Well, duty calls." He stands and glances down at me. He's taller than I thought while he was seated. Long legs give way to a muscular build he wears confidently. "Tell Payne I said hello and if he's changed his mind to give me a call."

Nathan

"I'm so glad I don't live here anymore, but I sure do miss you guys," Zeke says as he crosses one ankle over the other.

Gabby's perched on his lap, staring up at him totally dumbstruck in love.

"Missed you, too," Joel says.

We're sitting outside, just the four of us. Wes and Blair already left and Katrina's home with her son Christian. Joel doesn't stay at the house very often anymore, he splits his time staying at Katrina's, ninety-ten in her favor, but with Zeke in town for the night, we all dropped any other plans so we could see him.

I discreetly check my phone.

"Heard from Chloe?" Gabby asks with a smirk that tells me she's on to me.

"No." My tone is strained but upbeat. "She's out with the girls celebrating their win today."

She chuckles. "I like her."

"We know," Zeke and I say at the same time.

"What, like it's a crime to be excited that Nathan found someone that I really like? Can you imagine if one of us was dating someone the others didn't like?"

"You mean like when Zeke started dating you?" Joel asks, somehow keeping a straight face.

Gabby's mouth falls open, but Joel can't stop himself from busting out laughing. Zeke wraps his arms protectively around his girl. "He's kidding, baby."

She stands, glaring and trying to pout but her lips tilt up into a smile. "I'm gonna go get a drink."

Joel jumps up. "I'll come with you. Guys?" He lifts his beer to ask if we want another.

I wave him off.

"How've things been?" Zeke asks. He's going for casual, but Zeke never makes small talk. He wants to know if I'm still a mess, drinking to excess and waking up to nightmares that have me tearing apart my room. He had to deal with both on more than one occasion. He saved my ass more times than I'd like to admit.

"They've actually been good." Which isn't a lie. Things are good. The nightmares haven't magically gone away, but I've stopped using booze to try and escape them.

"Did you get the money situation figured out?"

226

I blanch for a moment. Being the guy who always needs help gets old, but wait, I never told him about that. Then it hits me. "Gabby told you."

"She tells me everything, man."

I shake my head. I should have known. I guess it's no secret. I've been struggling for as long as they've known me and looks like that's going to continue to be the case.

Giving Chloe the money back was the right thing to do, but it puts me in a bind. I had to borrow half of it from Joel and the rest I got from a cash advance on my credit card. Neither of those feel super but owing Chloe and thinking any part of her was still with me because of it was something I just couldn't live with.

"She worries about you. And I'm sorry about your dad. I wish you would have told me."

"Talking about it made it real."

He nods. "Well, if you're looking for a job, I might have something for you." I cringe inwardly, but before I can put my hesitation to words, he holds up a hand. "Hear me out. I met this guy."

twenty-five

Nathan

Coach leans back in his chair and swivels to the side so he's staring at the Michael Jordan poster on the wall. He hasn't said a single word since I unloaded on him.

I told him about my situation, leaving out the parts about my mom failing to keep a job but ensuring he understood it was imperative that I have income coming in.

And I told him about Lincoln, the guy Zeke introduced me to. I'd been hesitant, but I'm actually excited about the possibility of working for him after talking to him on the phone this morning.

"This isn't only my decision. I'll need to follow the chain of command, but I'm inclined to allow it as long as you and Lincoln are both crystal clear on the rules set by the NCAA and follow them to the letter."

My pulse quickens. Is this what it feels like to get a break? It's been so long since everything in my life felt so in order.

"To the letter," I agree and stand in a rush. I actually feel lighter.

"I'll let you know when I have a decision."

I nod and shift in my chair. "Also." I clear my throat. "I never apologized or thanked you. I put you and the team in a bad position. I know that, I see it clearer now. Thank you for believing in me enough not to toss me on my ass."

He huffs a laugh. "It was close." He motions with his head to the door. "Get out of here. I like you better when you're not sucking up."

I smile and hurry to the door. That makes two of us. Plus, I'm meeting Chloe for lunch, and I can't wait to tell her about the job.

"And Nathan?" Coach calls after me. I pause and turn back to see him smiling at me. "I hope it works out. It sounds like a great opportunity."

"Thanks, Coach."

I text Heath on my way to the dorms to tell him to call me after practice.

Sydney and Emily are leaving as I get to their room. I'm cheesing at them like a lunatic, and I can't even help it. I'm so damn excited. "Hey."

"Hey, Nathan," Emily says, holding the door for me. "Chloe's in her room."

I knock on her open door. "Chlo?"

"In the closet. Be right out."

I plop down on her made bed to wait for her. The closet door opens, and she steps through looking like a vision. Brown midriff t-shirt and jeans that come up high on her waist so only a sliver of tanned stomach is visible. Her blonde hair is up in a ponytail, and I don't think she has any makeup on, but she's still the hottest girl I've ever seen.

It's on the tip of my tongue to say something stupid like *I love you*, but she speaks and saves me the embarrassment. "Where do you want to go to eat? I'm starving."

"I was hoping I could convince you to stay in. We can order takeout. My treat. I finally found a new job." Maybe I'm counting my singles before payday, but it feels like this might actually happen.

She crosses to the bed and sits on the edge, one leg dangling off the side. "When did that happen?"

"This morning. It's perfect. I'll be working with this guy who runs an online coaching website. It's huge, every sport you could imagine." So many more details I want to tell her, but I pull her on my lap and take her mouth.

"I missed you," I say when she rests her forehead against mine. "We might need to establish some new rules."

"Rules?"

"Mhmm." I cup the back of her neck and run a thumb along the delicate spot between her ear and collarbone. "Rule number one, I need to see my girlfriend every day."

She kisses me then, and we fall back onto the bed.

"Say it again," she insists.

"Rule numb—"

"No, the part where you called me your girlfriend."

Her eyes burn into me with need and desire and hope. I'd give anything to keep that look on her face, directed at me, forever. No one has ever looked at me like I held the key to everything they ever wanted. I hope I don't royally fuck this up.

"My girlfriend is bossy," I tell her. "But it's hot as fuck."

Our clothes come off in between long kisses until she's down to just a pair of black panties with strings holding the front to the back and I'm in my tented boxers. She climbs on top of me, her boobs bouncing and the pink buds tempting as hell.

Leaning forward, I bring my tongue to one and lick it until she sighs her appreciation.

"Your mouth... Jesus, your mouth."

I'm about to give her other nipple the same treatment when she scrambles off my lap and strips me out of my boxers. She looks up at me through dark lashes, green eyes swirling with desire.

Wrapping a hand around the base, she takes me into her mouth. The tight suction and the warmth of her has me hissing out a shaky breath. She feels so damn good. I let her work me over until I can't take it anymore. I flip her onto her back and untie one side of her panties and then the other.

"Damn," I say after I've unwrapped her like a present.

I reach for my jeans and grab a condom out of my wallet. She takes it from me and covers me while I watch on, fascinated with how careful she is and how good her touch feels even over the latex.

We both groan with pleasure and need when I push

into her tight pussy. Her hands roam over my arms and chest. She feels me up as I fill her up and it's so fucking good.

"How's Chinese?"

I glance at the clock. "I have practice in an hour, I don't think we have time. Someone kept me busy for too long." I drop a kiss on the tip of her nose and sit up. "Wanna grab food from University Hall?"

Chloe nods, and we get dressed. Linking our fingers, I pull her hand to my lips and kiss it before dropping our still joined hands and leading her out of the dorm.

"Oh, I forgot to tell you," Chloe says excitedly, swinging our arms. "I met a guy at the football party. Frank, I think his name was. He said he knew you and you used to hang out or work together or something."

I stiffen at the name but force my feet and arms to keep moving. "I know lots of people, babe."

"Tall, dark hair and beard, he said to tell you hello and to call him if you changed your mind?" She looks at me quizzically.

"Oh, yeah. Frank. We have Econ together. Wants me to join his study group." The words physically hurt as they leave my mouth. How do you tell the girl you're dating that she just met your former boss, and oh, by the way, he's a drug dealer and so was I up until the day you met me?

Bri and Mallory are coming out of University Hall as

we approach. Bri waves and we walk toward them.

"We're going over to the courts early to work on passing drills. You wanna come?"

Chloe motions with her head toward me. "We were gonna get lunch."

"Go," I say, trying to sound like an understanding boyfriend instead of a shitty one who just lied and needs to flee to think through what I've done. I drop her hand and take a step away before she can try and change my mind. "I've gotta couple errands to run before weightlifting. I'll call ya later."

"Oh. Okay. You're sure? You still need to tell me all about the new job."

"Positive, princess." I kiss her cheek and then wave to her teammates.

I head to the gym early and go straight into warmups. It's an hour before anyone else gets here but I need to burn off some of the worry and guilt I'm holding.

I jog up and down the court with the ball, crossing over every third dribble. I try and think through the situation logically. I should go straight after practice and tell her the truth. All of it. My friends have stuck by my side even after they found out. Then again, I didn't lie to them, at least not outright. It was more of an omission.

I know I have to tell her. And I want to. I don't want to keep anything from her, but damn, I can't help but want to hold on to the way things are right now. She looks at me like I'm her knight in shining armor, swooping in to save my princess, when in reality, she's the one who saved me. Every day since the day I met her, she's made me want to be better, but I can't hide from the shitty things I've done, and I have to believe it won't be the end of us.

Tuesday morning, Coach gives me the good news that I've got sign-off to take the job and I call Lincoln as soon as I get back to the house.

"That's great news, Nathan." He pauses. "Do you go by Nathan?"

"Yes, sir."

He chuckles. "Don't call me sir, makes me feel old as shit. Lincoln or Linc is fine."

"Got it."

"The site is still in progress, but I'll get you an account so you can see what it looks like from the back end. Pretty simple really. Once a client signs up, they have access to view tutorials, read blog posts, and submit questions or videos, depending on their membership. The most basic level is free, and clients can submit questions that are sorted based on sport. That will be your job, answering the questions that come in through the basic package. So far, it's been a lot of questions on how they can get more advanced help. We've got some canned responses for that, but a few sports-related questions have come in too. It might be slow to start, but I'm confident it'll pick up as the full site goes live."

"It sounds great. I'm really excited. Thank you for the opportunity."

"Glad to have you. I saw you play in the Florida Gulf game last year. You're a hell of a player."

"Thanks." This conversation is trippy. Is this my life right now?

"Alright, I gotta go. Flying to Texas tomorrow to do an event with Tiger Woods at a college down there."

"No way, really?"

He chuckles. "Watch a bunch of kids with stars in their eyes as Tiger talks about his success and then he leaves and I get to try and tamper their expectations. Everyone thinks they're the next Tiger Woods and I get to break it to them that they're not. I assure you it sounds more glamorous than it is."

When I get off the phone with Lincoln, I text Heath. He has his college visit tomorrow so I wish him luck and then tell him to give Mom the phone so I can call her, hoping my good mood isn't about to come crashing down.

"Hi, honey," she answers on the first ring.

"Hey, Mom, how are you?"

"Oh, we're fine. How are things at Valley? Your brother tells me you got a job."

"Yeah, I did. Should be able to start sending some money again to help out with Heath's hockey stuff." I take a breath and add, "And whatever else you guys need. How's your job hunt coming?"

"I talked to an old colleague who might have a substitute job coming open. Their fifth-grade teacher is going on maternity leave starting in December."

She doesn't mention how her last interview went so I guess that's my answer on if she got that job. "That's great, Mom. Heath told me about his NMU visit. Are you going with him?"

"Uncle Doug is taking him."

I tread carefully. I never know if it's better to push or leave it be, but this is one of those moments I think she needs a push. "I know, but he still wants you there, too, even if he doesn't say it." We're both quiet until I add, "He needs you, Mom."

She huffs a small laugh. "Your brother won't even let me drop him off for school unless I park nearly a block away. Besides, your uncle Doug knows what questions to ask regarding hockey and the team."

Another retort is on the tip of my tongue, but Heath yells something in the background and Mom responds to him, her mouth away from the phone so I can't quite follow along.

Hopefully, he's looking for a razor and some deodorant. I say as much and then it becomes a back and forth of me barking orders and Mom passing them along, then Heath grumbles back and Mom and I laugh.

It feels good to be joking and laughing, and it's the first time since Dad died that I don't wish for things to be different. I'd still give anything to have him around, have him call me and talk sports, tell me he's proud of me, hear him and Mom be grossly sweet to one another, plan summer trips to see the Brewers play. I miss all of those things, but this moment feels like progress.

"Tell Heath to call me tomorrow night so I can hear about the trip and promise me you'll at least think about going with him?"

"I promise," she says softly.

"Talk to ya later, Mom."

When I hang up, I drop onto my bed and sleep the

The Fake

entire night. Dreamless, peaceful sleep.

twenty-six

Chloe

$\mathcal{N}$athan comes over Wednesday night as I'm staring at my Ethics homework. We'd planned to go out tonight with his friends to celebrate his new job, but I totally spaced on a test I have tomorrow, and I feel like crying as I look through my notes and can only make sense of a small portion.

Things with the roommates have been going really well since I got back, but the more time I spend with them, the less time I have for myself.

He takes a seat on my bed in front of me, and I shove the textbook away and lean forward so my head rests in his lap. "I'm never going to learn this before tomorrow."

Long fingers slide over my hair. "Sure you will." He grabs the textbook. "I took this class last year, I can help."

I sit up. "I totally forgot you'd already taken this class with Professor Penn. Can you help me with Utilitarianism?"

He flips through the pages until he gets to the chapter where I've stuck a piece of paper to hold my spot. He reads through for a moment and then snaps it shut and looks to me. "I'm gonna be real with you. I don't remember a single thing."

I groan.

"But I'll stay, and we'll figure it out together."

"No, we're supposed to meet Gabby at Prickly Pear in thirty minutes."

He shrugs. "She'll understand."

"No. I can't let you miss this. It's important and you should celebrate. How about you go, and I'll finish studying and meet up with you guys later?"

"Are you sure?"

I nod and scan through my notes. "Maybe if I read through all my notes a second time, it'll come back to me."

He takes my notes and pulls me on to his lap. I wrap my arms around him and kiss him. Since we got back from California, it's felt like we've barely been able to see each other. If we didn't have class together, most days we wouldn't. His phone vibrates in his pocket.

"That's probably Gabby," I tell him.

"She can wait." His lips move to my neck, and he brushes my hair back, giving him more access.

My eyes close and I lose myself to his soft mouth and the rough feel of his unshaven face. His fingers skim the hem of my t-shirt, teasing and stroking my skin. I reciprocate by lacing my fingers through his messy hair and tugging while I grind on his thickening erection.

His phone vibrates again and this time, I can feel the resolve to ignore the outside world crumbling.

"Shit, I should check and make sure it's not Heath or my mom," he says as he leans back to try and get his phone out of the front pocket of his jeans. "Heath had that NMU visit today."

Reluctantly, I scoot off his lap. He turns the screen so I can see as he shakes his head. *Gabby.*

"You should go," I tell him.

He groans and looks at me with longing. Enough so that I know he doesn't want to leave me. It makes it easier to let him go. "I'll text you as soon as I'm done."

He kisses me swiftly and then stands as he answers. "Hey, Gabs."

I walk him to the hallway, and he places another kiss on my lips while he keeps talking to Gabby. He mouths, "Later." And then he hustles to meet his friends.

I spend an hour reading through my notes and looking up the answers to study questions before I decide to break for a caffeine fix. I head over to University Hall, grab a coffee and muffin, and then spend another hour studying there. By the time I get back to my room, I'm exhausted but starting to feel like I'm understanding the material.

I lie on my side and start to read through the chapter again for anything I might have missed.

"Hey roomie." My eyes fly open at Sydney's voice. "Sorry," she says. "I didn't know you were sleeping."

I peel my face off the pages of the book and sit upright. "I must have fallen asleep while I was studying. What time is it?"

I reach for my phone at the same time she says, "Eleven-thirty."

"Shit. I was supposed to meet up with Nathan."

I have two texts from Gabby.

Gabby: Tick tock. What time are you going to be done studying?

Gabby: CHLOE!!!! I <3 you, come hang out!

I respond to Gabby to let her know I fell asleep and haven't finished studying and then I text Nathan.

Me: I'm so sorry. I crashed reading my notes. I'm not going to make it out tonight. Make it up to you this weekend?

Nathan: Absofuckinglutely. Good luck on your test.

The next afternoon, I turn in my test and breathe a sigh of relief. My late-night study session paid off and I knew every answer. I vow to do a better job of keeping a balance between my classes and everything else as I head back to the dorm.

I take a power nap then get up and work on a paper that's due next week before heading to practice. We have an away game this weekend, so practice is light and we focus on skills.

Nathan's still at his practice when I get done, so I go back and pack for our drive to State tomorrow. Sydney comes into our room freshly showered. "Hanging out with Nathan tonight?"

"I'm not sure," I tell her. "He's got a late practice, and we didn't make any set plans so I'm waiting to hear from him."

"I'm meeting Liv at TKE if you want to come?"

"I don't think I wanna drink tonight. I need to get up early in the morning and run through some mobility exercises before classes."

She shrugs. "I'm not really planning on drinking either, I just need to get out for a while. We'll come back early or if Nathan texts while we're out, you can catch an Uber to his place."

It does sound nice to spend a few hours not studying or practicing. My insides fill with anticipation, and I grin at my roommate. "Alright, let's do it."

I double-check my travel bag and load up my backpack for tomorrow's classes before Sydney and I meet Liv on the first floor of Freddy. I still haven't heard from Nathan, so I text him to let him know my plans and tell him I'm going to stop by later. I can't go another night without seeing him, so even if we have to literally just sleep next to one another, I'm going to see him.

Things have been great between us. I think it works out that we're both so busy; we understand when things come up. And that seems to be the case a lot. He never asks me to stay over at his place since he has to get up so early and doesn't want to wake me, but I'm thinking I'm going to have to get used to it if I ever want to see him.

Besides, more often than not, I'm up early to get extra conditioning in so it's not that much of an imposition.

Not at all an imposition when I include the perks of sleeping next to my gorgeous boyfriend.

Sydney, Liv, and I walk to frat row. It's still fairly early so we grab cups of Sprite—sans the vodka—and hole up in a corner to talk and people watch.

"You look ridiculous wearing your backpack to a party." Sydney smirks as I drop my bag to the floor at my feet.

"I need my stuff so I can go straight to Nathan's later. Preparation is key."

They laugh, but I'm completely serious. Juggling time with Nathan with school and practice is tricky, but I'm determined to make it work.

"Have you talked to Shaw?" I ask Sydney.

She makes a face. "I think I might have played that situation all wrong. I told him I wasn't going to sleep with him, which he was great about, but now he just invites me over to play Tecmo Bowl."

"I'm pretty sure that's code for make out."

"I thought so too." She leans forward and crosses her legs, then has to pull at the hem of her seafoam-green dress. "The first time he asked, I went over totally expecting him to make a move and he just handed me a controller. He was wearing sweats and hadn't showered after practice and he ordered pizza."

I laugh. "And he didn't try to kiss you or get handsy, anything?"

"Nothing," Sydney says with disbelief in her tone. "I did kick his ass in Tecmo Bowl though. Hell hath no fury like a girl who shows up to get some action only to be friend-zoned."

"You said you weren't going to sleep with him, Syd."

"I didn't mean never, just not before I got to know him."

"And since then, has he tried to hang out again?" Liv asks.

She sighs. "He's texted a few times to see if I wanted to come over and play video games, but I make up an excuse every time."

"I'm sorry."

She tosses her blonde hair over her shoulder and straightens, perusing the room. "It might be time to throw my five-date rule out the window."

"Five-date rule?" Liv asks.

"How many dates she makes them hold out for sex," I tell her.

"How many dates did you make Nathan wait?" Sydney asks, putting me in the hot seat.

"None, or well, technically, I guess one. I slept with him the first night I met him."

I've thought about how to break it to my roommates that I lied about Nathan being my boyfriend so many times with no clear path, and this feels like my chance. "We didn't really meet in the boy's locker room. He found me hiding out at that athletic mixer and we got to talking and drinking and well, one thing led to another. Our first time was the night he slept over and Bri almost had a coronary that he was in our living room."

"You two moved quick. See, that's how it's supposed to happen." Sydney breezes right past the lies I told her like they're inconsequential, and maybe they are. It feels good to tell her the truth, anyway. "I'm definitely getting rid of the five-date rule."

Liv and Sydney end up wanting to stay out later, but

at eleven, I hug them and send Nathan a text that I'm on my way.

Nathan: Left the front door open for you. Come on up, I'm in bed.

I'm grinning as I rush out the front of TKE and nearly collide with a group of guys just walking in.

"Whoa, sorry," I say as I bob and weave between them.

My Uber hasn't shown so I wait by the curb impatiently, pacing up and down the short stretch of sidewalk.

"Yo, Payne's girl. Chloe, right?"

I turn on my heel to see Frank walking up to the house. He's got an easy smile and friendly demeanor about him that has me walking toward him. "That's right."

"Where's Nathan?"

"Home. He had late practice today."

"Lame," Frank says. "I never see him anymore. You leaving already, too?"

"Yeah, I'm gonna go see my lame man."

He chuckles and scans the street. "Need a ride?"

I hold up my phone. "Waiting on an Uber. Should be here any minute." I glance down and see the estimated time has increased and the driver's Subaru has gone in the opposite direction.

"I could have you there and be back to the party by the time they get here."

"That's alright. Nathan's probably sleeping by now anyway."

Frank doesn't move from his spot. His smile falls so that only one side of his mouth is pulled up into a half-grin. "Alright, well, it was good to see you again." He starts to walk off and then turns. "Oh, hey." He pulls out a cigarette, offers me one, and then lights it when I shake my head. He speaks again after he's taken a long drag. "Could you give Nathan something for me?"

"Sure."

He walks toward the curb and unlocks a black Jeep. He opens the back-passenger side seat and pulls out a Microeconomics textbook. "You'll see that he gets it?"

I nod as I grab the thick textbook. "Sure. Did he leave it in class or something?"

Frank pauses a beat before nodding. I shove it in my backpack, and he closes the door and takes a step toward the party. "Thanks, Chloe, I appreciate it." He motions toward the blue Subaru pulling up. "Looks like your ride finally made it."

It takes forever to get to Nathan's. Okay, it only takes five minutes but I'm so anxious that every second of the driver trying to make small talk feels long. The front door is open as Nathan said it would be and I hurry through, only pausing to yell hello to Datson sitting on the couch watching a baseball game.

Nathan's room is dark, and I can just barely make out his shape on the bed. Quietly stepping out of my heels, I drop my backpack near the door and get in under the covers with him.

"Surfer Princess," he whispers gruffly and pulls me into him without opening his eyes. "You're a beautiful dream."

I wake up sometime later plastered against Nathan. I

lift my face from his sweaty chest and a deep groan from him startles me. His eyes are still closed, but his muscles twitch.

I move over a bit to give him some space and lie back down so I won't disturb his sleep, but the tremors get worse until I'm not sure if I should wake him up or shut my eyes and try to sleep. I turn on my back and inch closer to the edge in case my nearness is keeping him from falling back asleep.

When his forearm connects with my forehead, I wince and then laugh. "Owww, Nathan," I start, my voice laced with laughter that he's hogging the bed and ready to fight me for space. I turn to him and fling his arm back.

"No," he growls. "Stop." At the last word, he jumps from bed and stares down at it with blind fury and torment.

"Nathan," I try again, gently this time as I sit up in bed.

He rips the blanket off and then the pillow. His eyes don't seem to register anything as he tears apart the bed. I scramble across the mattress on all fours and stand on my knees to reach his face.

"Nathan, hey, wake up."

He groans again and his chest lifts and falls quickly. I'm panicked and have no idea how to wake him or even if I should, but I'm desperate to take away the pained look on his beautiful face.

I reach for him, place both hands on his face. "Honey, look at me."

He does, but his beautiful blue eyes are glossy, and I'm not sure he really sees me. I'm so scared my own fingers tremble. Without removing my hands, I move from the bed to stand beside him. "You're okay. You're just dreaming."

Words fail me so I step flush against him and press my lips to his. His hands go to my chest, and I think he might push me away. Slowly, his rigid body relaxes. When he wakes up, his eyes widen, and he steps back out of reach so fast I stumble back onto the bed.

He looks around the room and then back to me, running a hand through his hair as he catches his breath. "Oh, my God, Chloe. Are you okay?" He takes a step toward me and then retreats. "I didn't hurt you, did I?"

I shake my head. "Of course not."

My words don't seem to comfort him. He stands rooted in place, body coiled so tightly I'm not sure what to say or do. Since it worked to wake him, I hope going to him is the right move, and I throw myself into his chest and wrap my arms around him tightly. He crumbles, taking me with him to the floor. I climb into his lap and he squeezes me against his heaving torso.

"I'm sorry. I'm so sorry." The choked words spoken over the top of my head don't feel like they're meant for me.

"It's okay. Hey, I'm here. It was just a dream."

twenty-seven

Nathan

We lie on the floor in my room. Chloe must have grabbed the pillows off the bed at some point because there's one behind my head as I stare up to the ceiling.

I've been pouring my guts out to the point I should probably be embarrassed, but I can't seem to stop. All the things I've held onto about my dad and the guilt I feel, I share those with her because she's here and for the first time I believe she's not going anywhere.

"Wanna know what the worst part is?"

She nods, the slightest tilt of her head in the darkness.

"It's my fault he's dead."

Her eyes widen and then her brows pull together in confusion.

"About an hour before it happened, we got into a big fight. I'd blown off school to go to the lake with friends, which was bad enough, but I didn't have cell service so when the school called Mom to tell her I wasn't there, no one could find me. They'd thought the worst. Mom was in tears when I finally made it home and Dad was so pissed. I'd never seen him so mad."

"They were worried about you."

I nod. "Yeah, and I knew I was in the wrong, but my hot head couldn't own up to it, so I yelled back and then stormed out and went to my buddy's house. Last time I ever saw him."

"I'm so sorry."

"If I hadn't skipped school or if I'd just stuck around and been there…" I let myself imagine all the possibilities.

"It wasn't your fault. People argue and they say things they don't mean. He knew you loved him."

My eyes burn, and I swallow a lump in my throat. I guess that's the root of the issue. Did he die thinking I was an ungrateful punk who only cared about himself?

The wound is already open, so I keep going, sharing the darkest parts of me. "Ever since he died, I have these awful dreams. It's that night except I don't go to my buddy's house. My dad and I are sitting together in the living room watching TV. There's a baseball game on and he's glued to the screen and I know it's coming—I know he's about to have a heart attack, so I try and warn him, but it's like I'm not really there. I start off calm but then I get frantic until I'm screaming and waving in front of him, but he can't see or hear me."

Chloe squeezes my hand. Her slim fingers intertwine with mine between us. She hasn't spoken since I started talking. Just listens and holds my hand to let me know she's here.

"When I come to, I have to remind myself he's already dead. In the dream, he's alive. I always wake up before he dies so for a few seconds I think it was all just a bad dream. I can't fucking remember and when my brain catches up to reality... he's gone and I start the process of grieving him all over again."

Chloe turns on her side to face me, but I don't drop her hand—I hold onto it like a lifeline. Her teeth sink into her trembling bottom lip.

"I've never told anyone all that," I confess.

"How come?" she asks tentatively.

"It's fucking embarrassing. Joel and Zeke know I have the nightmares."

It feels weird to call them that, but I guess that's what they are. Reliving the worst fucking day of my life from an alternate point of view. I hadn't been there when my dad had a heart attack in his favorite recliner, but I've seen it over and over nearly every night since.

"Zeke used to come in and wake me up when they were really bad. Most of the time I wake up on the floor in the morning, my room trashed, and I have no memory of doing it."

Rolling on top of me, Chloe blankets me with all of her. Her hair falls around her shoulder into my face and I breathe it in. I breathe *her* in. She's an ocean of possibilities and hope that there's still good to hold onto. That there's still good in me.

"It's never happened twice in the same night, but if you want me to sleep somewhere else tonight, I'll totally understand." I run my hand over her hair and down her back. "Or if you want me to take you home."

She stands and holds her hands out to me. I get to my feet and she pulls me to the bed. "I'm not going anywhere."

And neither do I.

I'm dragging ass as I walk across the street to the fieldhouse at dark thirty. I left Chloe sleeping in my bed and damn it was hard to leave. As my muscles warm up and the fog from not enough sleep starts to ease away, I find my rhythm.

We split into two teams and do a light scrimmage to run through plays. We've got the exhibition game coming up and a lot of work to do before we show the university and local fans this year's team.

Basketball has become an escape, but this morning I try and push all that away and remember my love for it. I don't want to play to forget, I want to play for me and for the great memories I had practicing with my dad and Heath, memories I've made playing on this court for the past three years, and for the memories I hope to make with my team this year.

We may not make it back to the Final Four, but we're gonna fight to go as far as we can.

Joel and I bump wrists as we head to the sideline to grab water. "Nice fake back there. Datson was three steps in the wrong direction when you blew past him."

We sit down to take five, and I look out over the court. "Last year. Pretty surreal."

"Getting sentimental about graduation already?"

"Guess I am."

"Me, too." He tosses his towel on the floor next to him. "What are you thinking for next year?"

I glance at him in confusion. "Next year?"

"Yeah, next year, after graduation. Are you entering the draft?"

I laugh but he doesn't join me. "You're serious?"

"Hell yeah."

"I hadn't given it any thought," I answer honestly. "I just wanna see this year through first."

"Alright then, let's do it up right," he says and stands ready to go back out and get our team ready.

Chloe's already gone to her early morning classes when I get home from practice. I hop in the shower and get ready for Comm class.

When I slide into the seat next to her, I'm grinning like an idiot. She's smiling at me, and my chest fills with such happiness to have her. Really have her. I worried last night was going to make things awkward between us, but in some weird way, I think it brought us closer.

Professor Sanchez is on a rampage today, so we barely get a chance to scribble notes to each other and when class is dismissed, I groan because I know she has to hurry to make her bus.

"Don't go," I tease and hug her tight.

"I'll be back tomorrow, and I'll come straight over."

She tips her head up, her green eyes meeting mine. "I mean, if you want me to. I didn't mean to invite myself over."

I brush my lips against hers. "You can invite yourself over any time. Don't think I'll ever get sick of you."

"Chloe, let's go," Emily calls, and I loosen my grip on my girl.

"Good luck. Kill 'em.'"

She grins. "I will." She rushes to meet Emily and Sydney at the top of the stairs, and I watch her, feeling like a chump because I already miss her.

I sent Heath a couple texts to hear about his college trip, but he sent a meme of a little girl being dragged facedown around a carousel and told me he'd call tomorrow. Guess he's tired.

I head to Gabby's apartment later that night.

"Gabs?" I call, entering her place.

"I'm changing, give me one sec."

I take a seat on her couch to wait. She comes into the living room, practically bouncing with each step.

"You look happy."

"I am." Plopping down next to me, she pulls her feet under her on the couch. "We haven't hung out in forever. What do you want to do tonight?"

I lie my head back. "Movie?"

"You're such an old man. What happened to the guy who used to close down the party on the dance floor with me?"

"He's still in there. He's just tired. Chloe and I were up half the night."

Gabby's eyebrows raise.

"Not like that, perv."

She holds both hands up in front of her. "I don't need to know."

I grab a throw pillow and lightly hit her over the head with it. "We stayed up talking."

"You really like her." Gabby smooths her hair back from her face and smiles at me, showing all her straight white teeth.

I nod. "I really do."

"Good." She claps her hands. "I was going to ask her to be in the wedding so you can't break up with her."

It's my turn to be shocked. "The wedding?"

"I'm getting married. Hello?" She flashes her ring.

"When? I figured you two would be engaged for a few years first, I guess."

She shrugs. "Next summer. If it weren't for the logistics of me finishing school and Zeke's schedule, I'd do it even sooner. I love him, and I want to start our lives together."

"I'm happy for you, Gabs."

"Thank you." She uncrosses her legs and reaches over to the coffee table. "Okay, now you have two options. One, help me pick out wedding stuff?" She holds up a bridal magazine.

"What's my other option?"

"Go dancing with me."

I hold my hand out for the magazine, and she squeals before putting it in my hands.

"If anyone asks, we went dancing."

twenty-eight

Chloe

Nathan: Plans June twentieth of next year?

Me: Let me think, I'll have to check my calendar... nope, no plans. What's up?

Nathan: Wanna make sure I have a date to the elaborate wedding Gabby's planning. Do people really release live doves?

I'm lying in bed holding my phone over my head with one hand. Sydney's giving herself a pedicure on the bed next to me. Despite only getting a few hours of sleep last night, I'm wired and wide awake.

Me: Doves, butterflies... yeah, it's a thing.

Nathan: Weird.

Me: So there'll be no releasing of any wild animals at your wedding?

Nathan: Do I get a choice? The way Gabby's forging ahead over here I don't think Zeke's getting a lot of say in the matter.
Me: Let's pretend you do.

My chest squeezes as I wait for his response. I haven't given a lot of thought to weddings or marriage but talking about it with Nathan feels... fun and I find myself wanting to know exactly how he sees the future, including whether he's yay or nay to doves at his someday nuptials.

Nathan: I'm a simple guy. No doves, butterflies, or other defenseless animals should be harmed (or scared) in honor of my "special day" – Gabby's words, obviously.

Nathan: Ready for tomorrow?

Me: Yeah. A little nervous. State is tough. We lost to them last year.

I yawn and turn on my side. I plug my phone in and wait for Nathan to respond.

Nathan: You lost to them at Golden?

Me: I meant Valley.

I didn't face them at Golden, but I smile because I totally "we'd" myself like I've always been here.

Me: I should get some sleep.

Me: Night, handsome.

Nathan: Sweet dreams. Night, Surfer Princess.

I'm just about ready to crawl under the covers when there's a knock at our suite door. Sydney calls out, "Come in."

Emily and Bri come through the door that adjoins our rooms, arms full. Bri holds a two-liter of Diet Coke in one hand and the ice bucket in the other. Emily hurries behind her and unloads a bunch of mini liquor bottles onto the end of my bed.

"What's going on?" I ask.

"Away game ritual," Sydney says and walks over to my bed on her heels to keep her freshly painted nails from getting ruined.

Emily and Bri sit on the end of my bed, and I scoot over so Sydney can sit next to me.

"A drinking game?" I ask.

"Everyone picks a bottle to drink," Bri says. "First two to finish automatically lose. The other two chug a second bottle to determine the winner."

I sift through the bottles. Wild Turkey, Smirnoff, Bacardi Pineapple, tequila, schnapps, Jager, Jack.

"These are all awful." I glance up, and they're all

grinning at me.

"That's the point," Emily says and grabs the Bacardi. "You gotta take lots of small drinks and prolong it instead of taking it like a shot."

"Five minute time limit." Sydney grabs the tequila. "And you have to take a drink every time the person to your left does. No mentioning the game tomorrow, or any game, for that matter, or you have to drink."

"Pick your poison," Bri says and sits back as if to let me know I get to pick before her.

I take the Jack because it reminds me of Nathan and then Bri goes for the Jager.

Emily grabs glasses from both our bathrooms and adds ice and Diet Coke for us to chase the liquor.

After we all take our first sip and grimace, I look around at the setup. "I did not expect this. Especially from you." I glance at Bri.

She shrugs. "It helps with nerves and sleep. Plus, it's fun because I never lose."

She takes a drink, and it's like a domino effect until we've each taken another sip. We hold up our bottles to compare and sure enough, Bri has the most left.

"What can I say? It's a gift," she says triumphantly.

"Real sips, Bri," Emily grumbles. "Next time, I'm going to bring a Sharpie and draw a line before each drink to make sure it goes down."

"I'm drinking it," Bri says and takes another, forcing us all to go.

Without being able to talk about the game tomorrow, which is on all our minds, we fall quiet. Sydney is the first to break the silence. "I need a boyfriend."

Emily groans.

Bri rolls her eyes. "You don't *need* a boyfriend."

"Okay, fine," Sydney huffs. "I want one. When we get back to Valley tomorrow night, it's my new mission. Screw Shaw and his friend-zoning, video-gaming, sexy ass."

"You want me to knock him over the head with a controller next time I see him?" I offer.

She giggles. "Yes, please."

We offer her sympathy smiles, and she shakes her head. "Let's talk about something else. Chloe, tell them what you told me about how you really met Nathan."

"Oh." I take a drink without realizing it until the others follow suit. I look to Emily and Bri guiltily. "Nathan wasn't really my boyfriend the morning you walked in on us before classes started. I met him at the mixer the night before and one thing led to another."

Emily laughs. "You dirty skank."

"I'm sorry I lied. I panicked and then you guys seemed to warm up to me because of him." I shake my head. "It was shitty, and I'm sorry."

"But they're together now. Isn't that twisted and romantic?" Sydney asks and takes a drink. She holds her bottle up. "Shit, I'm out."

"Me, too," Emily says.

Bri and I look at each other as we take our final sips.

Emily motions to the remaining bottles. "Pick your bottle, ladies."

Bri holds out, waiting for me, and I take the Smirnoff. She grabs the Wild Turkey.

"You're full of surprises."

She grins.

Sydney holds up her hand between us. "On your

mark, get set, go!"

We both hurry to open our bottles. I have a slight edge on her as I get the bottle to my lips first, but I hesitate as the liquor hits my tongue. I fight to get the rest of it down, but it's Bri who slams her empty bottle onto the bed first. "Undefeated."

The next morning, I fall into line next to Bri as we do our team warmup.

"You ready for today?" she asks with only a hint of her too-serious captain tone.

"Ready," I say as we high knee across the sand. I raise my legs higher and then shake my head. She might be a pain in the ass, but Bri is effective in making us work harder.

"About Nathan," she starts, and my heart rate picks up and not because I'm lifting my legs to my chest.

"Yeah?"

Bri shakes her head. "You went to an insane level to try and be a part of the team."

I give her a shy smile. She's not wrong.

"I'm sorry you had to do that."

My head snaps to look at her to make sure she's seriously apologizing.

"As captain, I should have placed my personal feelings aside. And as a decent human being, I should have welcomed you. I'm sorry."

"It wasn't so bad. I did get the guy after all."

She smiles. "Well then, you're welcome."

Coach blows the whistle, and we hang back as the team gathers near her.

"You ready to kick some State ass today?"

"So ready."

Before our first match, we head to the locker room to relax and to get more individual plans from Coach. Coach is talking with Bri and Sydney first, and Emily and I take a seat in front of our lockers to wait. Nerves I'd been fighting all morning bounce to the surface, and I'm a ball of anxious and caged energy.

"You got any Tylenol?" Emily asks. "I don't do caffeine the morning before games, and I feel a withdrawal headache coming on."

"Yeah, in my bag." I stand and grab my backpack from the locker and hold it in my lap as I rummage through.

"Good Lord, what don't you have in there?" Emily picks up a box of tampons in one hand and a textbook in the other.

"Shit, I forgot to give that to Nathan," I say as I finally find the bottle of Tylenol at the bottom of my bag.

"The tampons?" She hands me those, and I stuff them in my backpack.

"No, the textbook." I hand her the Tylenol and take the textbook. "It's Nathan's. Crap, I hope he didn't need it this weekend."

I flip it open, more out of curiosity than anything. What the hell is Microeconomics, anyway? I freeze at what I see inside and fail to close it before Emily looks over.

"Holy shit, Chloe. What is that?"

Unfortunately, her outburst catches the attention of everyone around us, including Coach.

"I..." Words fail me. I don't understand, and there's ringing in my ears like someone knocked me over the head with a barbell.

I register Coach's harsh voice telling everyone to get out, but I can't manage to move or look at anyone.

twenty-nine

Nathan

*W*e've got late afternoon practice today, so Joel and Wes are over and we're hanging outside by the pool enjoying the day.

"Zeke's got his first home game in a few weeks. I talked Coach into giving us the day off practice. You guys in?" Wes asks.

Joel lifts his bottle of water. "Nice. You being the assistant coach is finally paying off, Dubya."

"I hate when you call me that."

"I know. That's why I do it." Joel smirks. "Dubya."

I pat my pockets for my phone. "Shit, I left my phone upstairs." I stand to go get it and the guys chuckle and yell after me. Something about being pussy-whipped, yadda, yadda. I don't let it get to me because, hello, pot meet kettle. Those two are the most whipped guys I know.

I take the stairs two at a time. Chloe should be done soon and headed back to Valley. They'll get in tonight around the same time we're done with practice, and I'm looking forward to seeing her. Twenty-four hours and I'm totally jonesing for some time with my girl. Yeah, okay, so I'm pussy-whipped. I'm not mad about it.

I've got a dozen new texts, but I skip them all and pull up Chloe's name. She hasn't responded since my good luck text this morning, but I go ahead and send another as I head back downstairs. I let her know what time I'll be back to the house and that I'm excited to see her. We've already talked about it so it's not really necessary, but damn, I just want an excuse to text her.

I take my seat outside and start scrolling through the other messages. Wes and Joel are talking about the team, so I tune them out as I read my missed texts. Heath sent me a picture of the NMU ice and locker rooms. Visit went well and I think he's getting excited about the prospect of playing in college.

Gabby sent me color schemes, which I ignore because I gotta draw the line somewhere on helping her with wedding plans.

The last text is from Frank. I open it, prepared for another job offer, but when I read it my stomach drops.

Frank: Get the book? No pressure, not expecting anything in return, I just wanted you to know I miss having you.

Confusion turns to unease as I read the message over and over. I'm in my room tearing it apart before I even realize I've moved from my seat outside.

"Dude, you alright?" Joel asks from the doorway. "You turned all pale and looked like you were about to puke before you raced up here."

"Have you seen a textbook?" I pull at my hair when they both stare back at me with puzzled expressions. A cold sweat breaks out over my entire body. "Frank. The textbooks. Have you seen any?"

Wes groans and then grits out, "You said you were done."

"I am." I turn in circles, but I don't see it anywhere. "Fuck, I am. I can't explain right now."

I give the downstairs the same treatment but don't find anything.

With no answers in sight, I call Frank... something I swore I'd never do again. It's not like I hate the guy, he gave me a job when I needed one and he was cool when I told him I was done, but he represents a whole part of my life I'm not proud of and would prefer not to ever think about again.

"Hey," Frank greets me cheerily.

I don't waste any time on niceties. "What book? Where did you leave it?" Mentally, I'm already thinking of everywhere he might think to put it for me, and I'm really hoping he doesn't say the locker room. Goodbye scholarship, goodbye basketball, goodbye Valley.

"I gave it to your girl."

Life as I know it flashes in front of me. Shame and regret make my knees buckle, and I lean against the nearest wall.

"Chloe," he says her name, confirming my worst nightmare. "I saw her at TKE on Thursday night as she was getting in an Uber to go to your place. She didn't give it to you?"

He keeps talking, but I hang up on him and turn to face Wes and Joel. They're hovering like two mother hens.

"Chloe has it."

"Maybe she tossed it and didn't wanna tell you about it. That's what I would have done if he'd given it to me," Joel says reassuringly.

I shake my head. "She doesn't know."

I read the judgment loud and clear on their faces. Fuck, I should have told her.

"Don't panic. It's probably just in her dorm. It looks like a normal textbook unless she opened it." Joel might believe that, but I don't. My gut tells me everything.

She knows, and I've already lost her.

Chloe

*H*ead leaning against the window, I find some solace in the cool glass. The promise of night and the end of this shitty, shitty day.

I'm sitting in the very last row of the bus all by myself. The seats across and in front of me are both empty. A glance up and across the aisle finds Sydney watching me with worry in her dark eyes.

The day was a success, at least regarding volleyball. Valley came out on top and the team looked good. The bus ride home should be filled with excited chatter, but instead it's quiet and an impending doom hangs in the air.

After Coach confiscated the textbook and informed Emily she'd be paired with Liv, I was dismissed to the sidelines.

Bri's gone back to hating me. She hasn't even attempted to speak to me. Emily either; I think she was more shocked than anyone. I'd nearly forgotten what it was like to live with people who were repulsed by my existence.

The silence around me is a reminder of what my life was like when I first got to Valley and how much things have changed. Gradual change feels like it isn't change at all until you compare it to where you started.

Two months ago, I wasn't sure who I was or what I was capable of. I couldn't reconcile which parts of my life had been earned and which had been bought for me. Now? Now I know I deserve to be here. I feel it deep in my bones and with every fiber of my being. Having something taken away when you've earned it hurts so much worse than when it's been bought.

My phone vibrates in my hands and I look down to see Nathan's name flashing on the screen. I'd been replaying the conversation with Frank over and over in my head all day for clues. Why was Frank giving Nathan a textbook filled with drugs? And why had Frank used me as a proxy? And the last one that bothered me the most, did Nathan know?

He'd called at least a dozen times, which was enough to doubt his innocence. Then there was the single text that told me everything and nothing.

Nathan: I'm so sorry. I can explain.

I sit up straight as the bus pulls into the parking lot outside Ray Fieldhouse. Sydney offers me a reassuring smile that I try and return. Everything is going to be okay. I didn't do anything wrong. I repeat those things hoping I'll believe it by the time I face Coach. But when it's just me and her left, I give up on hope and force myself into action.

Silently, I follow Coach inside and through the locker room to her office. She flips on the light illuminating the small space in a fluorescent haze.

She drops her shoulder bag on the desk and removes the sunglasses and visor from her head. I take a seat while she gets settled in. I interlace my fingers in my lap and squeeze to let out some nervous energy. When she finally sits down, I brace myself for the worst but am prepared to fight to stay on this team. I deserve to be here. I know that now, but I also know that some things are out of my control. There are consequences for every action, fault or not.

"Chloe, I don't know where to begin. I didn't expect this from you." She sighs. "Aside from the obvious infraction of possessing illegal substances, you put the team at risk. The type of scandal and bad press this could bring to Valley is the sort of disruptive PR that can kill a program."

She gives me a look that says I, of all people, should know better and she's right. I should. It's not the first time I've brought scandal to a team.

"It's not mine. I know how it looks, but I need you to believe me."

Her pinched expression tells me she doesn't and why should she?

Everything I've worked for—transferring schools, the extra workouts, the dedication and determination I put into it all—it's disappearing before my eyes.

"Wait." Sydney pushes into Coach's office unannounced. She's breathless, hair wild, still in her team colors. Emily is two steps behind her and then, astonishingly, Bri appears.

"Ladies, this is a private meeting."

"That wasn't Chloe's book," Sydney insists, totally disregarding Coach's not-so-subtle hint to get out of her office.

Tears prick behind my eyes. I can't believe they showed up for me.

"Chloe isn't even taking Microeconomics. Ask her."

Coach glances from them to me, weighing their words and trying to decide to entertain it, from the look on her face.

"If it isn't yours," she asks me. "Then whose is it?"

My stomach drops. "I can't tell you that, but I swear it's not mine."

She presses her index fingers to her temples and rubs with a pained expression.

I'm so mad at Nathan and myself too for getting swept up in a guy I clearly don't know. This is what happens when you live in a make-believe world—reality eventually crashes down.

Murmurs from the doorway brings my attention back to where Sydney and Emily stand. Bri pushes past them into the office, looking angrier than I've ever seen her. "The textbook doesn't belong to Chloe. The truth is, it's my fault. I put it in her bag."

"What?" I ask, shocked by every word that came out of her mouth.

She doesn't look at me as she continues. "I found it

271

near Chloe's things and I just assumed it was hers. I put it in her bag, but I had no idea what was inside." Her gaze flits to me, but she doesn't quite look me in the eye. "My bad, Chloe." She shrugs and looks back to Coach. "Emily and Sydney were with me, they can vouch for her."

Emily nods, and Coach looks to Sydney. "That true?"

"Definitely," Sydney says a little too enthusiastically. She might be overselling it a bit.

I chance another look at Bri but her hard expression is pinned away from me.

I fix my gaze back on my lap while Coach mutters about being too old for this drama and nonsense.

"I've half a mind to suspend all four of you."

We're like stone as she studies each of us.

"Next time, I will."

Sydney gives a little squee of excitement, but I keep my own joy shoved down because nothing about this feels like a victory yet. My teammates finally had my back and I want to be happy about that, but it's shrouded in the reality that because of my friendship I nearly took them down with me.

Nathan

Coach holds Joel and I back after practice to talk

about how things are going with the freshmen. I let Joel do most of the talking. I'm too amped, too nervous, too anxious to see Chloe and explain. She hasn't responded to my calls or texts, but I know they'll be back soon. This conversation is really better in person anyway.

I need her to see the sincerity on my face. I want to wrap her in my arms and hold on forever, let her feel the apology in my touch. Because I am so fucking sorry and I know words won't be enough.

"Nope," I say, a little too eagerly after Coach asks if I have anything else to add to Joel's summary. "That it?"

He chuckles as he shakes his head. "Hot date, Payne?"

"Something like that," I say as I jog backward a few steps and then turn and run the rest of the way to the locker room.

I swap my shirt for one that isn't soaked in sweat, but that's all I make time for. If the bus isn't here, it should be any minute.

I jog to the other side of the building. As I get close to their locker room, a few of the volleyball girls are walking out but Chloe isn't with them. But she's here. The panic and relief wreaking havoc on my insides tells me she's nearby.

Shaw steps away from the wall and in front of me. I'd been so focused on finding Chloe I didn't see him. "She's in with the coach now."

"I gotta get in there." I try to step past him, but he moves with me.

"Negative." Shaw knows a very short version of what's going on since he came out of his room to see why I was freaking out and terrorizing the place when I was looking for the textbook. "Sydney and a couple others are in there with her. They'll take care of her. Sydney might look sweet and innocent, but she'd throw herself overboard before letting someone she cares about go down."

"You don't understand. I can—"

"You can what?" He steps closer. "Say it's yours? Take the fall?"

"Exactly."

"And do you really think they're going to believe her boyfriend put a textbook filled with drugs in her backpack and she had no idea about it?"

"That's not what happened."

Shaw raises both eyebrows waiting for an explanation.

"It doesn't matter if they believe me or not. I have to try."

"Alright, let's say they do. What then? You'll be out on your ass and I'd bet my left nut that Chloe will be too. Guilty by association... well, and possession."

I flex my jaw as I admit to myself that he might be right. But there has to be something I can do. Toss me out, fine. I'll gladly take whatever punishment they want to throw at me if it means keeping her safe from my dumb mistakes.

"Listen to me, man. You love her? You care about her?"

I give him a hard look, but he doesn't relent.

"Fuck, of course I do."

"Then the best thing you can do for Chloe is to go home. You've already done enough damage."

thirty-one

Nathan

I jog up three flights of stairs to get to Chloe's floor. An hour run did shit to clear my head. I can't quit replaying Shaw's words in my head. *You've already done enough damage.*

He's right. I've done damage. I've made mistakes. More than I can count. I've repeatedly hurt the people I care about. I can't take any of it back, but I can apologize, come clean, and hope like hell it's enough.

Sydney opens the door wide and lets me in. Emily is on the couch and the TV is on. Chloe is nowhere in sight, but the door to her room is closed and light filters out from underneath.

"How is she?" I ask. Stalling and maybe hoping for some reassurance.

"Sad, mostly. I think," Sydney says quietly.

I nod. Nope, no reassurance there.

I texted Chloe to let her know I was coming. I knew she wouldn't respond, but I didn't want to ambush her. I knock on her door once and then open it a crack. "Chloe?"

She makes a sound that's not quite a greeting and I step inside and close the door behind me. Her hair is wet and her face clean of makeup giving me a good look at her red and puffy eyes. She's running a brush through her hair while sitting on the bed, unshed tears threatening to spill over.

"Princess." I rush to her and wrap my arms around her, pull her into me and breathe in the smell of her shampoo and just her — summertime even on the darkest and coldest day. "I'm so sorry."

Her shoulders shake and she cries into my t-shirt. Silent sobs that prove Shaw was right. The proof of my damage is in my arms.

Eventually her tears quiet and she sniffles. "Why?"

When I don't answer, she pulls away and looks up at me. "I've been replaying it over and over and I still don't understand."

"I'm so sorry." It's all I can manage. No idea where to start or what to say and knowing there's likely not an explanation she's going to like.

She wipes under her eyes. "Are you using?"

"No. Hell no." I'd like to be offended she'd think that, but I can't really blame her. I take a deep breath. "I worked for Frank, Chloe. For almost two years, I sold for him. It's how I sent money back to my family. I was desperate and reckless. Coach caught me with drugs in my locker right before the school year started and I stopped. I haven't dealt at all since you've known me, and I didn't know Frank gave you the book until today when he texted me. I would never knowingly put you in a position like that."

"But you would put yourself in that position?"

"Not anymore. I have too much to lose now. I screwed up. My life before you…" I shake my head. "I did a lot of dumb things that I can't take back, but it's not who I am anymore. Please tell me you know that I'm not that guy."

"Honestly." She lifts both shoulders and lets them fall. "I don't know anything right now."

"Yeah." My voice sounds like I swallowed razor blades — my insides feel like it, too. "I guess I deserve that."

"I think I just need some time and space. We jumped into this so fast. What do we really know about each other?"

"Everything that matters."

She tilts her head to the side and regards me seriously. "You know that's not true."

"It is true, though. You might not know my past, but you know me. I've never been more myself than I am with you."

"Even when you were lying to my face?" Her words twist in my gut. She smiles sadly. "I know that you didn't mean for this to happen, but it did, and you can't take it back."

"What can I do?" Gabby asks from my doorway the next afternoon. I was up all night, but I'm not tired.

"Take this away from me. It's not helping." I hold out the bottle of Jack without getting up. I'm flat on my back in bed, staring up at the ceiling. I thought I could drink away the pain and then pass out and forget it ever happened. I was wrong or maybe I can, but I don't want to. I need to figure out how to fix this.

She takes the bottle from my outstretched hand, sets it on the floor, and then climbs onto the bed and lies beside me.

"I screwed up, Gabs," I say, choking up as I admit it both to her and myself. "I screwed up, and I don't know how to undo it."

She rests her head on my shoulder and takes my hand.

"I love her. I can't lose her."

"You won't."

"You didn't see her face." I turn my head and look Gabby in the eyes. "I've disappointed a lot of people in my life. My dad used to lecture me for hours when I'd get a bad grade or fight with my brother, my mom would send me to my room or ground me when I was in trouble, Coach yells out his disappointment, but Chloe she was calm, resigned even. You know who reacts like that? Someone who has given up on you."

"Then you have to believe in yourself enough for the both of you." She stands and tugs on my hand. "Come on."

"Where are we going?"

"We're going for a run."

"Now?"

"Endorphins, Payne. I've got world domination and a wedding to plan and you need to figure out how to win back your girl."

thirty-two

Chloe

$\mathcal{M}$y mom calls me the next morning to let me know she and my dad are in town. Their timing on a spontaneous visit couldn't be worse. My mother sees through my bullshit like a dollar store shower curtain, and right now, I'm about as confused and emotional as I've ever been. Still, I haven't seen them in months, so I shower and put on some makeup, prepared to go about my day with some sort of normalcy.

That is until I get to communications class. I'm not sure if he'll show up after how we ended things last night, but he does looking as handsome as ever and hesitantly takes the seat beside me.

"Hi." His voice washes over me like a rogue wave, slamming into me and pulling me under. He drops a brown paper bag from the café on the desk. I don't even have to open it to know there's a bran muffin inside.

"Thanks."

He nods.

Class starts and the first of the presentations are slated to start. A trio walks up to the front of the room and begins. They start in on their sales pitch for adult diapers, and I shudder and tune them out. Easy to do when Nathan pushes his notebook in front of me.

I miss you is scribbled in his small messy penmanship. I want to run my fingers over the words and trace his letters. Instead I stare down at it and wonder how those words can possibly make me feel sadder. When I don't move to write back, he adds another line. *I'm sorry.*

I take my pen and write, *I miss you, too.*

I miss him so much. One day without him and I feel emptier inside than I've ever been.

After that, I keep my eyes glued to the presentation, horrifying as it is, and Nathan doesn't try to get my attention again. We stand with the rest of the class when it's over and shuffle up the stairs and outside.

"Do you want to get together tonight and work on our presentation? Gotta make sure it's not going to be as painful as that one was." His voice is light, but I can see the uneasiness in his posture.

"I don't think we need to. We're ready."

He shoves his hands in his pockets and nods. "Alright. Well, can I see you tonight anyway?"

Falling back into a routine with Nathan would be easy, but it still hurts too much. "I can't. I'll text you later. Okay?"

I start to walk away, and he calls after me. "Wait. I have something for you."

I turn to find his hand outstretched and a piece of folded paper with my name scribbled on top. "I know I screwed up and I know that I don't deserve you, but I'm going to keep trying anyway." He places it in my hand and leaves me standing on the sidewalk staring after him.

When I get back to my dorm, I collapse on my bed and open the note. My heart flutters at the sight of the page nearly completely filled with his small, messy penmanship. There's something intimate and special about a handwritten letter.

Surfer Princess,

Yesterday I was going to drown my sorrows in a fifth of Jack and do everything I could to forget about the mess I made. It's what I did before I met you. Numb the pain and sting of failure until it felt trivial.

Then you came along.

The way you looked at me that first night made me believe I wasn't really the guy I'd become. That the clusterfuck of my life was just crappy circumstances and plain bad luck. I lied to myself because what I really didn't want to admit was that I was scared you wouldn't like me if you knew the truth about who I was.

I don't know how things would be different if I had, but I hope that I'm not too late.

When I was nine, I told our next-door neighbor that things were really bad at home and my parents were fighting a lot just so she'd feel sorry for me and let me come over and watch cable any time I wanted.

In sixth grade, I walked into the girl's bathroom. I told everyone it was a dare, but really, I just wanted to see what it looked like in there. I thought there must be something cool since the girls spent so much more time in there than we did in the boy's bathroom.

I downloaded porn on my mom's computer and when she found it, I told her it was Heath's and that she shouldn't say anything because he was trying to figure out his sexuality.

I hate fishing, but my dad loved it. Every year he'd insist we wake up early on opening trout weekend. He got so excited about it I could never break it to him that I didn't really wanna go.

When I started dealing, I told myself that it was just a job and that I wasn't hurting anyone.

I got so drunk one time I peed on Wes' bed and blamed it on Joel.

I met a girl, a stunning and perfect girl, and I hurt her because I was too selfish to own up to my past. Everything else — the time we spent together and the way you make me feel, it was all real.

You're my truth, Chloe.

Nathan

I read the letter at least a dozen times before I have to put it away and hustle to practice. I don't think it's my imagination that Coach is extra hard on us. We do twice the number of conditioning drills.

Then, she holds Bri, Sydney, Emily, and me back after practice and informs us the supply closet needs to be cleaned out before the weekend. I really want to get out of here so I can go meet my parents for dinner, but as far as punishment goes this one seems pretty reasonable, so I keep my mouth shut and send my mom a text that practice is running late.

Sydney puts some music on while we take out every box from the supply closet so we can go through them. Emily devises a two-day master plan to get the closet cleaned and the rest of us just go with it, letting her be the leader of this venture. Typically, Bri would be the one stepping in and coming up with the plan, but she's barely spoken and not at all to me.

We pull out boxes and boxes of old stuff. The Valley U beach volleyball program is one of the oldest in the NCAA, and we find tons of merchandise dating back to when it was called sand volleyball instead.

"Look at these tanks." Emily holds up a yellow sleeveless shirt with blue horizontal stripes. "It looks like a bumblebee costume."

"Ooooh." Sydney yanks it out of her hands. "I love it."

Emily rolls her eyes. "Of course, you do."

Over the next hour, we condense twenty boxes to eight and sweep out the closet. Tomorrow the plan is to wipe down shelves and organize and label the boxes. All things considered, not a terrible way to spend an afternoon.

"You guys wanna grab Chinese and watch *New Girl*?" Sydney asks, and I want to hug her for trying to act like things are totally normal.

"I can't. My parents are in town. Heads up, they're probably going to want to stop by and see the place."

"Must hide dildo. Got it." Emily smiles. "Bri?"

She shakes her head. "No thanks, I'm going to stick around and work on some drills."

Emily groans. "I couldn't even if I wanted to. My whole body hurts."

She and Sydney look like they're waiting for me to walk out with them. I wave them off.

When it's just me and Bri, she gives me the stiffest

smile ever and heads toward her locker. I follow behind her and wait while she rummages inside and pulls out her phone and headphones. She catches me out of her peripheral and raises both eyebrows. She still doesn't speak though.

"I'm sorry and thank you. I really appreciate what you did."

She nods and brushes past me.

"Wait."

She pauses without turning around.

"Can I do some drills with you? We could work on some passing."

"Look, you don't need to do this." She turns and motions between us. "Make nice or whatever. I didn't do it for you."

"Okay."

She crosses her arms at her waist. "The best thing for the team is having you on it, as much as it pains me to admit it. Plus, I knew even you weren't dumb enough to bring drugs to an away game like party favors."

I stay silent but hold my ground and finally she relents. "Fine, but we're doing blocking drills not passing."

I hide my smile. "Whatever you want."

My mom laughs as I hug her. "You smell like a locker room, but I've missed my baby too much to care."

"I'm sorry." I pull back to check for damage, but she

looks perfect as usual. "I didn't have time to shower. Bri and I were working on some partner drills." I turn to my dad and throw my arms around him. "I missed you guys so much."

My dad motions to the host to let him know we're ready to be seated, and we're led to a table in the middle of the restaurant of the same Italian place we came for the team dinner. The waiter takes our drink order and we settle in.

"Despite needing a shower," my mom says with a teasing smirk. "You look good."

"Thanks, Mom."

My dad plays with the wine menu, not looking it over but holding it and tapping it lightly against the table. "Your mom said you weren't allowed to play Saturday. Sounds like your coach is an idiot. You're the best player they've got."

So this is it… jumping right into it. My chest squeezes, and my face warms. "It was a misunderstanding. Coach did what she thought was right."

He scowls.

"Wait, you think I'm their best player?"

He gives me a look that says *don't play dumb with me*, but when a big smile stretches across my face, he caves and gives me the grin that tells me he means it. "Of course, you are. They're lucky to have you. Damn idiots at Golden don't even know how badly they screwed up losing you."

After everything that happened, I often wondered if my parents really believed I was good enough to make it on my own. I've been stuck in limbo, deciding if they paid my way into Golden because they thought it's where I belonged or if they didn't think I could do it by myself.

Maybe they were just doing everything they could to ensure I got my dream. I don't like what they did, and I'd never condone it, but I can't say I don't get it. If I could pay to have all Nathan's troubles erased wouldn't I do it? Isn't that what I tried to do in a way?

"Thanks, Dad."

"So this is it, huh?" my mom asks.

I know she's referring to my decision to stay at Valley and if I hadn't been one hundred percent sure before, I am now. Each bump in the road has solidified it. I don't want to run. I want to prove I can handle everything thrown my way.

"Yeah, Mom, this is it. This is where I belong. At least for now."

The waiter brings our drinks and my dad takes a sip of his red wine. "I know it's hard for you to understand, but we just want you to have all the opportunities you deserve. We're sorry we interfered and cost you your spot on the team."

"Actually, I think I'm starting to understand just how much people will do for the ones they love, but I appreciate the apology."

Conversation is easier after that. I fill them in on classes and all things Valley, and they tell me about a new hotel opening and renovations they're doing to the house.

"Do you guys want to come see my dorm before you leave?" They're heading up to Scottsdale for the rest of the week and then coming back this weekend to watch our last fall scrimmage against New Mexico.

I can tell my mom doesn't totally understand why I'd want to live in the dorms when I could have an off-campus apartment, but she keeps her comments mostly positive as I lead them up the stairs and to my room.

I introduce them to Emily and Sydney, who are sitting on the couch watching TV. A glance around the room, and I can tell they picked up for my parents.

Bri is closed up in her room so it's a quick tour of my room and the living area, which only takes a few seconds to really see. I'm just about to usher them back out so we can say our goodbyes when there's a knock at the door.

"I'll get it." Sydney leaps from the couch to answer it.

"Thank you for coming," I say as I hug my mom tightly.

Sydney calls out from the door, "Chlo, it's for you."

thirty-three

Nathan

$\mathcal{S}$haw and I'd been playing video games for the better part of two hours when I couldn't take it anymore. No texts, no calls. Shit, I'd take communication by pager right now. Morse code. An owl. I just want to know I didn't screw things up beyond repair. Gabby told me to be patient, but I'm failing pretty miserably with that virtue.

Which is how I end up standing in Chloe's dorm with her parents looking me over. *Shit.*

"What are you doing here?" Chloe asks. Her eyes widen, but she walks toward me.

I smile a little too big to cover the panic strumming through my veins. Meeting the parents was very clearly not on the list of to-dos tonight. Mine or hers.

"I…" I start to make an excuse, but I've told enough

lies to last a lifetime. "I wanted to see you."

She blushes and smiles as she turns to her parents. "Mom and Dad, this is Nathan, my boyfriend."

My heart stops beating for a second at the word boyfriend. It's the second time she's shocked me by using it. The first time was the morning after our one night together when she was trying to please her roommates. I gotta wonder if right now she's using it to please her parents. But when she glances back at me, her eyes dance with amusement and I know she means it. I haven't lost her yet.

"Meet my parents, Ellie and Jeff Macpherson."

I don't miss the slight quirk of her dad's eyebrows.

Her mom, however, isn't so subtle. "Chloe Marie, you didn't mention a boyfriend."

I step toward them with my heart beating a million times per minute. "Nice to meet you."

I extend my hand to her dad, and he shakes it wordlessly with a nod. He's wearing a polo shirt and jeans like he's trying to give the appearance of casual, but he's all upper class and money. Finally, he says, "Pleasure to meet you."

Chloe rolls her eyes when her mom gives her a thumbs up like she approves of me.

"I'm sorry to interrupt, just wanted to give you this." I hand her the note folded up intricately like a heart, courtesy of Wes and his random origami skills.

"Thanks." Chloe takes the note and we stand there awkwardly until I back away. "I'll talk to ya later. It was nice to meet you both."

I stop outside her closed door and bring my palm to my forehead. *Stupid. Stupid.*

She said she needed time and space, and what do I do? I stop by unannounced like some creeper. I just want her to know how I feel and what's at stake for me.

She's so much more than a girl I'm dating. I call her my princess, but I'm not the white knight. She is. She saved me.

"Hey." Chloe slips out of her room and shuts the door behind her.

"I'm so sorry."

"It's fine. You would have met them eventually, right?"

"I would have?"

She looks at me with a curious stare. "Yeah, of course. I guess we haven't talked about it, but they're my parents. Don't worry, they aren't expecting marriage and babies just because I introduced you."

She has no idea that those things with her don't really scare me. With her, nothing does.

"Honestly, I didn't know where we stood so I was surprised you introduced me at all, let alone as your boyfriend."

Her features soften.

"You said you needed time and space and here I am crowding you."

"I get it. It's hard to stay away for me too. Look, Nathan, I do need time to process everything, but it doesn't mean I've deleted your number or that I'm going to pretend there's nothing between us."

"I'm so sorry. I know I've said it a million times, but I am. I need you to know that I'm sincere. I never wanted to hurt you."

"I was thinking about that tonight, about how

everyone does dumb shit they wish they could take back. Look at me and the situation with my parents. The thing is, knowing we all do it is comforting in a way. Someday I'm going to do something stupid. I may not even know it at the time I'm doing it. I might think it's the best thing for me or for someone I love, but I'll hurt them the most in the process. The point is, I'm going to screw up and I'm hoping when I do, you're still going to be around. I don't need time away from you because I'm trying to decide if I want to be with you, I need it because I do. And that means I need to accept what happened and forgive you so we can move on. My feelings for you haven't changed. That's not how this works."

I have so many things I want to say, but I keep them in for now. I don't want anything I say to be perceived as my trying to win back her forgiveness or speed up her timeline for forgiving me. I owe her that. I bring my lips to her forehead. "Thank you."

She holds up the note. "More truths?"

"Oh, uh, no. I may or may not have re-written the lyrics to 'Ice Ice Baby'." I clear my throat. "All right stop, please forgive me, and listen, Payne is back with a brand new…"

I stop after the first few humiliating words and give her a sheepish smile, but when she returns it—I'm not the least bit embarrassed about the lengths I'll go to prove how much she means to me.

The rest of the week is torture, but I do my best to give Chloe space. We see each other in class and text a little, but I'm basically sitting on my hands and rocking back and forth to keep myself from pushing too hard. I'm losing my mind.

My phone rings and I dive for it, only deflating a bit when I see it's Heath and not Chloe.

"What's up, little bro?" I answer.

"You're never gonna guess who just called me."

"Ariana Grande? She finally get all your fan mail?"

"Fuck off."

I hear Mom scold him in the background and I chuckle. "Busted."

"Coach Meyers called. The head coach of the Valley U hockey team."

I sit up straighter. "Really?"

"So, you didn't do this?"

"No, man, I swear."

He repeats that info back to Mom, and I can tell they're both excited. I didn't know he was even considering coming here.

"When are you coming out?"

"I don't know." He talks faster now, no longer able to hide his excitement. "He wanted to set a date on the phone, but Mom said she wanted to talk to you first so we could coordinate my visit with one of your home games."

My mom and brother at one of my games? The idea of looking up into the stands and seeing them makes me beyond excited. "I'll shoot you the link to my schedule."

"Cool. Alright, gotta go. Talk to ya later."

I walk into the theater room where Joel and Wes are

watching some game footage from last season.

"What did you do?" I ask, standing in the doorway.

Joel presses pause on the game. "You're going to have to be more specific."

"I just got off the phone with my brother. Coach Meyers called and invited him out for a visit."

Joel looks to Wes, who gives us both a sheepish smile. "I'm sorry, man. I didn't mean to overstep. I just told him there was a kid in Michigan he might want to take a look at and shot over some videos of him playing last season." He pauses. "Are you pissed?"

"Thank you."

He relaxes and smiles. "He's good. Really good."

"Still, thank you."

He nods. "Any time, man."

thirty-four

Chloe

I've officially reached the end of my sanity while making sure I've given myself time to process everything. I've forgiven Nathan and I want to move forward, but I'm still hesitating.

I've started arriving at our Communications class fifteen minutes early so I can be there and soak up every second together. I think it's time to call off the time apart. I miss my man.

"You're overthinking it. Just call him," Gabby says as she refills my wine glass. The coffee table in the apartment she shares with Blair and Vanessa is filled with bridal magazines and the four of us flip through them looking for ideas.

"Have you forgiven him?" Blair asks.

I nod. "Yeah. It wasn't as much about forgiving him

as coming to terms with the things he's done. I know he's still the same guy, but I can't pretend he didn't do those things."

"The real question is, do you think he'll do it again?" Vanessa asks.

"No way," Gabby and I say in unison and then smile.

"He learned his lesson," she adds, and I nod in agreement.

Blair points to a bridal bouquet.

"Oooh, I love it." Gabby's eyes go wide with excitement. "Mark it."

Blair adds a sticky tab to the page. "Have you given any thought on how you're going to tell him you're ready to move forward?"

"Two words," Vanessa says, holding up two fingers on her right hand. "Trench coat."

I laugh at that image. "Can't I just go over there and tell him?"

"You could," Gabby says and rolls her eyes. "But what fun is that?"

Blair looks up to the ceiling like she's thinking hard. "What could you do to show him you're ready to move on? Special places, inside jokes... that jog anything?"

"You know what? Actually, it does."

"Alright, Wes says Coach is in his office and everyone is mostly dressed. You ready?" Blair asks. "Joel's distracting him, but you gotta get in there soon."

I'm definitely rethinking my plan, but Vanessa opens the locker room door and I'm pushed inside. No one bats an eye at my being in the boys' locker room. I don't know if Wes told them or if they just don't care, and I try not to give it too much thought as I avoid looking up or making eye contact with anyone in their varying stages of nakedness.

"Nathan," I call out, keeping my head down.

"Chloe?" His voice comes from my right, so I angle myself in that direction and glance ahead at feet and legs until I find him. As my eyes slowly sweep up his body, taking in his long basketball shorts and bare chest. He chuckles, but his voice is concerned when he asks, "What are you doing here? You know this is the boys' locker room, right?"

"I'm adding some truth to our first meet-cute story."

He smirks and crosses both arms over his chest. The pose makes him look stronger and hotter than usual, which is a feat of epic hotness proportions. "The one where you walked in on me naked?"

"Mhmmm, but I thought it through, and I like the real version of how we met so this will have to be the start of a new story. Like, maybe it's not how we met, but how I came to tell you something important."

"Such as?" The muscles in his throat flex.

The locker room has fallen quiet, and I can feel all eyes on us. I breathe and don't take my eyes off his. "Nathan Payne, I am in love with you. I miss you, and I was wondering if you wanted to hang out tonight?"

He smiles and the locker room erupts in cheers from his teammates. He starts to speak, but it's so loud I can't hear a thing.

"Maybe I didn't think this through."

"What?" he yells and leans forward.

Coach Daniels yells over the others, "Payne, you and your girlfriend could maybe take this outside?"

"Yes, sir." He starts toward the door.

"*After* I talk to you and the rest of the team about the schedule for the rest of the week."

Nathan groans and looks helpless.

I take a step back since I'm about five seconds from being asked to leave. "Sorry," I whisper and take another step backward.

Conflicted emotions pull his face into a grimace until he says, "Fuck it."

He reaches me in two long strides and cups my face in both hands. His soft lips press against mine, and my ears thunder with the hoots and hollers of the locker room. I put everything I have into the kiss. God, I've missed him. This is right, and I know exactly who Nathan is. He's flawed. He's imperfect. He's my forever.

"By all means, keep me waiting," Coach Daniels sounds as much amused as he does angry, but we pull apart.

His teammates crowd around him, giving him shit. He stands up on his toes to look over them. "I'll call ya later."

I wait for five minutes outside the locker room, but I can still hear Coach Daniels inside talking about a change in the weightlifting and practice schedule and he doesn't sound like he's going to stop any time soon. I text Nathan that I'm going to my dorm, and it's an hour before he finally texts.

Nathan: Longest after practice talk EVER. I think he dragged it out just to get back at me. I'm so sorry.

Me: Maybe wasn't the best plan, but I have no regrets.

He sends me the meme of the guy with *No Ragrets* tattooed on his neck.

Nathan: Totally worth it. I can't wait to hang out, but can I raincheck until tomorrow? I have something I need to do tonight.

Disappointment deflates my excitement and the build-up to tonight, but I try not to let it show. He knows how I feel and that's all that matters. We've got time.

Me: Of course. See you in class tomorrow. We can go out tomorrow night and celebrate finishing our project. You ready?

Nathan: I will be.

I'm more nervous than I thought I'd be when Nathan and I make our way to the front of the classroom to give our communications presentation. I introduce our product, its current selling features and target audience.

When it's time to make our pitch and try to sell our pricey pen to our peers, Nathan leans over and whispers, "Roll with it."

He turns to the class. "Now I know you may be thinking, any old pen is fine. Why would I want to spend seventy dollars on anything when I could use that for alcohol or new kicks?"

The class plays right into his hand and murmurs their agreement.

"Because there are moments in life when any old pen just won't cut it. You want a pen that writes clearly and most importantly, one that has backup ink in case you run out. Some moments require a guarantee that only a seventy-dollar pen can give you."

He holds up the pen and the extra cartridges and then walks to my backpack and pulls out my notebook. Then he pulls two chairs that I hadn't noticed pushed off to the side to the front. He motions for me to sit and he takes the other chair. Flipping open the notebook, he crosses one leg over a knee and uses it to write on.

On a blank page, he writes, *Will you go out with me?* He hands it to me, and I read it aloud so the class can follow along while I write *Yes*.

"Like getting a date," he says to the class and they laugh.

He scribbles something else on a new page and hands it to me.

The Fake

"Nathan 867-5309," I read.

"Exchanging numbers."

I look up to the class as he starts writing again. They're totally hanging on every word. It's so much better than what we'd planned, and I have no idea how he came up with it or why he didn't tell me. It's genius. This time he hands over the whole notebook instead of a single page.

I start to read and then stop when I realize it's the notes we exchanged back and forth at the beginning of the semester. I find my voice and read Nathan's messy scrawl. I've looked at it so many times since that day, I practically have it memorized.

Things I've learned about Chloe:
   1. Likes Bran Muffins (yuck)
   2. Likes my mouth ~~on her fingers~~

I roll my eyes when I get to number three where he's added,

   3. Loves Nathan

"Keep reading," he urges.

Things I've learned about Nathan:
   1. Likes blueberry muffins
   2. Likes your mouth. Period.
   3. Likes PDA.

My eyes prick when I see the new addition. I swallow around the lump in my throat and read it.

4. Loves Chloe.

When I meet his blue gaze, he smiles and speaks to the class without taking his eyes off me. "Or telling a girl you love her for the first time."

He stands, holds up the pen, smirks, and tosses it to

a guy in the first row. "Invest in a good pen and get the girl."

The class applauds. He pulls me to his feet and shields me from the class as he says, "I love you, Chloe. I wanted to tell you yesterday. Hell, I wanted to tell you weeks ago. You're everything. My princess, my knight, my dragon. Every fairy tale I ever heard rolled up into one and so much better because you're real."

"Kiss me already, Nathan Payne."

He does and the class gets louder. I think Professor Sanchez might try and settle them down, but I just keep kissing my man because he loves me and I love him and right now, it's all that matters.

thirty-five

Nathan

"Girlfriend."

Chloe walks into the kitchen with Emily and Bri. She rushes to me and throws her arms around me.

"God, you two are obnoxious," Shaw says from beside me.

We had our exhibition game tonight and a party at The White House after is protocol every year.

"Want something to drink?"

She nods, and I grab her a cup.

"Where's Sydney?" Shaw asks my girl.

"She's coming. She had a date with that tennis guy she met last week."

Shaw mutters under his breath, takes his drink, and storms off. Damn, something went sideways there.

I nod to Emily and Bri. "Can I get you guys

something to drink?"

"I got it. I got it." Datson sweeps in front of me and winks at them. I chuckle but leave him to it.

"Come on, Gabby's outside. She's been waiting for you to get here."

I hold her hand tightly as we join my friends outside. They've pulled chairs into a circle off to the side of the party. Blair and Wes, Joel and Katrina, Mario and Vanessa, and Gabby all greet us as we join them.

As I predicted, Gabby tries to steal Chloe, but I hold on tighter. "You're not stealing her tonight."

Gabby pouts and I give in. I love that my best friend and my girl are close, but she gets five minutes before I'm taking her back.

Gabby talks a mile a minute about our upcoming trip to watch Zeke play, and I just watch them, completely in awe that this is my life. Great friends, great girl. Even the family situation has improved. Mom's still struggling more days than not, but she's showing up more and when I told her I was going to start talking to somebody about the nightmares, she agreed to talk to someone too. Everything is moving forward, and I'm finally looking ahead more than one day at a time.

I take the flask out of my pocket and catch Chloe's eye. Lifting it, I give it a little shake. Haven't pulled this thing out in a long time, but I think tonight might be the night to get stupid. Tomorrow, she's definitely not pulling a fast one on me and kicking me out. Or vice versa. She fakes left; I'll be waiting right to catch her.

She walks toward me, eyeing the flask with humor and mischief. "Whatcha got in there? Everclear?"

"I want you to remember how awesome I'm going to

be later when I fuck you senseless, so I went for something a little less potent."

She takes it from my hand and tips it back so the liquor flows into her mouth.

"Champagne?" she asks after she's had a taste.

I nod. "Everclear is for forgetting; champagne is for the nights you want to remember."

She wraps her arms around my neck and kisses me. Our tongues tangle, and I can taste the sweet alcohol lingering between us.

"Mmmm." I pull back and nip at her bottom lip. "Could blow off the party early."

"Can't," she says with a smile.

"Why's that?"

"I have a little surprise for you."

"A dirty surprise?"

She laughs and wrinkles her nose. "Definitely not and when I tell you what it is, you're going to regret saying that."

"Alright, I give."

She checks her phone. "Ah, perfect timing. Come on."

I follow her back into the house and toward the front door. It opens and Heath steps through.

Chloe turns to check my expression, which has to be shocked because I'm totally blown away.

"How? When? What?" I ask as Heath steps to me. We hug and then I pull back and look him over. I haven't seen him in months. I get home once or twice a year because the flights are so expensive, and driving takes damn near forever. "Damn. Little bro, you got tall."

Chloe steps forward and hugs my side. "Hey, Heath."

Heath gives my girl a once over and blushes. "Hey, Chloe. Thanks for getting me out here."

"Were you at the game?" I ask him.

"Yeah, got in this afternoon. After the game, I went by to talk to Coach Meyers. He's going to let me skate with the guys tomorrow morning."

"That's awesome."

He nods.

I squeeze Chloe and look down at her smiling face. "You did this?"

She shrugs like it's no big deal.

"Thank you." I take her mouth. My heart beats so wildly I think it might bust out of my chest to get to the owner. And she fucking owns it. "Fuck, I love you."

Heath groans. "Can I at least get a beer before you two suck face?"

"No booze for you."

"Lame."

"Come on, let me introduce you to some people."

Chloe

Watching Nathan and his brother together makes me happier than I imagined. And I imagined it being pretty great.

"Guys, this is my brother, Heath." Nathan introduces him to everyone, and the pride in his eyes is easy to see.

"Baby Payne." Joel stands and shakes Heath's hand. "Let's get you a beer."

"Negative," Nathan says.

"Come on," Heath whines.

Joel adds, "One beer isn't going to hurt him."

"Oh, okay. Let me just give Michelle a call and see if she wants to join him."

"Leave my little sister out of this." Joel puffs out his chest, and I bite back a laugh.

Nathan hands me the flask discreetly. "Shit. I gotta stay sober and look out for him, don't I?"

I sneak another look at Heath. He looks so much like his brother. Not quite as tall as Nathan, but he's already filled out more than most guys his age, probably from the hockey I know he plays. His hair is darker than Nathan's, but they have the same bright blue eyes.

"You're a good brother," I tell him.

"Yeah, yeah." He takes the flask back and takes one last drink. "Wait, where's he sleeping?"

I bite down harder on my bottom lip, and Nathan shakes his head. "Cockblocked by my own brother."

I press against him. "Tomorrow night, I'll make it up to you."

That brings a smile to his lips.

I leave the party a little early and head back to my dorm to give Nathan and Heath some time together.

"What are you guys doing back already?" I ask as I spot Bri and Emily in the living room. They've got the couch pushed away from the wall, all but blocking my way into the living room.

"Rearranging," Sydney answers as she appears from our bedroom.

"We were thinking the TV should go on that wall." Emily points.

"What happened to your date?"

"It was fine." She pushes past me and sets our speaker on the coffee table.

"*Fine*," Bri mocks. "A ringing endorsement."

"Can we just focus on the living room?" Sydney looks to me. "Chloe, where should we put the chair? And where'd you put the rug you bought? I couldn't find it."

"Under my bed."

Her eyes light up, and she runs to get it. We try every piece of furniture in every spot before we get it just right and collapse down in exhaustion.

"It's perfect now." Emily drops on the couch.

Sydney falls to the other end and Bri sits in the chair.

"What do you think, Chlo?" Sydney asks, and they all look at me.

I jam myself into the small space left in the chair next to Bri. "Feels like home."

thirty-six

Chloe

"There he is!" Gabby screams and jumps up and down as Zeke takes the court.

He's easy to spot since Gabby has shown me about a million pictures of them together, but even if she hadn't, the way he's looking at her would have clued me in.

Nathan hands me my loaded fries and rings and takes the seat next to me with his hot dog.

Our group is taking up most of an entire row. Zeke got us floor seats behind the team and it's exciting. I don't know a lot about the players or teams, but the energy at sporting events feeds my soul.

Nathan and I switch seats two minutes into the game because Gabby is killing my eardrums. The girl can yell, and she's making sure the entire place knows how proud she is of her man. It's adorable... from a distance.

At the half, Nathan's boss Lincoln comes over to say hello. I gotta admit, I'm not exactly sure what it is Nathan's doing for him, but he loves doing whatever it is.

Lincoln extends a hand when Nathan introduces me. Tan skin and dark hair, tall and athletic build. He's a little older, but he's a good-looking guy. He doesn't hold a candle to my man, but I'm not blind.

"Nice to meet you."

"Same."

Nathan makes introductions all the way around, and my boyfriend looks so proud and happy amongst his friends. *Our* friends. They've become so much more than people I know because of him. I'd love them regardless because of how good they've been to Nathan, but I love them even more for how good they've been to me.

We told them all the truth about our fake relationship, and they took it in stride. Gabby was a little hurt, I think, that Nathan didn't trust her with it sooner, but when he told her that it was because he didn't want to admit how much he really wanted the girl—me—she forgave him and we both swooned a bit.

Lincoln shakes Nathan's hand as the buzzer sounds, signaling the start of the second half. "I'll call you this week. Enjoy the game."

"Boss seems nice," I say after he's gone.

"Yeah, I think so too."

"I thought his specialty was golf. Why is he at an NBA game?"

Nathan shakes his head. "He's everywhere. Last weekend, he was at a Brewers game in the executive suite."

"Fancy."

He pulls me to him and wraps his arms around me, resting his hands on my lower back. "You wanna hang in the executive suites, princess?"

"I want to hang wherever you are."

Nathan

I watch Chloe make her way out to the aisle with Blair to hit the ladies' room.

Gabby leans over, following my line of vision. "So, when are you going to ask her to marry you?"

"What?" My head snaps around to meet her grinning face. "I'm not… We're not…"

Gabby bites back a smile while I spiral. It's not that I don't see a future with her but it's so soon.

"You're blushing, Nathan Payne."

My cheeks do feel warm, so I take a sip of my Coke and try to focus on the game. Of course, Gabby is having none of that. She nudges me with her elbow. "What? I see the way you look at her. She's it for you. Your whole damn world. It's the same way Zeke looks at me."

Her eyes flit to the court and if that look she's talking about is anything like the one she has on her face right now, I can see how my feelings are so transparent to her.

"We're not there yet," I tell her. "The only ring I can afford to buy her would have to come out of one of those cheap quarter machines."

"She doesn't care about the size of the ring."

I glance down at the rock on her finger. Zeke went a little overboard, but I get it now. He wanted to make a statement about how much she meant to him. I want that, too. "Maybe I care."

She pulls the ring from her left hand and holds it out to me. "Here." She tries to push it into my hand. "Take it. We could trade it in and get her something else, of course."

"Of course," I mock like that's the ridiculous part of this situation. I shake my head and thankfully, she puts it back on her finger.

"Glad you didn't take it. I'd miss it." She holds it over her heart. "But don't let money be what stops you. When Zeke proposed, I didn't even look at the ring until after I'd said yes. And even if it'd been made out of paper, I would have still loved it."

Chloe and Blair return, and we watch the final half of the game. The Suns win, and we're ready to celebrate.

We're meeting Zeke at his apartment, so Chloe, Vanessa, and I pile into Mario's car. Gabby is riding with Wes and Blair, giving me and Chloe the backseat to ourselves. I pull her into the middle, and she buckles but has to swing her feet to the side. It's not roomy, but I'm completely okay with her being up in my personal space.

Vanessa reads the directions from her phone to Mario, and they go back and forth on the best routes. Zeke's apartment is nice. One bedroom, one bath with

The Fake

an awesome view. He and his teammates arrive just after Gabby gets the music going.

"Nice game," I tell him. "It's going to be a rookie season for the record books."

He tilts his big head to the side. "Still early." He introduces me to his teammates Kevin O'Stark and Jason Harris.

"Nice to meet you," O'Stark says. "I'm looking forward to seeing you out there next year."

"Me? You mean Joel?" I tip my head to where my buddy is talking to Katrina and Chloe, using his hands with a big animated expression.

He and Zeke chuckle before he responds, "Yeah, *you*. You've got some nice handles and a good sense of the court."

"Thank you," I manage, shocked that this guy has seen me play.

He nods and the conversation turns to their upcoming road trip to Denver.

As much as I'm trying to enjoy college and not look too far ahead, being in Zeke's place and seeing the life and friends he's made since graduating makes me excited about the possibilities of the future.

I find Blair and Vanessa in the kitchen.

"Blair, do you happen to have a piece of paper and a pen?"

Vanessa rolls her eyes. "Probably varying colors and sizes."

Blair shoots her a pretend dirty look before admitting, "She's actually not wrong."

She produces options and I pick one, tear out a sheet, grab a pen, and thank her.

I hole up in the bathroom for a good ten minutes. A weird place to be writing a love note to your girl, I realize. When I'm done, I pocket the pen and paper and go find Chloe. She sits on the couch between Vanessa and Katrina, but as I approach, Vanessa stands, giving me a perfect opening to take the seat next to Chloe.

"Hey," she says with a big smile and her green eyes light up. "Where've you been?"

"Around." Placing a hand on her thigh, I lean into her space.

"It's weird to think, in a few months this could be you. Living in Phoenix, or wherever, and playing in the NBA."

"So weird," I agree. "Also, weird, Gabby tried to talk me into proposing to you tonight."

Her eyes go wide, and I think she's holding her breath. Shock and maybe excitement plays out on her face.

"Don't worry, I'm not going to. Not because I don't want to marry you someday, but because I want to do it the right way. With a big rock." I use my hands to give her an idea of the size—roughly the size of my head—and she laughs. "And in the perfect spot with all the right words."

I produce the paper ring I made from the paper Blair had in her purse, take her hand, and place it on her finger. "I wrote all the things I love about you on there. Barely a blank spot on either side."

She inspects it, turning it around and trying to read the small scrawls and drawings.

"I don't really expect you to wear it. It's likely to fall apart before the end of the night, but I want you to know how much you mean to me and how excited I am about every day. Not just the future where we have jobs and fancy apartments, but even today when all I can give you is this."

She holds it up over her heart, just like Gabby did with her giant engagement ring. "I love it and you."

And the thing is, I know she does. Paper isn't as valuable as diamonds, but when filled with sentiments from the one you love, it's just as precious.

epilogue

Chloe
Six Months Later

"You want a drink?" I offer Bri a cup.

She raises one eyebrow and makes no move to take it. Finally, she says, "No way, I want to be impossibly fresh when we land in Bangkok tomorrow. Three days, MacPherson, and then I finally get to kick your ass."

"Oh, God, you're going to be impossible to live with this summer."

She smiles smugly, and I pour myself a double. Tomorrow Bri, Sydney, Emily, and I all fly to Thailand for the first in a series of international tournaments. Camilla and Jill will be there, too. One last summer to play volleyball and have fun with my friends before I "join the real world" as my dad keeps phrasing it.

"Chloe!"

The Fake

My name being yelled across the room causes me to look up and see Gabby craning her neck and standing on her tiptoes to be seen.

"See you tomorrow morning," Bri says and gives me a little condescending wave that I know is in good fun. Well, she really does want to kick my ass in match play this summer, but it's only because she sees me as real competition and that makes me smile.

"Come on, we need you." Gabby takes my hand and pulls me toward the stairs.

"Who is *we*?" I ask, laughing as her short legs pump quickly, and she tugs me behind her.

"You'll see."

When we reach the second-floor gym, I'm not surprised to see it shut. The room is usually locked during parties, but the small window on the door is covered with black paper so I can't see in. That's new. Gabby knocks three times so hard her little body bounces back from the impact. I can hear music and people inside. Joel and Vanessa are the only voices I can pick out.

The door swings open, and Nathan appears. He smiles big, wearing his blue graduation cap from earlier today with his usual jeans and a plain t-shirt. His hair has grown out and is tucked behind his ears. Flashes of color dance around the room from the party lights hanging from the ceiling.

"What is this?" I ask, laughing as I look to the group. My graduation cap is forced onto my head by Gabby, who now wears hers as well.

"It's our graduation party."

"And what's that downstairs?" I ask, amused. The

house is jam-packed with people who came to celebrate the end of another school year.

"That," Joel says, pointing down. "Is for them. This is our party." The music gets louder, and he dances around. Katrina laughs at him until he sweeps an arm around her and then dips her backward.

A flask is pushed in front of me, and I quirk a brow at Nathan as I take a drink.

"Tequila?" I ask, coughing from the burn and handing the flask to Gabby.

"Someone let Vanessa choose," Blair says and shudders to show how much she dislikes it, but she takes a drink when Gabby hands it to her anyway.

"Hey, Zeke," I say to the big, quiet guy hanging back. He's got a basketball in his hands and he and Wes are the only ones without caps since they graduated last year.

"Good to see you, Chloe."

"Alright, are we doing this now that everyone is here?" Joel asks, taking the ball from Zeke.

I look around, trying to discern what *this* is as the guys huddle together.

"How are we dividing teams?" Wes asks. "Boys versus girls or are we splitting a couple to play five on five?"

"A basketball game is how we're celebrating?" I question Blair.

She sighs, a dreamy look on her face. "It's fitting, really. One last game before we all leave."

"You and Wes are staying in Valley, right?"

Her eyes slowly meet mine and she nods. "Yeah, I'm going to grad school, and Wes signed a two-year assistant coach contract." She shrugs. "It's going to be sad with everyone leaving, but Gabby will only be a couple of hours away and with the wedding this summer, we'll get to see everyone at least one more time. But I know these guys; they'll be finding excuses to see each other and if they don't, we will." She hip checks me playfully.

"Definitely," I agree.

"So, what do you say?" She nods her head toward the group.

"I'm awful at basketball."

"I find that hard to believe, but you can be on my team because I'm the reigning PIG champion."

She links her arm through mine, and we head toward the guys.

"Girls versus guys," she states confidently. "We get the ball first."

The girls spread out, and the guys match up to defend their respective partners. Nathan walks toward me, all swagger, with a competitive gleam in his eyes.

"You can't handle this, Payne."

"That so?"

I nod, head held high with false confidence.

Blair checks the ball to Wes and so it begins. I think the guys are going easy on us at first, but when Gabby and Blair pull off some pick and roll play and actually score, their shocked boyfriends up their defense.

Vanessa shoots and it bounces off the front of the rim. Zeke rebounds and tosses it with one hand to Nathan. I square off, blocking his direct path to the basket. He dribbles left to right, behind his back, between his legs. He's showing off, and I'm enjoying every second of it. I lunge for the ball and come up empty, but instead of blowing by me, Nathan keeps taunting me.

I narrow my gaze and deepen my stance. I mean business. One side of his mouth pulls up, and he leans down so that our faces are only inches apart.

"I'm sorry to have to do this to you," he says right before he spins to my left and takes the basketball to the hoop and scores.

The guys fist bump him, and I move to the top of the three-point line. "Give me the ball."

"Ah, shit," Blair says as she bounces it to me. "Chloe is pissed."

Nathan walks up toward me with a rueful grin. "Sorry, princess, had to be done."

"Mhmm, too late for apologies."

Wes chuckles. "Don't you know you're supposed to let your girl beat you, Payne?"

"That's not what you do, is it?" Blair asks, her voice going up an octave with each word.

Everyone laughs except Blair. Wes pulls her into a hug and shoots us all an "oh, shit" look over the top of her head. "Of course not."

I dribble, concentrating hard. I don't have any mad skills to do anything fancy, so I decide to go with brute force. I step on his left foot with my right and I *may* throw an elbow in the process. It all happens so fast it's hard to say.

Whoopsies.

The rest of the guys part to let me through, and I manage to make a shot right under the basket. When I turn around, Nathan is sprawled out on the floor on his butt. He's got both eyebrows raised, but he smiles as I approach. I offer him a hand, and he pulls me down on top of him.

"I scored."

"Where was the back-up D?" Nathan asks the guys as he squeezes my waist.

"Everyone was afraid to get in her way." Joel approaches, ball tucked into his side. "You're dangerous, Macpherson. Let's keep him in one piece."

"Sara'll kick your ass if you show up to train next week with an injury," Zeke adds with a smirk.

Nathan's signed with Zeke's agent, Sara Icoa, and he and Joel are heading to a training facility in Phoenix this weekend. I'll be traveling the world playing volleyball while he's there and then meeting him in New York for the draft. Then? Who knows? I'd follow him anywhere, which is the plan. It's as good a plan as I can imagine. I can get a job pretty much everywhere, but there's only one Nathan Payne.

We don't continue the game after that. Sitting on the hardwood floor, we pass the flask around and share memories from college. They have more stories with one another than I do, but I love listening to every one of them, even the ones I've heard a dozen times before. Their friendships and relationships have withstood a lot, and this may be the end of one story, but it's just the start, really. Our happily ever after is just beginning.

Nathan

One Month Later

"There's a Chinese place two blocks away that delivers or we could try that Italian place that has the toasted ravioli." Chloe shuffles through a stack of takeout menus and produces the one she's talking about. My mouth waters.

"Whichever can get here the fastest. I'm starving."

She calls and places our order while I dig through a box. One of three we still haven't unpacked. We arrived yesterday in Florida with six boxes between the two of us—mostly hers, and the floral chair from her dorm.

The apartment came furnished, courtesy of my new team, but Chloe wouldn't move without it. And let's be honest, I'd have bought and packed anything she wanted to have her with me. I still can't believe we did it. I got picked up early in the second round of the NBA draft, and Chloe has two interviews next week before she heads back out for another month abroad playing volleyball.

"Do you know which box has my phone charger in it? I'm at five percent, and I want to call Heath."

"I think all the cords ended up in the box with your clothes, but isn't he working at that hockey camp in Wisconsin?"

I nod. "Yeah, I want to make sure he didn't do anything stupid."

Chloe raises an eyebrow like I'm being overbearing. My job with Lincoln turned into a friendship, and he got

Heath the assistant coach position at a youth hockey camp this summer to help with expenses before he goes to college.

Money isn't an issue anymore, but I think it'll be good for him. He's heading to Valley and it's sorta trippy to picture him on my old stomping grounds.

"Lincoln has done a lot for me and him, I just want to make sure he respects that."

"Lincoln and Heath can take care of themselves."

I find the charger buried at the bottom of the box and plug in my phone before I join my girl on the couch. She climbs onto my lap and straddles me and any ideas I had of talking to anyone are forgotten.

"Food will be here in twenty minutes."

"How do you suggest we kill the time, princess?"

She leans forward, her blonde hair tickling my face as she presses her lips to mine. "Should probably unpack the last of the boxes."

"Absolutely," I agree between kisses as I move both hands to her hips and slide them up under her tank. I move to stand, and she wraps her arms around my neck and legs around my waist.

"Where are we going this time?" she asks with a note of humor.

"We haven't christened the bed yet."

"The three times last night didn't count?"

"I meant in the daytime."

Walking her to our room, I lay her on the bed. She props herself up on both elbows to look at me. "Well, in that case."

I get rid of my shoes, shirt, and shorts in that order. Grabbing her ankle, I tug gently so she falls back flat and climb over her.

"You're not naked, and we're down to eighteen minutes before the food gets here."

"Guess you better undress me quickly then." Her eyes glimmer with excitement and want.

I'm not above showing how eager I am. I strip her down like my life depends on it. My next orgasm does, so close enough.

There's something supremely satisfying about making love to her in this bed, the first one we've shared in a place for just the two of us. It's only been a day of living together, but it feels so good and right to share our lives totally and completely like this.

I want to wake up and watch her drink coffee while sitting on our small balcony. I want to come home every night and order takeout and hear about her day. Weekends exploring our new town, sex in every room and on every surface of the apartment, days that start and end with her. The sweetest dreams and an even sweeter reality.

When I push inside her, those green eyes lock onto mine. She takes another little piece of my soul every time she looks at me like this. Love and respect and strength reflect back at me and somehow seeing right to the very core of me, too.

I handed her my heart long ago, but I won't be satisfied until I've given her all of me and anything else she wants in this life and the next.

The past few days driving across the country and taking on all these new experiences together has been its own brand of foreplay. Each of the half dozen or so times we've had sex since we arrived has been frantic and quick, and this one is no different. Pumping my hips faster as her moans get more desperate, I watch her unravel beneath me.

Stunning. Perfection. Home.

My release follows hers, and we're just limbs and panting breaths as we lie together sprawled out on top of the comforter.

The doorbell rings, and I groan even as my stomach growls in anticipation. "I think this is the first time ever I've been disappointed the takeout arrived so fast."

"I'll get it." She sits up and starts to get dressed.

"Let's take it to the beach."

"Craving a little sand in your General Tso? It'll take us forty-five minutes to get there."

"Someplace else to be?"

She rolls her eyes and then brushes a kiss onto my lips. "No, I just thought you were starving," she mocks before jogging out to get our food.

We decide to eat first and then drive to the beach, which has us arriving right at sunset.

It's all too new for us to be annoyed by the tourists or the traffic and chaos of trying to find a place to park. I take her hand and we walk along the water's edge and watch the sun start to descend. Chloe takes off her shoes and smiles as her feet squish in the sand.

"I'm glad we ended up so close to an ocean," she says.

She pauses and closes her eyes like she's trying to capture the moment. The salt air kissing her lips, the breeze off the water whipping blonde hair around her face, sand and waves and love. So much love. I never thought it was possible to feel this way.

I couldn't have planned a better moment, but I definitely imagined it just like this. I drop to one knee with my heart racing like hurricane winds. It's only part nerves; mostly I'm just so anxious for everything that comes next.

When her eyes open and she finds me kneeling in front of her, she looks confused until I take the ring box from my pocket. Her eyes sparkle and her mouth opens to speak but she just closes it and pulls it back into a big smile instead.

"It had to be on the beach," I tell her.

Tears fill her eyes, and she nods.

Emotion deepens my voice and makes it hard to remember all the things I want to say to her. The things I want to promise. The life I want to build with her. It's all clear and yet so hard to describe. The words aren't enough. It's moments and glances and every second in between all the important ones. Days counting down the seconds until I can see her when I get home and nights tangled up together. It's just life, and I want to spend mine with her.

"Chloe, I… fuck." I grimace. "Shit, I mean…" I groan low in my throat. I'm bungling this spectacularly. I flash a sheepish smile. "Of all times to be at a loss for words."

"I don't need the words. I just need you."

The confirmation of her love and devotion gives me new purpose to tell her just how important she is to me.

"The first time I saw you, you were wearing a red dress and standing alone in a crowd of people. You looked so gorgeous. Part surfer girl part princess. I don't think I ever would have had the balls to approach you if

I hadn't recognized something in you. You were hiding away just like me and that made me feel less alone. I was trying to escape my life that night and instead, I stumbled into it. You changed my life and then became it. I love you. Marry me?"

She laughs as she nods but doesn't speak.

"And no pressure, but if you say no, I'm probably going to take off swimming. Find a nice island to live on, grow a beard."

"Yes," she says, and it sets my soul on fire.

I stand and frame her face with my hands as I kiss her.

"Say it again."

"Yes, I'll marry you, Nathan Payne, or we can swim out to that island together. Me and you. Forever."

the end

Thank you for reading *The Fake*

Please consider leaving a review!

Coming Soon

More jocks are coming in 2020! Sign up for my newsletter to be notified of release dates and other book news:

www.subscribepage.com/rebeccajenshaknewsletter

Join my **Facebook Reader Group** for behind the scenes, exclusive excerpts, and more:

http://smarturl.it/RadRomantics

Playlist

- "Simple Things" by Miguel feat. Chris Brown & Future
- "Ghost" by Badflower
- "Nights Like This" by Kehlani feat. Ty Dolla $ign
- "Let Me Go" by Hailee Steinfeld feat. Alesso, Florida Georgia Line & watt
- "Heroine" by Marc E. Bassy
- "Undrunk" by Fletcher
- "I'm So Tired" by Lauv feat. Troye Sivan
- "If You're Gonna Lie" by Fletcher
- "Wow." by Post Malone
- "Hate Me" by Elle Goulding feat. Juice WRLD
- "Takeaway" by The Chainsmokers feat. ILLENIUM and Lennon Stella
- "Wasted Youth" by Fletcher
- "Woke Up Late" by Drax Project feat. Hailee Steinfeld
- "Goodbyes" by Post Malone feat. Young Thug
- "Cold" by Maroon 5 feat. Future
- "Fuk, I'm Lonely" by Lauv feat. Anne-Marie
- "How Do You Sleep?" by Sam Smith
- "Easier" by 5 Seconds of Summer
- "The Way I Are" by Timbaland feat. Keri Hilson and D.O.E.
- "Come As You Are" by Nirvana
- "Creep" by Stone Temple Pilots
- "Call You Mine" by The Chainsmokers feat. Bebe Rexha
- "One Thing Right" by Marshmello feat. Kane Brown
- "You Need To Calm Down" by Taylor Swift
- "Rescue Me" by OneRepublic

- "I.F.L.Y" by Bazzi
- "Post Malone" by Sam Feldt feat. RANI
- "Sunshine" by Charlie Heat feat. Ant Beale
- "Cross Me" by Ed Sheeran feat. Chance the Rapper & PnB Rock

Acknowledgements

A massive thank you to everyone who took a chance on this series. I hope the Smart Jocks felt like putting on Jock Jams and having a dance party with friends.

I LOVE sports. All of them, really, but especially college basketball. I did a ton of research while writing this series and injected some of my own collegiate experiences, but at the end of the day—it's fiction, baby! Thank you for letting me take liberties like having Spring Break in April (because, come on, it's only fair that my NCAA champs get a spring break too!) and making every guy on campus insanely hot. Creating the Valley U world was an absolute blast and I never want to leave.

So many people had a hand in helping me along the way. Special thanks to Amy, Ann, Brooke, and Louise for beta reading throughout the series. ALL the love to the bloggers, bookstagrammers, and readers who read, loved, shared, and reviewed.

XOXO

Also by Rebecca Jenshak

About the Author

Rebecca Jenshak is a self-proclaimed margarita addict, college basketball fanatic, and Hallmark channel devotee. A Midwest native transplanted to the desert, she likes being outdoors (drinking on patios) and singing (in the shower) when she isn't writing books about hot guys and the girls who love them.

Be sure not to miss new releases and sales from Rebecca – sign up to receive her newsletter
www.subscribepage.com/rebeccajenshaknewsletter

www.rebeccajenshak.com

Made in the USA
Monee, IL
14 August 2022

11651022R00187